SEVEN-X

MIKE WECH

DEDICATION

To my wife, Ana Maria,
whose love and support always gets me through my
roughest moments.

To our parents
Mike and Diane Wech
and Mary and Robert DuFour.

They are a blessing to us,
and their contributions to our lives
have helped us achieve our dreams.

ACKNOWLEDGMENTS

Special thanks for the contributions of
my friends and family,
and the mercy of God,
who rescued me from the depths of darkness
and showed me His grace, love, and kindness.

Thank you to Rachel Kirsch for her editing work
on this edition of SEVEN-X

TUESDAY, DECEMBER 7, 2010 – 9:00 PM

I feel like I'm signing away my life. Literally. I just read through the consent forms I need to sign to cover this story. A story that has to be told. A story I uncovered as part of my investigation into seven missing death-row prisoners in the state of Texas.

My name is Eddie Hansen. I'm a freelance reporter. This journal, along with my audio and video diary, is my record of the Uphir Behavioral Health Center in Uphir, Texas. An unofficial ghost town that's completely off the grid. A place without a zip code or mailing address.

My best guess is that this is a privately funded asylum where experimental procedures are being conducted without the consent of its patients.

While conducting this investigation, I will be voluntarily under the care of Dr. Alan Haworth, a clinical psychologist, and Rev. William H. Billings, a local minister who will act as counselor in charge of my spiritual condition.

It's my theory that Annette Dobson, the SIDS Killer, is being held in Uphir, at the asylum, under the care of Billings and Haworth.

In case you missed the news, here's her story. Over a thirteen-year period, five of Annette Dobson's children died before they reached their first birthday. Each time, SIDS was determined as the cause of death and no wrongdoing was suspected.

When her sixth child, Anthony died less than three months after his birth in March of 2009, evidence suggested a homicide. A lengthy investigation ensued and Dobson finally broke down and confessed to all six murders.

After a speedy trial, Annette Dobson received the death penalty from the great state of Texas, with her execution scheduled for Friday, May 13, 2011.

While on death row, Dobson became pregnant. A media nightmare broke out when Dobson requested her execution be moved to November 19, 2010. No media, no family, and no outside witnesses were to be present. She stated that her privacy was to be respected, and she alone would suffer the consequences of her actions.

Right to life advocates protested believing Dobson would be consenting to a late term abortion by the time the court made its ruling. The state could not execute her if she was pregnant, but on November 19th the execution proceeded as scheduled.

Annette Dobson left no last statement. A death certificate was filed with the state and her case was closed.

Her infamous husband, Kevin Dobson vehemently denied knowledge of the murders. He told me in our interview that Annette was afraid to die and she would do anything to stay out of hell.

When the state informed Kevin that Annette's wishes had changed, he knew something was wrong. So he came to me. He begged me to find answers.

So here I am sitting in the only diner in Dell City, Texas, a booming bastion of 413 people and the last vestige of civilization before venturing into the asylum at Uphir.

Dell City is the town infamously named after the children's song "The Farmer in the Dell," and it's the last place I'll have phone service or Internet access for a while. It's imperative I get my documents and journal in order and leave a digital trail of breadcrumbs to my whereabouts should something go wrong.

I feel like Michael J. Fox in *Back to the Future*. It's as if I punched 1955 on the dashboard of my DeLorean and crashed into this world. A far cry from my bungalow in Hollywood, California.

Hearing people talk about hunting elk with a White Onyx, double barrel, is refreshing compared to the endless chatter of wannabe Spielbergs gabbing about their latest film project over a half-decaf double latte.

The fashionable beauty of missing teeth makes every smile a picture worth a thousand words, and I'm stuck in this moment, enjoying simplicity. Everything seems so appreciatively simple, yet this hunger in me is pushing me to sign my life away for my shot at glory.

These people don't give a shit about glory. They're not crying to become the next reality star or rock legend. They're not spending their last dollar on plastic surgery, desperately trying to maintain fleeting youth.

No. They're going to take their toothless asses out into the woods behind me and shoot a deer or elk or rabbit, and some primal urge within them is going to find unlimited satisfaction in dragging that carcass back home on top of their pickup truck and ripping it apart to eat.

I'm the same animal, but with a more sophisticated palette and better dental coverage. My unlimited satisfaction is coming from the hunt too. The hunt for truth, for my story to be seen by the world. I'm going thirty-two miles away from what these Dell folks call civilization, heading into nowhere to hunt.

Or maybe I'm the poor elk, wandering into the path of the White Onyx, staring stupidly into that double barrel, wondering what the hell I did to deserve this fate.

As a precautionary measure, my assistant, Melody Swann, is transcribing my tapes and piecing this diary together from my journals.

You read that right. Her birth name really is Melody Swann, and as fate would have it, she came to Hollywood to be a singer. Five American Idol auditions later and a part-time job at Dimples Karaoke Bar and here we are together.

Anyway, should anything happen to me, Melody will retain authorship of this work, and she has instructions for its completion. All my entries will be assembled in chronological order and transcribed as given. Entries may be placed together to provide clarity, and descriptions of my recordings may be added as needed.

As I wrote those words, *should anything happen to me,* the gravity of this situation claws at my mind. I've assessed the risk, and the rewards far outweigh any potential problems I may encounter.

Speaking of rewards, my greatest one is calling. I see her face on my phone screen and it warms my heart.

"Hey, baby girl."

"Daddy!"

The sound of her voice melts any remaining fear that haunts me. "How's my Pebbly?"

"Daddy, I'm eight," she scolds.

"I know, sweetie. You're a big girl… I just… want you to know that I love you."

"I love you too… Guess what?"

"What?"

"I got the Virgin Mary, Daddy! I got her."

"Wow. Where is she?"

"Silly!" She squeals. "In my school play. I'm the Virgin Mary. I got a solo. Singing in front of the whole school."

"Wow. Are you scared?"

"No, Daddy. I love singing. But then Mommy goes and puts me in ballet class. I hate it. The music is boring, and they say French stuff, which is so annoying. I told her like a hundred times I like hip-hop. But she says ballet makes me cultured. I don't want to be like yogurt."

"You'll be peachy,"

"She makes me eat it too, you know. I only like vanilla with Cheerios. But Todd licks his fingers, then sticks them in the box. And Mommy doesn't even hit him. If I did that, I'd be so dead."

"Me too, sweetie."

A moment of silence sweeps in. I know her little brain is churning with possibility as she softly says, "Daddy?"

"Yeah, baby," I answer, sensing what is coming.

"Promise, if I tell you…"

"Sure, honey."

"Promise you won't tell Mom."

"I won't… I promise,"

"Okay," she says, choking back her words. "First you have to come to my play."

"I'll ask your mom."

"No, Daddy. No! You have to come. You have to! Then you can spend Christmas with me."

"Christmas with whom?"

Those words pierce my heart through the phone. I know the voice of my ex-wife Jamie too well. *"Christmas with whom? Who are you talking to, Kennedy?"*

"Nobody. My friend," Kennedy says defensively.

"Give me the phone. Give me that phone! This is not the phone I bought you, is it?"

Silence hangs on my nerve endings as I wait to hear her next words. *"Is this the phone I bought you?"*

I can hear Kennedy sob as she is ordered outside. The energy is sucked out of my body and the upcoming shit storm is about to hit land.

"Son of a bitch! I warned you not to buy her any more phones."

"Sorry."

"How stupid are you?"

"Really?"

"Yeah, really stupid, Eddie. You're violating a court order."

"I'm not with her, okay? You got sole custody. You win."

"That's not the point, Eddie," she rambles. "It's been four years. Move on. Let go. She would have forgotten about you by now, and I'd have peace in my family. Not some child who doesn't acknowledge her father."

"I am her father!"

"You're nobody's father. You blew that privilege. Move on with your life!"

"It's not final. You know it."

"You brought this on yourself. You bring everything on yourself, Eddie. That's you! You're responsible for your actions. Now you have to pay for them."

"I am paying!"

"No, you're not. Did you pay alimony? Child support? You thought you had the upper hand. You made your play for her and you lost."

That's bullshit. She knows it. I know it. But her mind won't process it. Jamie doesn't rationalize. She never did. But I'm going to let her know the truth.

"I followed court orders. I gave you everything I had. I wanted to work this out."

"You never thought Scott would beat you, did you, Eddie? You thought you'd get your big story and ride off into the sunset with my daughter."

"I never said that. I tried to work this out."

"It's worked out. Read your court documents. I better not catch you within fifty yards of my daughter or your next call will be for bail money. Understand?"

And with that, she hangs up. That was it. Jamie always has to have the last word. There's no use calling back. Nothing I can say will fix anything.

"Need a fill?"

That's my waitress, Aida Mae, stalking me with coffee for the eighth time today. Her wild red hair and gap toothed smile sneak up behind me while I'm deep in thought then spring into conversation startling me back into this reality.

"You all right, hon? Your face just flippy-flopped all happy to sad."

"Sure, fill me," I say, stretching out my cup, watching her watch me. "See, I flipped back. All smiles."

"Well that's better. People digest better when they're happy. You've been sitting here all day, and your face keeps changing like the clock."

"I've got a lot going on," I tell her as I organize my documents.

"I see. All them papers."

Aida's face suddenly changes to a look of wonder. "I know you. I do. You were here before. 'Bout a month or two ago, weren't ya?"

"You got me." I smile.

"I 'member you now." She scans me with curiosity. "Said you were headed up to Uphir." She pauses for a second as a look of confusion settles into her face. "You made it back here."

"Guess so," I say, smiling as I notice the sudden change in her demeanor. A frightened cognizance seems to crawl over her.

"How'd you do that?"

"Do what?"

"Get out," she groans, fighting something building up inside her. "Never seen anyone go up that way and come back. Maybe they do. But they don't stop here."

Then, with a sincere look, she gazes back at me and asks innocently, "Is it my food?"

"No, the food's great," I respond, trying to be polite.

She smiles back, relieved, and her next words pour over me like hot coffee. "Well then, it must be the devil!"

"What do you mean?"

She stops cold and looks around as if someone else besides me is listening. Then she leans into me and whispers tentatively, "You can't say nothing. Promise?"

"Sure."

"Promise!"

"Yeah. Go ahead," I say as she walks to the window and looks out, making sure no one is within audible distance.

Then she turns and slowly walks back toward me, acting nervous with the coffee pot shaking in her hands. Clenching the pot, she lets out a strong sigh.

"'Bout ten years ago. They came here looking at land. Asking questions. Mostly about the water, 'cuz we feed El Paso, and they wanted to run pipes out there too."

"Who?" I ask, perking up.

"I don't know. Corporate. Government folk. The kind with money. Anyhoo, all the sudden, the whole town went crazy, fighting over everything. Money mostly. 'Cuz they spent a lot up there. Then once that hospital got reborn, it all got worse."

"How?" I ask, feeling her nervous energy puncture me.

"You know, the folk in the wood who lived up there all moved out. Or disappeared. Some we just never heard from. And nobody says nothing."

"Why?" I ask, seeing her hesitate for a moment before scurrying to the window again, looking out carefully for signs of trouble.

She takes a deep breath, then slowly walks back and sits down across from me, staring at me with eyes that remind me of a wounded animal.

In choppy breaths she continues her story. "They were scared to death… Evil things go on… Some folk say they heard hell rising. Demons running wild… You can never…tell anyone…I told you this. Promise."

"I won't. You can tell me anything," I say, touching her hand gently to reassure her of my intentions.

"All right. You have kind eyes." Aida stands up and nervously takes out a rag to wipe off the coffee that missed my cup.

"Anything else peculiar you notice?" I ask, feeling there is something beneath her charred surface.

"Well… I did see prison trucks roll on by late at night. Mostly down that back road," she says, gesturing with her head cocked toward the back door.

That perks me up more than the coffee, knowing the clues to my investigation are bubbling up all around me. She finishes wiping the table and begins to make her way past me when I stop her and ask, "You know if any came through here recently?"

She hesitates, trying to read me for trust. "Not that I recall," she whispers. "But a man did come by in a uniform awhile back, looking for that hospital. You know… No one can figure out them roads up there, all curvy and crisscrossed. They don't want nobody up there. That other one, he ain't been back."

"Was he Spanish?" I ask.

"I think so… Yessiree!" she exclaims excitedly.

"Was his name Renaldo?"

Aida pauses for a moment, thinking hard, then scans the room again like she is trying to listen for the answer.

"Rings a bell," she flutters. Then her eyes bug out as she bursts with this vein of knowledge. "Know what?"

She bends down and looks me dead in the eye. "I just heard him. Jose. His name is Jose!"

"You what? You heard what?" I say, trying to gauge her sanity.

She squints as if listening to someone whisper in her ear. Then she closes her eyes softly and squats down in front of me as we engulf this ominous breath of silence together.

After a moment, she responds, "No. Sorry... He said Ose. Not Jose." She pauses again, listening carefully. "Yep. Ose! He called you. I just heard him."

"What?" I ask, confused.

Aida zeroes in on something. Her eyes dart into mine. "Listen! He's saying, 'Eddie. Hey, Eddie.'"

"I don't hear it," I tell her, not tipping my hat to signs of her lunacy.

"Well he said it again! Eddie. That's you, right?" she asks.

"Yeah. That's me."

Then she breaks contact, gets up, and walks to the back door. "Maybe he's round back."

"Sure you heard that?" I ask.

"I swear, I did! I heard a voice say 'Eddie. Hey, Eddie.' Then he just said, 'It's Ose. I'm coming for ya.'"

"Okay," is all I can say as she walks out the door, carefully peering around the corner.

I get up to follow her. As I go out the door and make my way toward the back alley, I hear something crash against the ground. Aida Mae rushes past me like a deer through the woods. She quickly runs back into the diner and locks the door, leaving me standing in the brisk winter air as the howling wind bites at my face.

Aida's petrified, staring at me as I calmly tell her.

"It's okay. It was just a trashcan. The wind blew it over. Nobody's out here."

Her body is shaking. She can't move. Her eyes glaze with fear as I look around for any intruders. There is no one in sight. Just the empty black horizon that stretches out into the frigid woods for miles in every direction.

"Aida, please… It's freezing."

The temperature feels like it dropped another ten degrees. I look around again.

"No one is out here. I checked."

She doesn't move. She just stares at me with a look of torment.

"All my papers, they're inside. They're very important to me. My life depends on them… Can I please come in and get my papers? I really need them… Please. I promise, no one is here."

I smile gently, trying to break the wall around her. She timidly scans the empty lot, then finally unlocks the door.

I hurry in with a gust of cold, dark air and snow, trying not to alarm her. As I get inside, she quickly jams the door shut behind me.

Turning back to me, she coldly states, "That place is the heartbeat of hell. You be careful."

I sense true fear in her eyes. Imaginary or not, an icy fear covers her.

I walk back to my table and begin to pack my things. But she just stands in a dark puddle of melted snow, clenching her teeth and squinting her eyes.

"I'm not saying it," she begins repeating to herself.

I finish packing my documents and notice she still hasn't moved. She rambles to herself, "He's a good man. He has kind eyes."

She's beginning to concern me. Her whole persona has changed. I cautiously approach.

"Are you okay?"

"I'm not saying it," she repeats.

"Not saying what?"

"What he wants me to tell you," she mutters, becoming increasingly agitated. "I'm not telling him."

"It's okay, Aida. You don't have to do anything. Whatever you want."

She trembles, breaking down. "He's here! He won't stop touching me."

"No one's here, sweetie."

She pauses, listening to the air again, panting in sobbing tones, "Yes! Ose is here."

Dark tears slide out her eyes.

"I'm sorry... I'm sorry... He's making me say it."

As I inch closer she moans, "I have to tell you."

"Go ahead, tell me," I say, hoping it will calm her.

She pants, holding back before relenting. "Ose. He's coming for your soul."

And with that she breaks down. "I'm sorry. I'm sorry," she cries, excusing herself, rushing into the kitchen. "If you want more coffee, just holler."

And with that she disappears. All I wanted was coffee and Internet service. But Aida Mae, my psychic waitress, hears voices coming after me.

She wasn't this scattered on my first visit, or was she? I don't remember. I was focused on getting answers to my investigation and I'm not going to get any more here. It's time to move on. I've got what I need. I know what I have to do.

I'm signing my Consent of Voluntary Commitment and my Liability Release and heading into what Aida Mae calls the heartbeat of hell.

JOURNAL ENTRY/AUDIO LOG: WEDNESDAY, DECEMBER 8, 2010 – 2:13 P.M.

My rental car must be a DeLorean because the deeper I disappeared into these woods, the farther back in time I traveled.

If Dell City was *Back to the Future*, ushering me into the 1950s, then Uphir is *Back to the Future Part III*, because I just time traveled back into the 1880s. Hidden between mountains in the heart of nowhere stood this massive colony of Gothic architecture, sprawled across acres of dead land, forgotten in time, but rediscovered with my own eyes.

As I drove into the compound, awe and respect swept over me to see millions of stones laid on top of each other, creating a historical landmark from the age of mad scientists, lunatic asylums, and bloodletting. A remnant lost in time, but restored to the glory of the spirit that still lives inside. A spirit or a feeling that somehow took hold of me.

As I walked up to the main building, I felt its force, its power, and its majesty. I felt the building breath as if the stones longed to speak with me and tell me their story.

Long before I was born, this place birthed unspoken tales of terror. I still feel it as I write this.

Every part of my body trembled with anticipation as I reached the massive arched doorway that welcomed me inside.

An elderly nurse greeted me, ordained in the uniform from that golden age. This was more than by design; it was by choice. Her forced smile led me to believe something was quite different in here.

My heart was telling me to turn around, but my inquisitive nature forced me to step inside.

As we walked down the long, cold hallway, she was silent, and I could think of nothing to say to break the awkward sound of our pounding footsteps echoing down the corridor.

I merely observed the architecture with reverence. I could see my breath pour out before me with each footstep. Clouds of smoky air reminded me that my body was alive and much warmer inside than in my new environment.

Soon enough I felt the air begin to grow warmer, and the rumbling sound of a heater filled the room I was about to enter.

"Take a seat. The doctor will be with you momentarily," the nurse told me. And with that, she left me in a room of wonderment, staring at the ghosts of this place. Pictures and paintings of people I neither knew nor had ever heard of adorned the walls.

A warrior, a philosopher, a family, all dead now, and the only memory of them were these portraits, painstakingly painted by hand, not some digital flash of random numbers that create the instant images we see today.

One particular painting called out to me. It was created by someone who spent endless hours closely observing their subject, applying precise strokes of paint in patterns to replicate what their mind said was the essence of the person who modeled before them.

With that thought, in walked Dr. Alan Haworth.

I was finally face to face with him again. This time inside the heart of his domain.

"Sir Richard Andrews," he told me, pointing at the picture above me. "The designer of this magnificent structure. We strive to maintain his spirit, to restore to glory such a time when men would adhere to more noble causes. Wouldn't you agree?"

"Sure," I told him, not fully comprehending his statement, but playing along.

"Please come in." Haworth stated as he led me inside his personal office. It's the kind of room that is purposely designed to make you feel inferior.

I took a seat at his command, a bit below him, on a plush nineteenth-century crimson chair, which looked across his massive mahogany desk. I had to shift myself to see him clearly past all his impressive credentials and a peculiar statue of a leopard attacking a man.

There he sat, draped in the finest linens of that bygone era. Like Daniel Day Lewis in *Gangs of New York*, Haworth is indeed a character of great magnitude.

He has this lean, gray-haired sophistication that's wrapped inside green eyes that dart into you.

I only spent a few minutes interviewing Haworth on my first visit to Uphir, before being escorted away. Speaking with him was a chess match more than a conversation. He interviewed me more than I did him. He wanted to know, what I was doing there? How did I find him? What did I truly want?

I played his game, but didn't get the answers I wanted out of him. I'm not sure if he got what he wanted out of me either.

I usually get something, some sort of clue that helps me unravel the real story. But this fellow is brilliant. He has that power of diversion where unconsciously the conversation always seems to tip in his favor.

About a week after my initial visit with him, I received a Minnesota Multiphasic Personality Inventory in the mail with instructions to return it to a PO box in Dell City.

This thing was about fifty pages with a few hundred yes-or-no questions, and it was highly repetitive, like a dumb-ass corporate job application.

Needless to say, I knew who it was from and what he wanted, so I filled out Haworth's MMPI and mailed it back to him.

Then three days ago I received an "open house" invitation to come to Uphir to cover his story. So here we were, face-to-face.

"Your papers, please," beckoned Dr. Haworth as he leaned back authoritatively in his chair. I placed my signed consent forms on his desk while he quietly observed me.

Ready to capture the moment, I pulled out my digital recorder and asked, "Do you mind if I turn this on?"

"Not at all," Haworth responded, acting colloquial, but I knew he had motives behind everything he said.

"Welcome to Uphir, Mr. Hansen," he continued. "During your stay, you may record when given permission and at no other time. Do you agree to this?"

"Sure," I told him, gaining the sudden realization that I had no other choice.

"Then let's begin," he replied, staring at me. As soon as I dropped eye contact, he picked up a pen and maneuvered his case file just out of my line of sight.

I turned on my recorder. "This is Eddie Hansen. It's Wednesday, December 8, 2010. I am at the Uphir Behavioral Health Center in Uphir, Texas, speaking with Dr. Alan Haworth."

"Correct," Haworth interrupted, making sure to control the conversation. "Edward Thomas Hansen," he bellowed. "You are of sound mind and body. You are currently not under the influence of medication, alcohol, or drugs. You enter this facility voluntarily and under your own free will. Is this true?"

"Yes," I replied, watching him read between my answers.

Haworth continued, "And you will submit to my procedures for your care during your stay here?"

"Yes."

Here's where the audio gets weird. Parts of my interview are not on this memory card. As I play back my recording, all I hear is hissing from this point on. Every once in a while, I hear this low rumble, and a muffled voice breaks through the static.

As I sat there with Haworth, I felt eyes on me. More than just the hundreds of cameras that seemed to be planted in every corner of the institution. There was a presence or a strong feeling that someone else was in the room with us. Maybe it was Rev. Billings watching, because about five minutes later, he came into the room fully informed of not just my conversation with Haworth, but of our past meeting and my present agenda with the Dobson case.

This guy spooked me. If Haworth was looking into me, Billings was looking through me. He looked more like a football player than some minister. He had this hulking stillness wrapped inside a pinstriped suit, which hung off him in direct defiance to the whole nineteenth-century theme Haworth had going on.

Rev. Billings looked as if he had seen it all and nothing was going to faze him. He was eyeballing me hard, trying to penetrate me deeper than my emotional or mental cognitive capacity. Billings was examining my essence, or "spirit man" as he called it.

I'll be honest; I was uncomfortable in that room with these two playing good cop, bad cop, dissecting my mind and spirit like it was a game.

Haworth said they needed a comprehensive assessment of my total being if I were to be allowed full access to this facility. From my childhood memories to my family medical history, they drilled me on it all.

Then Billings told me I would see and hear things that I wouldn't be able to explain or rationalize with my senses and that I needed to trust them and their procedures completely. Finally Haworth concluded that I must be fully prepared to protect myself in case of...

Protect myself? Seriously? I thought.

At that point I felt like slapping Haworth. His even-toned psychic probing of me was bashing my nerves, but I kept my cool as they continued interrogating me.

Sitting there, the lingering scent of sulfur burned through my nostrils, waking me to the fact that I needed to fight to maintain control of this situation and never let my guard down. So I began to dissect their strategies and formulate my plan to get the answers I needed to break this case.

I'm thinking, and stop me if I'm paranoid, that they have some sort of white-noise generator, like inside a military facility, to control any digital communication in and out of the facility, including my recordings. After about fifteen minutes of hearing this static, our conversation just came back as clearly as I remember it. My memory clenches to the subject matter as I listen to Rev. Billings speaking.

"The gateway to demonic forces is a thin veil covering a realm that influences most human beings," he told me. "Do you believe that a mere thought can act as a core element in the infiltration and possession of demonic hosts?"

"No," I answered firmly.

Then Dr. Haworth interjected with his air of superiority. "Would you care to elaborate, Mr. Hansen?"

"Not really," I told them. "I don't get myself crazy over this whole God-devil debate. I like to separate church and state, especially in a mental institution."

"But what if it's the place they come together?" Billings responded.

Seeming to know I wouldn't answer that, Haworth proceeded. "Mr. Hansen, would you say the core of evil is rooted in our experience, a chemical imbalance caused by instability in the world around us?"

"Maybe. Could be partially true," I responded, noticing Haworth purposely thumb through the file he created on me. He subtly revealed a picture of my ex-wife and daughter that seemed to accidentally slide out from under his file. A pulse of fury rushed through me.

He did his homework on me. He has the power to get that kind of information on my personal life, and I can't help but wonder what else he's dug up from my past. There I sat, his guinea pig. All I could do was smile and play along when he asked, "What's the worst evil you've ever committed?"

I know I had a response, but my recording just went static again. As I listen back, all I hear is a static buzz. Maybe it's the white noise, or they're trying to jam the frequency or modulate the sound, because now I hear this low, gravelly voice saying something. I can't make out the words. It doesn't sound like it's in English.

I just listened back to the recording a few times, trying to accurately define what I heard. It's difficult to decipher what this voice is communicating, so I broke the words into segments where the voice paused, and wrote it down.

"Ego Animo Habitant Quemadmodum Habitarunt Hoc Recording."

I have no idea what that means. Let's break that into smaller segments, maybe it will make sense.

Ego Animo Habitant.

Could be something about an animal, a habitat. Animal house? A living animal? Something like that.

Quemadmodum.

That sounds weird, but I'm sure that's what the voice said. I keep listening to the way it's spoken, fast and sharp.

Quemadmodum. Quemadmodum.

What is that? *Que* means "what" in Spanish. Maybe it's *what*? Mod modem? A modular modem? A listening device? I know they're listening to me.

Habitarunt. House. *Hoc Recording.* For recording.

An animal lives in this house or in this recording. Could that be right?

Is this a clue to something? Maybe it's just some software that garbles the frequency or pitch shifts it, creating this weird voice effect. I don't know, but I have a strong feeling this voice is trying to tell me something.

Where's Google Translate when you need it? Because the more I listen to this recording, the more this voice pierces through me. I can feel that voice resonate deep in my chest every time I listen.

It has some kind of power over me, like it's warning me, trying to communicate some vital message. Right after the voice finishes speaking "*Ego Animo Habitant Quemadmodum Habitarunt Hoc Recording*," the audio from my conversation with Haworth and Billings returns crystal clear.

I hear my own voice cracking with emotion. "I got him to the ground and kept kicking. In the head, chest, face. Blood was bouncing out of him with every shot."

I was telling Haworth and Billings about a fight I had back in college, in the woods behind campus. I remember it now. We were talking about the type of evil within us that allows us to do things that bypass through filters of our reasoning. What I'm talking about on this recording is part of that conversation.

Dr. Haworth kept pushing me, testing me. He kept trying to engage me, get me to go deeper and talk about the worst things I've ever done.

I clearly remembered the day of the fight. It was this unconscious recollection that surfaced as Haworth kept digging to my core.

After seeing the picture of my ex-wife, this adrenaline rushed through me, pounding me with thoughts.

I thought about Haworth playing games, prying into my personal life, trying to get the upper hand with every question.

This is my investigation, not his inquisition. But I let him push my buttons, explore my boundaries and gauge my reactions.

I had to stop looking at him because with every breath this rage within me grew. So I sat there and focused on the statue on his desk of the leopard attacking the man.

I pictured myself like that animal, ruthless and without conscience, destroying my victim. It all seemed to pour out of me as I recalled this long-forgotten attack.

I feel a swell of adrenaline pushing into my nerves again as I listen to myself on this recording.

"I kicked him, watching his face pop back. Then I went for his ribs. I felt my feet crack through him as his breath burst out. I wanted to keep going, but I stopped. I just stopped and watched him struggle to get air,"

"What stopped you, Eddie?" Billings inquired.

"I don't know… I just… The blood soaked into my shoes and I thought…"

"Go on," Billings chided. "We're almost there. What were you thinking?"

"I thought…maybe the cops would come. I don't know. I just... I just…needed to leave."

"Did you regret hurting another human?" Haworth asked.

"Yeah… No. I don't know. I didn't remember anything. It happened so quickly. He spit on me. Took a swing at me… I just…"

At that moment I was blank. I had opened myself up to these men and that set something off in Rev. Billings.

Billings got up and walked over to me and said, "Do you understand that this type of behavior may be the result of a demon working though you? You surrendered to his will, enabling his power over you."

"I don't believe that!" I laughed, not mockingly, just uncontrollably, which got Billings inflamed. He fired back.

"You stated that you had no self-control while fighting and you couldn't remember anything that happened."

"I was a kid. I was drinking. That's how we settled things!"

Then Dr. Haworth arrogantly assessed. "So was it a chemical reaction? A cerebral imbalance brought on by alcohol intoxication and external stress? An imbalance so intense and so acute that it would cause you to engage in unpredictable and violent behaviors?"

"It is what it is. Two drunk kids fighting over a girl. No devils, chemicals, or psychosis. Human nature!" I concluded.

I took a breath composing myself in the midst of their assault. I don't know why I felt so agitated, like a trapped animal being hunted.

Taking note of my response, Haworth continued his monotone assessment. "Do you often swear when you're upset, or is this part of your normal vernacular?"

"Is that another demon at work? Little Focker, the swear demon," I stated in my best Texas accent. "According to your ass-nalysis, he's working through me right now, huh? With all them devils looking for homes 'round here, you boys should be in the real estate business."

"I wish it were a joke, Eddie," Rev. Billings said, solemnly backing away from me.

Dr. Haworth continued taking notes as an unsettling silence engulfed the room. Finally Haworth looked up, stating coldly, "Mr. Hansen, we would like you to take a few tests now, along with some precautionary vaccinations."

I thought, there's no way I'm submitting myself to this. After more silence, Rev. Billings quietly excused himself, submerged in deep thought and perhaps a sense of disappointment in my answers.

Dr. Haworth casually leaned to me and shut off my recorder. Then the office door opened, revealing my security escorts.

JOURNAL ENTRY:
WEDNESDAY, DECEMBER 8, 2010 – 9:45 P.M.

I can't believe I spent three hours being tested like a lab monkey. Height. Weight. Blood pressure. All the usual shit, and I say that having provided my personal samples to the staff for review. If this is a pissing contest then Haworth got my first shot in a cup, ready for examination.

They're probably drug testing to see if I'm lying about using. I'm clean!

No stone was left unturned in there. I got the full physical with all the bells, coughs, and whistles.

At least one of the nurses was kind of hot. A young blonde in her mid-twenties. She didn't say a lot, but she helped pass the time, and it kept me from feeling anxious.

I'm not the type of person who likes being poked and prodded with needles and medical equipment, especially when it's against my will. I felt as though I was on display the whole time, a guinea pig being set up for a treadmill run.

I knew they were watching me to see how I'd react. It felt like my nurse was part of this experiment too, waiting for my reaction.

She'd do something ditsy, drop cotton balls, bend over, whisk her hair, laugh at my stupid jokes, then I'd catch her look over at one of the cameras. I didn't care because she was the only one with any semblance of a personality. Everyone else robotically attended to me as if I were a lab rat. At least she smiled.

Now my arm's sore and I feel woozy. I'm a little nauseous too. I feel like something's off.

Maybe it was the vaccinations. Or it could be that I'm starving and can't eat anything. They're forcing me to fast so they can take my blood in the morning. There's not even food in this place.

I'm shacked up in a little cottage about a half mile from the institution. I'm still officially on their property because I'm fenced in and the guard's gate is about a quarter mile up the road. It keeps me isolated from the madness of the facility.

You've got to see this décor, shabby-chic mystique. There's a leopard print blanket on this old iron bed, which looks like the patients put together because the cross is upside-down. The blood red pillows and sheet set are straight from the Martha Stuart Insanity Collection at K-Mart.

A deer head is mounted on the back wall with a beautiful hand-carved table below. The table has this bevel of circles going across, and each one has a little stone dot in the center, almost like an eyeball.

On top of the table is a crushed velvet liner and circle of black candles that surround a black bowl filled with herbs. Of course, no room is complete without an obligatory leopard statue.

Dr. Haworth must have this weird leopard obsession, because I see them everywhere. This one is bronze, sitting, staring at me. The more I look at it; the more it feels alive.

He looks like he's waiting for his prey. Observing me in a calm but powerful position, in total control. He's even watching me closely as I type. The more I look back at him, the more I feel like he's moving toward me ready to strike.

The most unusual part of this place is the only window looking out. It's shaped like a triangle and catches the glow of the lights from the institution.

You can see straight down Madness Avenue. I'm sitting, hidden inside these purple walls, desperate to entertain myself and escape my thoughts from this excruciating day.

But the ancient TV in here doesn't have cable. I can't even make any phone calls to the outside world. There's no cell reception, and the antique phone only connects to the guard gate or the receptionist in Ward A.

I do, however, have a vast array of psychology and religious books at my disposal, all tucked into a little bookcase, which has the same circled carvings as the table.

But I'm not in the mood to read. I want to chill out and watch Comedy Central. I need a laugh. I need something funny to knock me out of my anxious mind-set.

What back-ass town has no cable, no Internet, and no cell phone reception? The Beverly Hillbillies were more technically advanced than this primitive tribe of lunatics.

On the little counter of this kitchenette is an old boom box with a cassette player. It looks nostalgic. Let's see if it even works. I'll check the radio first. See what's out here…

Static… Static… Damn, I got nothing. No radio stations come in out here. Go figure.

Why would they even put a radio in here? Do they want me to know how isolated I am?

There's got to be something. Let's try the AM band. Still nothing…

Wait. Wait. I think we got something. 660 AM…

You got to hear this. It sounds like two hillbillies out in the woods killing something.

I'm getting my recorder. Listen…

"If you don't plan to mount the head, you got to keep cutting all the way to the hollow, fleshy junction of the neck and chest cavity."

"Short strokes right. I'm using my fingers to push that belly open as I cut, right?"

"Once most of the organs are exposed. Sever the diaphragm."

"Got it."

They're ripping the flesh open. The sound is nauseating. I think that animal may still be alive. I hear a sad, pained moan. There's another animal digging around. It may be a hunting dog.

I think they shot a deer. What the hell is that pounding?

"I use a camp axe to separate the rib cage and pelvis. Wedge the lower edge of the axe into the sternum, then pound the back of the hatchet with the sledge hammer."

That hick is pounding open the ribs. That sound is turning my stomach. I'm turning this off, taking a shower, and going to bed. I've had enough stimulation for one day.

"This is Eddie Hansen signing out from the Uphir Behavioral Center, December 8, 2010."

It's two AM. I can't sleep. My body feels agitated. My heart's pumping so fast I feel like I could have a heart attack. I'm not sure if it's my nerves, a panic attack, or something worse.

I feel something pulling on my heart, trying to rip it through my chest. It's a gnawing pull that won't let me rest. I'm trying to walk it out.

Looking out the triangle window at the institution, the moonlit glow makes this feel like I'm in some horror movie. Like some nut job will come busting in here any minute in a hockey mask or holding a chainsaw. It's surreal, this feeling. Everything is heightened, oversensitive.

Maybe that's why I can't sleep. Self-preservation, my instinct is taking over before Freddy comes in my dream.

I have a feeling they're watching me. I never feel alone in here. I already did a clean sweep for hidden cameras, took down the mirror, checked the deer head, the lamps, the clock. I didn't find anything.

But I'm going to type instead of recording anything until I know it's clear. I don't want to give them the upper hand on what I'm thinking or doing.

I've got to give them credit for trying to rattle me. The Reverend even left a Bible in the top drawer of the nightstand like a cheap motel. He personally inscribed it:

> *"To Eddie. <u>My words are spirit and life</u>.*
> *Use them and live. John 6:63"*

What's that supposed to mean? Is this a warning? Is he threatening me?

The good minister also took the liberty to highlight in yellow more verses about demons.

I noticed this as I looked for that John 6:63 reference. This one is a couple of pages after that verse. Page 1,898 in this book. He highlighted this:

"At these words the Jews were again divided. Many of them said, "He is <u>demon</u>-possessed and raving mad. Why listen to him? But others said, "These are not the sayings of a man possessed by a <u>demon</u>. Can a <u>demon</u> open the eyes of the blind?"

He underlined *demon* each time in pen. Feeling curious, I continued thumbing ahead to see what other clues he left me.

The next one is on page 2,077. 1 Corinthians 10. He's got verses 20-21 circled"

"No, but the sacrifices of pagans are offered to <u>demons</u>, not to God, and I do not want you to be participants with <u>demons</u>. You cannot drink the cup of the Lord and the cup of <u>demons</u> too; you cannot have a part in both the Lord's table and the table of <u>demons</u>."

Let's figure this out. In this story, someone is demon possessed and raving mad? But people around him are divided to what his problem is. There are two sides to every story, right? Arguing opposite points about demon possession.

Could this be Billings and Haworth?

Both men keep trying to get me to see their side of the story, this argument they are presenting or maybe even experimenting with. Is Annette Dobson the sacrifice? Could she be the subject of this debate? That's it!

"THE GREAT DEBATE."

Picture this. The minister and the psychologist, puppeteers of humanity, squaring off over Annette Dobson!

If she is here, why is she here? What do they want from her? What's the subject of their experiment?

"What's the worst thing you've ever done?"

That's what comes to my mind. Haworth asked me that yesterday. He and Billings were so intent on exploring my dark side, crawling into my head to find the worst things inside me.

What creates evil in me? Evil! That is our common denominator. So that must be our theme!

"The Core of Evil!"

They ping-ponged this off my head all day. We spoke of unrestrained violence, fits of rage, and outbursts of passion. The things we do so easily without thinking or remorse.

So what's the catch? What's their motive?

To find the origin, the core of evil? To discover its birth! I think that's it! Follow my reasoning.

Annette Dobson was supposedly twenty-four weeks pregnant when she had her abortion before the execution, but no one really knew. The right-to-life protestors were enraged, but since the court ruled it legal, no one could do anything about it.

Public sentiment was against Annette Dobson, so when she makes this plea to have her execution moved up, no one asks any questions. It's what the people wanted. Slay the monster! But to quell any controversy and hide her pregnancy, her execution needed to be closed.

Why?

If whoever is behind this can keep the media out, there's no trace of her body. No trace of a baby. They send her husband some ashes, a few personal items and a handwritten letter explaining everything, and this case has closure. No one looks for anything.

We're satisfied. Justice was served. A few weeks later people move on to the next monster.

So they remove Mrs. Dobson from prison and ship her here, where she can be forced to give birth. This is the perfect case study for this asylum. That kid has the blood of a stone cold killer. How is he going to react to that? Is he a natural-born killer or an innocent baby? An ANGEL or DEMON?

Dr. Haworth wants his mind. Rev. Billings wants his spirit. They can raise him any way they want without question. They can influence him. Study him. Mutilate him if they want to. He's nothing more than a lab rat because he doesn't exist. He's got no birth certificate. No social security number. Out here, no one would ever find him. No one would ever look. Except me!

If there's a chance in hell I'm right, then Annette Dobson is here, and she's about thirty-eight weeks pregnant. So the baby is due in a week or two. Which means—

VIDEO LOG:
THURSDAY, DECEMBER 9, 2010 – 2:13 A.M.

"Somebody's out here. I saw someone run past my window when I was typing, so I grabbed my camera and ran outside.

"This place is freaky… Damn it's cold. Sorry, you can't see shit here in these woods. Until we get down the hill. See the lights. That's the asylum in front. The medical ward is to the left down the road. Housing wards are on the right.

"Listen… Hear that weird droning noise. It's
pulsating, like a heartbeat, like the building is
groaning. I think it's coming from behind the medical
ward. I'll go over and—"
"Stop! Don't move. Hands up! Hands up! Up!
Turn!"

I turn and see this pudgy Mexican kid about twenty years old,
wearing a security uniform. He shines a flashlight in my eyes.

"Put it down! Down!"
"Okay. It's just a camera."

I set my camera down. As I duck under the light I can see that
he has a gun under his flashlight. He's shaking. He's nervous.

"Put it down. Step away. I'll shoot! I'll shoot!"
"Okay. Okay. It's down."

He slowly movies toward me with the gun pulled, stuttering.

"Hands. Hands! Who…who are you? Why you
here?"
"I'm Eddie Hansen. I'm a guest of Dr. Haworth."
"No. No. Nobody told me at the gate. You got no
permission."
"I got my badge, my ID, right—"

I reach for my wallet. He cocks the trigger.

"Step back! I—"
"It's in that guest house. Up there. My ID.
Everything's there!"

His face turns ghost white, shaking in disbelief.

"No! No. Nobody goes there. For five years. Nobody."

I try to gauge him, but he's too antsy. Finally, I make a friendly move to pick up my camera, but he fires his gun into the air warning.

"No! Hands up. You can't tape nothing!"
"Dr. Haworth agreed. I'm here working on his story."

He stares at me for a second, wanting to believe. Then he carefully picks up my camera still pointing his gun at me.

"Nobody said… You follow rules. Nothing without permission. Nobody. Never!"

JOURNAL ENTRY:
THURSDAY, DECEMBER 9, 2010 – 4:30 A.M.

Lesson #1

If you ever want to be seen again, never walk around a mental institution without credentials. I learned this from Santiago, the night security guard whom I had the pleasure of just meeting.

While I was writing my last journal entry, I saw someone run past my window. It freaked me out, so I went outside to take a look.

It was Santiago. Nice guy, but not the sharpest tool in the shed. Maybe he's smarter than me, because I'm not sure if he was messing with my head or being serious. He's got this nervous tick in his eye, and he shudders every few minutes, like a Chihuahua in the snow.

His whole vibe is off. On our whole walk back here, he had this friendly but agitated demeanor. About every fifty feet he would stop and take a deep breath, like he was asthmatic, but when I confronted him, he said he was good.

Then we get to the door and he freezes. It took me a minute to catch on because I was looking for my badge. When I found it I called over, but he was staring at the floor with this intense glare. Completely still, frozen there, shivering.

I told him to come in. It felt like a minute before he finally blurted out, "The last guy that was here killed himself! Right there." Santiago said this pointing at the very bed I'm typing in now.

Apparently, suicide boy ripped the cross off the bedpost and gutted his throat with the pointed end before he bled himself out on the bed. The stains soaked into the wood floor are supposed to be his blood.

I couldn't tell if it was an act or not. Before scurrying away, Santiago nervously mentioned that this room would make me "loco."

That's "crazy" for us gringos. This room has the power of the demon Ozzy or Ose, or something like that. I couldn't tell by his accent, but that demon is assigned to rule here. Santiago said he's not supposed to tell me this. He begged me not to mention anything to Dr. Haworth.

So is this a coincidence, or is this the same little devil Aida Mae, my psychic waitress, was rambling about in Dell City? Maybe it's all a setup.

What I need to do is figure out how to get information on Annette Dobson. When I mentioned her name to Santiago, all I got was a blank stare and stupid shiver. The same came with the mention of any pregnant woman.

He's seen nothing. That's his story.

It's almost 5:00 a.m. I've got to get some sleep. Good night, faithful readers.

שלי היא שלך הנשמה

JOURNAL ENTRY:
THURSDAY, DECEMBER 9, 2010 – 7:00 A.M.

Don't ask me what that symbol writing thing above is. I have no idea. I left my computer on. I think I hit a keyboard key or something before falling asleep. Maybe the font changed. I was so wound up and exhausted, I thought I turned it off. Anyway, I left that up there just in case it means something.

I want to make sure everything I type, say, or find is accurately recorded. I want clarity to my investigation. I promise not to leave anything out.

I have to go get my blood work done now. They are really working me over here, maintaining total control and to get this story I reluctantly consented to testing.

My reward for this: I finally get to eat! Breakfast is at eight over at the nuthouse cafeteria. Then I'm off to a meeting with Rev, Billings, a facility tour, and I cap my day off with another visit with Dr. Haworth.

It should be an eventful day. I'll keep you plugged in.

AUDIO LOG:
THURSDAY, DECEMBER 9, 2010 – 8:05 A.M.

"Good morning, Uphir Behavioral. It's Eddie Hansen. Thursday, December 9th, five after eight this beautiful morning. I'm sitting in the cafeteria eating breakfast with some new friends. Donald here told how much he loves my recorder. He wants to say something. So buddy, tell us how you're doing here?"

Donald laughs in this weird maniacal tone, and then slowly lowers his head into his cereal bowl. His eyes peer up at me, making contact, but he's disconnected from reality, looking through me with this smarmy grin.

"Listen real close. Hear it?"
"Do I hear what?" I ask.
"Quiet! You need to listen."

Donald touches his ear to the bowl. The other patient at the table giggles. I guess his name is Rudy, or they call him that because he looks like that guy in the movie *Rudy*.

"Quiet, Rudy! Everyone. Quiet! Shhh! He's talking. Keeeeeeee. Keeeeeeee. Pop. Pop. Pop... Pop. Pop. Pop. They're all talking."

I lean in to give Donald attention as if the possibility of talking cereal existed. He twists his head around the bowl.

"They call me every morning. They snap, crackle, and pop, but sometimes they tell me secrets."
"Okay." I tell Donald before he snaps back up in his chair. His eyes flutter. This unsettling vibe crawls over my skin.

"I know your secret!" Donald says as his body contorts into a distorted position awaiting my response.

"Really?"
"Yes... Listen. Snap. Crackle. Snap... Oh. That's bad."

Rudy leans over the table, sniffs the bowl, teasing:

"Oh. That's bad!"
"Tell me, Donald," I respond.

Donald closes his lips tightly, twisting his head with a grunt. A fiendish voice spews out that's not quite his own.

"Edward Thomas Hansen. Grandma called you ET, but you didn't like it; 'cuz you were scared of aliens. You thought they touched you funny, but that was Mr. Greeley, your science teacher. I made him do it. I made him…touch you!"

"Mr. Greeley touched you. Mr. Greeley touched you, "Rudy laughs. Mr. Greeley touched you."

"He always listened to me," Donald calmly states before taking a bite of his cereal.

I calmly get up noticing the security guards eyeing me. As I excuse myself from the table, Donald innocently asks in his own voice:

"Where you going, Eddie? Don't you want to eat Crispies with Ose and me?"

JOURNAL ENTRY:
THURSDAY, DECEMBER 9, 2010 – 8:15 A.M.

I just listened to my recording again. Before I meet Rev. Billings, I need to get this off my chest. I'm not erasing that recording because I said I'd be honest with my investigation, and anything may be a clue. So I guess I have to deal with everything that happens to me here, right? I just have to deal with it. So let's deal with it! I only have one question.

How?

How could Donald have known about Greeley or my Grandma calling me ET? Who set me up? How far could Haworth pry into my private life?

I never talked to anyone, ever! I never, not once, ever talked about my abduction! Not to my parents, schoolteachers, friends, girlfriends, priest. No one. EVER!

I feel a lot of things "bubbling up" inside me, for lack of any better words. My whole body is pulsating with:

Hate! Rage! Pain! Shame! Guilt!
I feel violated! I feel helpless! I feel violent!

You know how many times I fantasized about killing Greeley? Taking a knife and ripping out everything he stole from me? Son of a bitch pervert took advantage of an innocent kid.

I was eight. Only eight years old and even now, I still smell that Old Spice and feel those wet, clammy hands that started sweating with excitement after that door clicked shut. I still hear that rattling air conditioner drowning out his demented moan.

And I see the chalk dust dancing in the air. It didn't want to fall to earth and feel that cold, hard floor. It just wanted to be free and float in the sunlight, fly out the window into the playground and laugh with the other children and forget about the fact that it became chalk dust because it was crushed.

Crushed against that blackboard.
Crushed against that wall.
Crushed against its will.
Crushed in the hands of a monster, until it wasn't even chalk anymore!

AUDIO LOG:
THURSDAY, DECEMBER 9, 2010 – 8:30 A.M.

"This is Eddie Hansen. I'm with Rev. William Billings. I have permission to tape this interview."
"Yes. You seem a bit disconnected, Eddie,"
Billings says, taking a long hard look into me.
"I'm fine. How long have you been here, Reverend?"

"Since September of 2009. Let me ask you, Eddie. Do you believe the Bible is true?"

"I'm asking the questions, Rev. It's my interview, right?"

"All right, Eddie. Go ahead."

"Why are you here?"

"To seek the truth."

"Good. Me too."

"Good."

"Then you believe the Bible is true?"

"Why's that matter?"

The irritation of his piousness seeps into my skin.

"Because you chose to enter into a world, or more carefully put, enter into a spiritual dimension that is experiencing warfare. And you are not equipped to be on the field, much less fight in this battle."

"If I were you, I'd be the one who was worried. People know why I'm here and have proof to back my theory about Annette Dobson. If she's here, you're the chicken cooking in shit stew."

Rev. Billings stands up, taking a deep breath. It isn't a nervous breath, but a patient one. He's trying to get me to see his point, but I'm not the type who gets brainwashed by preachers and politicians. He turns to me and calmly explains.

"Eddie, you have to understand that human beings in the mental, emotional, and spiritual state of Mrs. Dobson require care which is not yet recognized by the state or federal municipalities. In the process of regulating such alternative therapies, there is a certain amount of testing and research needed to prove beyond a shadow of a doubt these treatments are safe and effective."

"So she's here."

I'm wising up to the fact that I'm on to something big.

"People *like* Mrs. Dobson," Billings interjects.

Billings isn't giving weight to my inquiry as he continues.

>"Nothing will be held back from you. But I need to make sure that you are safe under my care."
>"Safe from what?"
>"Demonic oppression, or in a worst case scenario, possession."
>"I am possessed. Possessed with the desire to find the truth."
>"And the truth shall set you free."

Billings leans toward me so I can see the intensity in his eyes.

>"'For our struggle is not against flesh and blood, but against the rulers, against the authorities, against the powers of this dark world and against the spiritual forces of evil in the heavenly realms.'"
>"Harry Potter?"
>"The apostle Paul, actually. He wrote that in Ephesians chapter six, verse twelve. I suggest you read the chapter. He was a man very much like you, Eddie. He didn't want to believe, but God had a way of revealing His truth."

I remain calm. I get up, scanning the room.

>"God... That's what you believe."
>"Because of what I've experienced," Billings replies. "And what you will experience will alter your life too."

"Will it? Then let's videotape this life-changing event." No! Wait. I can't because my camera was hijacked at gunpoint by one of your security guards last night."

"I'm sorry about that," Billings replies sincerely. "We'll get it for you. Follow me."

VIDEO LOG:
THURSDAY, DECEMBER 9, 2010 – 3:12 A.M.
RECEIVED BY MELODY SWANN

This is Melody Swann. In the process of compiling Eddie's story from these logs, I received this video file dated December 9, 2010, 3:12 a.m. that I'm about to transcribe.

A package was mailed to me at Eddie's address. The note inside said from, "A Friend," so I don't think this came from Eddie.

Inside this package was a compact flash drive containing the video file. Eddie asked me to arrange all these entries by date and time for this book so it would go here. I will add my notes.

The camera is on, but it's really dark, pitch black. I can't see anything, but hear something moving. The camera is rattling. I hear water dripping. Now a voice speaking with a Spanish accent.

"This Santiago. I want everyone see this. I can't take no more. Listen, you hear the woman. Crying, screaming. Someone hurts her, bad. Sometimes many people, yell, fight, speak crazy in other language. I don't tell what they say"

I think he's in a tunnel or a basement. I see a large iron door in front of him. It's sealed shut. He's breathing really heavy. He's nervous.

"This is far as you go with no keys. Listen."

I hear it! I hear a woman screaming. It's awful. She sounds like she's being tortured.

"Hear. You hear?"

There's a gurgling noise, like something sick or growling. The camera's shaking. I see a dark shadow. Something I can't tell what's there, but I don't think that guy sees it. He's backing away from the door. The camera is shaking.

It moved! Something leaped out at him. The camera spun fast. The man's running, freaking out, screaming. The camera bangs off the stairwell. He runs up the stairs, crashes through the door. He falls and knocks the camera over.

I only see his leg. His pant leg, it's ripped open. It looks like a claw mark or a big bite. Something tore into him good. It's bleeding badly. He's in pain. I don't think he can move.

"Help! Please. Jesus, please!"

His leg is shaking. Blood's pouring out. He drags himself toward the camera.

"I promise. I promise. I never go here. God, please, help me"

I hear something clawing the grass. It sounds like a wolf or a leopard. I can't tell what kind of an animal, what that is. That guy is still lying on the ground, not moving.

"Jesus. Please! I don't want to die!"

I hear something. A voice. It said something. Oh my God, I think that animal said something.

The camera is shaking. That thing must have picked it up. It's moving across the field fast. That's it. The camera broke or dropped. That's the end of the tape. That was freaky. Why did they send this to me?

Why do they want me to see this?

That voice. I heard it say Hansen. Something about Eddie. I need to write down what that voice said. It could be important.

Something in my heart says write this down. That voice on the tape felt sinister. It wasn't English, except for the word Hansen. I'm playing it back. *"Avatar Hansen Key O Say E C."*

That's what it sounds like when I play the video back. I feel sick. My stomach's churning. I'm listening again. This could be important.

That was weird. I felt pressure on my fingers as I tried to type. *Avertir Hansen que*

I never felt anything like this. So much pressure on me. Like my thoughts or these voices are telling me this, moving my fingers across the keyboard, like a Ouija board. I want to stop but I can't. *"Avertir Hansen que Jose."* It's like the universe is trying to tell me this. Is this Spanish? That guy was Spanish! Maybe he's trying to tell Eddie something. I feel more pressure on my hands to finish. It's doesn't want me to write any...

I'm going to close my eyes and give in- *"Avertir Hansen qui Ose est ici."*

As soon as I wrote that down, I felt relieved. I can't describe it. Like I burst out from under water. My head was pounding. My heart was pumping. I could barely breathe. But these words released me.

"Avertir Hansen qui Ose est ici."

JOURNAL ENTRY:
THURSDAY, DECEMBER 9, 2010 – 12:30 P.M.

Some idiot busted my camera. My six-hundred-dollar lens is cracked, and there's a big dent in the back. We couldn't even get it turned on. Plus I can't find my flash card with my recordings.

I got no answers from the security guys, and Santiago hasn't picked up the phone at the gate. So I don't know the real story.

Rev. Billings got called into some emergency meeting that was hush-hush. There was no way they were letting me tag along.

He rescheduled my tour, which was fine with me because it gave me some time to leave the asylum and explore the surrounding area.

There are a few isolated cabins out here off Williams Road before you get to Route 180. Most are lined with deer pelts, skinned and hung like Christmas ornaments to welcome in the holiday season.

It looks like there's no running water out here and limited electricity in most areas. So I'm not sure I want to meet my neighbors, though I think I may have heard them on the radio last night.

Dell City looks good now, and that's about thirty-two miles away. Add another seventy-four to get to El Paso, which looks like the only place I can get my camera fixed, and I'm a long way from getting anything done today.

I'm 908 miles from my former life and I need this story. I can't afford to fail. I need a game changer. But for some reason, the only thing that pops into my head is failure.

I could picture every colossal screw-up in my life as I drove down that empty dirt road back here.

First it was my wreck of a marriage. I knocked up Jamie when she was twenty-one. I was twenty-five, barely surviving as a copywriter, slugging out descriptions of health products by day and playing in a cover band on weekends.

By the time my daughter Kennedy was five, Jamie and I were night and day. She wanted stability. I wanted sanity. If I spent another day extolling the virtue of lotus seed and papaya enzyme, I would go postal and she knew it.

But living in Los Angeles with a kid, I didn't have time for my dreams, much less a family. I was working nights too, writing copy for a pharmaceutical company to make ends meet. It seemed like we never had enough.

The first three years are the toughest with a kid, and we were not doing well. Jamie barely talked to me, and if she did, it was just ordering me to do something. Every time I looked into her eyes, all I could see was resentment, disappointment, and unmet expectations.

Nothing I did could be enough to make her happy. It felt like she gave up on us.

I heard voices in my head constantly telling me she hated me, that we had nothing. And nothing would ever be the way it was when we were in love.

I couldn't find anything to fill that void. I felt like the Walking Dead. I couldn't live another day like this. So I quit my shit jobs when I got this offer to do some investigative reporting.

It was exciting and dangerous. It made me feel alive, worthy of something. I got some tough cases too, and began to make a name for myself. I was good at this, and I was finally making decent money for once in my life without hating life.

But the better I felt, the worse Jamie got. Now I was putting my family in jeopardy. I was irresponsible, dangerous, addictive, an adrenaline junkie.

When I went undercover to expose child drug runners in the inner city, Jamie went ape shit. She nearly blew my cover, and we never had a moment of peace from that day on.

One night I got fed up fighting with her and took off to a local bar for a few hours. I had to get away from her, from everything, before we did something we'd both regret.

Next thing I knew, the cops pulled me over on the way home.

To make a long story short, Kennedy had fallen off her swing set that morning. Jamie took pictures when I was out. Then she beat herself, took some drugs I had stashed as evidence in my investigation, spread them around the apartment, and called the cops.

She made up the whole story about my abuse, and somehow got the court to believe her.

Jamie took custody of Kennedy while I was in prison. She got remarried to this vineyard owner, Scott Davis, your wine guide to Temecula. He's a total douche bag. He's even got those cheesy-ass business cards with his shit-eating grin on the front.

Anyway, she moved my family out there. Now I haven't seen my daughter in over four years. They figured it was better for Kennedy to have a stable family without me in the picture. So I'm the odd man out.

I look around at these patients. I could be one step away from being them. Who isn't?

When one bad thing happens after another, what's the one thing that finally breaks us? What's the tipping point?

I feel like I'm boiling inside. My body feels hot, and it's probably twenty degrees outside and sixty in here. I took my sweater off, but I'm still sweating.

Here comes Billings to take me into the big show.

JOURNAL ENTRY:
THURSDAY, DECEMBER 9, 2010 – 1:05 P.M.

I really need Internet service here, because I swear I'm staring at Timothy Nathan Tyler. I'm on the other side of a two-way mirror getting ready to record this group therapy session, and I'm staring right at him. I'm staring at Tyler.

Billings was afraid the patients would feel uncomfortable if I was present in the room recording them.

He told me that I may "enter when given permission," but I can't bring anything inside with me. I'm going to be introduced as a new patient. I think that's better for me because I'll be able to gain their trust and get information more easily.

If this guy is Tyler, then I am looking at a ghost. According to the Texas Department of Criminal Justice, Timothy Nathan Tyler is Executed Offender #363, with the date of execution registered June 6, 2006. That's right – 6/6/6.

It's not the date that freaked me out as much as the "last statement" from Tyler. It was never published.

But I got the audio recording of it from the prison guard who took the statement, Renaldo Gonzalez.

Renaldo is the man I asked Aida Mae about. He tipped me off to this whole investigation. He brought me Tyler's last statement tape in May of 2010.

Renaldo was scared, but he felt "convicted," as he put it, to do the right thing, because it was going to happen again. He told me he was "praying," and God gave him my name. God told him about me… Please!

I had to follow through on this just to appease my sense of humor and morbid curiosity. So I listened to the tape.

"Don't worry, Mama. You know I'm already dead, but I'm being resurrected tonight. Ose is taking my soul. He'll let me live as long as I do what he says. I'm gonna make it back to you. And take care of you the way I should have. I love you, Mama. So stay strong until I return. Love, Timothy."

Gonzalez swore to its authenticity. It seemed like Tyler's voice. Gonzalez even confessed this whole conspiracy to me. He said that Tyler's death was staged, and they were going to ship him out of the prison.

Guess where? Uphir! The town that doesn't exist. It makes perfect sense with Aida Mae seeing prison trucks. Renaldo Gonzalez wasn't sure where Uphir was because they had a driver who wouldn't talk for fear of his life.

Gonzalez had an idea of the general area based on some phone calls he overheard and information he dug up.

So he and I took a trip, but never found anything. We weren't even close to here, so I figured he was lying and gave up on the story.

Then the first week of September, Gonzalez comes to me a second time insisting he's got a good tip on the location and wants to check it out with me. I declined. That was the last I heard from him.

He disappeared off the face of the earth, and the investigation of his disappearance slowly faded from the headlines. After rummaging through his place, I found where he had hidden a handwritten note with the name Dr. Alan Haworth, a few photos, and a map of this area.

Then in early October, Kevin Dobson came to me upset about his wife's request. "It's an uncharacteristic change," he said.

Coming from the guy who didn't know his wife murdered six of their kids, I didn't put much stock into uncharacteristic. But after reviewing news clips and doing a little investigative research, I found this.

Every few years going back to 1982 when the death penalty was reinstated, someone's record slipped through the cracks. Paperwork was missing, there was an accidental cremation, some mistake was made filing the case, or complaints were filed by family members with suspicion of misconduct. Nothing seemed highly unusual until you put all the pieces together and could see the pattern. It piqued my interest, so I followed up on this lead.

Following Gonzalez's tip, I found Uphir and made my first uninvited visit. Trying to get into this fortress was difficult, but when I mentioned Haworth's name, the guard at the gate called in.

When I mentioned Renaldo Gonzalez to Haworth, the gates opened. I didn't get to see much that visit. Haworth kept me at a distance, and we chatted in the main lobby for a few minutes.

When I mentioned I was a reporter, I could hear his breath shorten. He danced around clearances being needed to enter the facility and proper channels of authorization; consent and disclosure regarding information I might want.

When I mentioned Timothy Nathan Tyler, I guess that's what stirred the cauldron, and my hint of Annette Dobson visiting probably warranted my official invite.

So if this is Tyler I'm looking at, then the good doctor wants me to see him. Tyler's tattooed neckline is a very distinct calling card, and his eyes are unmistakably cold. In fact, he's frozen like a corpse, sitting straight up, barely breathing, locked in a straitjacket with his legs in restraints.

He's so stiff you'd swear he's dead. He hasn't moved in at least five minutes.

I think they're doing some weird ritual. Everyone looks catatonic in there.

Three of them are in the room with Billings.

Next to Tyler is that freak Donald from breakfast, rocking back and forth rhythmically, murmuring to himself.

And finally there is this skinny old lady. She reminds me of the lady in that Wendy's commercial, "Where's the beef?" It would take a cattle prod to snap her ass back to life.

She is actually the most disturbing to look at. Her eyes are wide open. She hasn't blinked in over a minute, and there's no emotion on her face at all. She's completely in another world. I seriously have to go in and get a gander at this freak show. I'll turn this speaker up and put my recorder next to it and hop into the fun.

> "Test one, two. Test one, two. This is Eddie Hansen getting ready to join the cast of *Trancing with the Stars*!"

AUDIO LOG:
THURSDAY, DECEMBER 9, 2010 – 1:35 PM
RECEIVED BY MELODY SWANN:

This is the first audio recording I received from Eddie on December 13. It came a few days after our first phone conversation. I will add descriptive notes as needed.

PLEASE NOTE: I took this recording to the Beverly Hills Lingual Institute for translation and to verify the accuracy of the transcript.

A door slams shut. Footsteps cross the room. Someone's moaning like they're in a lot of pain. Another door just creaked open. I hear a man's voice.

> "Quiet. Sit down. You were supposed to wait."
> "Why are we whispering, Rev?" Eddie asks.
> "They are in a deep meditative state. It's dangerous if they come out of this improperly. Stay quiet. Sit here and observe. Please don't move."

It's silent except for these snorts and moans coming from various places. Some sound sadistic. Some sexual. Some painful. It's been going on about a minute. A woman with a raspy voice says something. She isn't speaking English. She sounds like she's dying.

>   *"Gnorízoume o énas ton állon."*
>   "What was that?" Eddie asks.
>   "She's speaking Greek," the minister responds.
>   "What'd she say?"
>   "She said, 'We know each other.'"
>   "What?"
>   *"Íê moun maz sas ótan* Jamie *aristerá,"* the old
> lady groans.
>   "Feel free to translate," Eddie tells the minister.
>   "'I was with you when Jamie left.'"
>   "Excuse me?" Eddie interrupts.
>   *"Sto motél éxi sto San Ntiénko,"* the old lady
> continues.
>   "'At the Motel 6 in San Diego,'" the minister tells
> Eddie.
>   *"Nomízate óti tha érthei píso se sas."*
>   "You thought she would come back to you."
>   *"Allá eseís me epélexe."*
>   "But you chose me."

Something screeches across the floor, then bangs hard against the wall. I hear the minister.

>   "Sit down! Eddie, you have to respect them!
> We're not dealing with flesh, here. Watch carefully."

Something clangs in his hands.

>   "Gloria. May I speak with Gloria?"
>   *"Den,"* says that creepy voice.

"I want to speak with Gloria."

"Den! To ónomá mou eínai Achlys."

"She said, 'No! My name is Achlys,'" the minister tells Eddie.

"Eímai dystychía."

"I am misery."

"Sýntrofós sas, Eddie.*"*

"'Your companion, Eddie.'"

"Aftó pou agapáte."

"'The one you love.'"

"Fuck you," Eddie yells.

"Eddie!"

The minister pauses before speaking to the old woman:

"I want to speak with Gloria."

"Den!" she replies, spitting.

The minister yells, "Achlys. *Sto ónoma tou Iisoú, anachoroún apó aftín."*

That was the most disturbing sound I've ever heard. A sick shriek that ran right through me like acid. I just heard this disturbing, flapping noise, like a bird. But it's in my room as I play back this file. It's the same noise on the tape, but it feels like it's in here.

"The demon left her. She's circling. Feel the room change?" the minister asks Eddie. "Feel the air? It's dry. Arid. It's void of spiritual substance. Achlys can't survive like this. She's looking for a home. A mind to feed on. Gloria!"

"Yes," she answers with an expressionless voice.

"Who are you?" commands the minister.

"Gloria Casey King."

My laptop shook. I feel this pulse in the air. Some kind of energy, maybe a power surge.

> "Feel that, Eddie?" the Reverend asks.
> "What?"
> "She's hovering over you."

I feel something in this room with me. Hovering over me. Watching me listen to this recording. I want to turn it off. But I can't. I don't know what that minister is doing, but I wish he'd stop. His voice is calm, but it terrifies me. Something is moving through me.

> "May I speak with Donald?" the Reverend asks.
> "Yes," says another voice.
> "Who are you?" the minister commands.
> "Donald Allen Lambeck."

That man, Donald, he's older. His voice is slow and choppy. Something is moving, flapping around.

> "May I speak with Timothy?"
> "Yes," says another voice.

He sounds demented, growling like a rabid animal.

> "Who are you?" the minister asks.
> "Timothy Nath— *aaaaa...*"

He gasps for air. Like someone's choking him. It's deep and guttural. Demented. His voice is rushing down my spine. I feel it penetrating me as he moans.

> "Kennedy *den sas leípei.*"

My hair stands on end. I feel his voice right behind me in this room, ripping through me. My body is tightening. I feel pain burning through my chest.

"Kennedy *chreiázetai éna pragmatikó patéra*."
"What'd you say about Kennedy?" Eddie fumes. "What the fuck did he say?"
"She said. It's Achlys talking through him," says the minister.
"Tell me what he said or I'll beat it out of him," Eddie orders.
"Kennedy doesn't miss you. Kennedy needs a real father."

There's a moment of silence, then I hear that voice hiss.

"Kai Scott *eínai ó, ti den eínai."*
"'And Scott is everything you are not,'" the minister translates.
"Den boreíte na deíte. Den agapás."
"Can't you see? We don't love you."
"Thé loume eseís dont sti zo í mas."
"We don't want—"
"Want you in our life!"

Eddie screams back, finishing the minister's sentence with a storm of violence. I hear screaming, fighting, shrieking like an animal being attacked, struggling to breathe. That minister is yelling in Greek. Something broke.

"Stop! Eddie, stop!" he yells.

The door bursts open. Someone grabbed Eddie. He's furious.

"Let go. Let go of me. I'll kill you. I'll fucking kill you!"

The minister is praying, mumbling something. He's not speaking English. They drag Eddie out. The door slams shut. That's it. That's the end of the tape.

But I hear that voice. The old lady, the Greek voice. She's talking to me. Saying something in Greek. The same words over and over. The same Greek words. It's not coming from the computer. Her voice, I think it's in here, in the room with me. I feel it.

Stop! Stop!.

She won't stop repeating the same thing.

No one's going to believe me. Am I hearing things or is this real? I'm taking out my phone. I'll record what I hear; I'm just going to say it.

As soon as I did, the voice was gone. When I took my recording in for translation, this is what came back.

> *"Egó eímai o Theós tou myaloú sas tha Eímai pánta mazí sas."*

It translates to, *"I am the god of your mind. I will always be with you."*

Why did you get me involved in your crazy shit Eddie? I don't want to do this anymore!

JOURNAL ENTRY:
THURSDAY, DECEMBER 9, 2010 – 4:33 P.M.

Guess where they put me? Seclusion! I'm waiting for someone to let me out. It's disgusting in here. This is the kind of place where you really can go crazy, so I'm writing to keep my mind off everything.

Haworth told me if I touch anyone again, I could become a patient here against my will. The sad part is, I think I may be at their mercy.

I signed away consent and liability. I screwed myself. I should have thought about my escape route better. I'm in a self-contained town with no police, no contact with the outside world and an hour drive for help.

By foot in this cold, it's probably a day's walk. And at night the temperature drops below freezing.

When the dust settles, if I get out of here, I'm taking off to Dell City to check in with Melody. I need to send her my tapes and email these notes. Then I'm going to El Paso to get my camera fixed. I don't trust making phone calls from Dell City anymore.

I know they listen to everything. They have complete control out here. And they're playing with me. The demonic circus act scared the shit out me. They all looked possessed. But they probably rehearsed that all, a one-act play presented by the Haworth Theater Company.

The last hour I've been replaying that whole scene in my head and these guys did their homework. They probably found my divorce records filed online, got credit card statements and followed up on Jamie's new last name from her marriage license. Almost anything can be public record on the Internet if you pay enough money. If anyone knows that, it's me. And yet, I still fell for it.

The only thing that really bothers me is how Tyler said exactly what Jamie told me in the hotel room five years ago.

That's what put me over the edge. It was the way he said it, just like her, with the same inflection, the same disdain she vomited to me with those exact words, "We don't want you in our life."

I felt that moment of complete emptiness again. Like someone was pulling my heart out of my chest and holding it mockingly in front of my face.

How Jamie got complete custody and used my DUI to seal it shut was heartless. The woman I loved for so long suddenly had this disdain for me and took away the only person who gave me unconditional love.

I know Scott was in on it. He was so jealous of me. He was never going to be daddy with me in the picture. She probably doesn't even know that I'm aware she had another kid with him last year.

Now they're the perfect little family. That pisses me off! I can't stop thinking about them. A couple of breaks, better timing, and that's my family!

All of it hit me in that instant again, and I don't know why, but I just snapped. I got Tyler to the ground and his eyes rolled back in his head.

He went limp. I could feel this energy around him. Like something was pulling me off him. I felt someone grab my ear and pull me up hard.

Everything happened fast. The next thing I knew, two guards tackled me and put me in restraints. They shackled me up like a rodeo bull, and it was pretty much over. I couldn't fight back.

The crazy old lady scratched me across my arm with her nails as they pulled me out of the room. She got me real good, took my skin with her. I still feel my arm burning.

I think they shot me up with something because one minute I was bound and being carried down the hall and the next thing I remember, I'm here.

I woke up to the sound of dripping water just outside this confinement room. There's one tiny window, but it's sealed from the other side.

They left me with a ham sandwich, some potato chips, water, and my thoughts. No silverware. No metal or glass. I can't even eat this crap because the smell in here is so nauseating.

It's dirty walls and a fluorescent light outside that flickers like a silent movie, reminding me how far back in time I'm trapped. Who knows how long they'll hold me here?

I know they're watching to see what I do, so I have to stay calm and not let my thoughts rule me. I'm trying to think of something happy, but I can't. Is that weird?

Every thought I have is so pathetically sad. Maybe it is Achlys, misery, haunting me.

"You here, bitch?" I'm going to sing happy songs. Happy songs will keep you away.

> *"Flintstones. Meet the Flintstones.*
> *They're the modern Stone Age family.*
> *From the town of Bedrock,*
> *They're a page right out of history...*
> *Ba pa... Da da da da. Da da da.*
> *When you're with the Flintstones*
> *You'll have a yabba dabba doo time,*
> *A Dabba doo time,*
> *We'll have a gay old time."*

Why'd I think of that? Why *The Flintstones*? Why did I think of *The Flintstones*?

It was my favorite cartoon as a kid. Then I got Kennedy hooked. We used to watch *The Flintstones* together all the time. She loved it. I even bought her this Pebbles outfit for Halloween one year and took her trick-or-treating. I went as Kazoo. That was my favorite Halloween ever. She'd say "Bam! Bam!" every time she got candy.

Why am I thinking about that now? I close my eyes. I can picture Kennedy like she's here with me. Dressed in that cave girl suit with her little pigtails, and me in my green football helmet with the mask taken off wearing those crazy green spandex tights. Jamie was laughing so hard she nearly peed herself.

My little girl is so precious, and I don't even know what she looks like now. She's growing up without me. Thinking of that makes me feel worthless. It makes me want to cry or slit my throat or kill someone. My nerves are battering me. Every sound is piercing.

That water:

drip, drip, drip
drip, drip, drip
drip, drip, drip
drip, drip, drip

It's maddening.

drip, drip, drip
drip, drip, drip
drip, drip, drip
drip, drip, drip
drip, drip, drip
drip, drip, drip
drip, drip, drip
drip, drip, drip
drip, drip...

"Sunny Day. Sweepin' the clouds away,
On my way to where the air is sweet.
Can you tell me how to get,
How to get to Sesame Street?"

I forget the rest of that song. My mind is blank.
I feel the silence. Then thoughts come darting through me like a razor cutting into my skin.

"It's all my fault."
"I'm evil."

"I'm cursed!"
"I'll never see my daughter again."
"Give up."
"Die"
"Kill yourself!"
"End the misery."

It is you, Achlys crawling into my head! Get the fuck out of here!

"Why are there so many songs about rainbows
and what's on the other side?
Rainbows are visions,
but only illusions, and rainbows have nothing to hide.
So we've been told, and some choose to believe it,
I know they're wrong, wait and see.
Someday we'll find it, the Rainbow Connection.
The lovers, the dreamers, and me."

I took refuge in Kermit the Frog. Why? Why'd I do that? Why did this come into my thoughts? What is it trying to tell me?

I think I remember.

I had a Kermit stuffed animal when I was a kid. It was like a hand puppet. You'd stick your hand inside to make Kermit's mouth move. We talked a lot. Kermit and me.

It's hard to remember what we said. Most of my childhood is a blank. Most of my life is blank. I'm always trying to forget my past, but this time I want to remember.

I hear Kermit speaking to me. I see this memory, as if a cartoon was being projected on the padded walls in front of me. I see—

A child alone in his closet.

Liquor bottles smash against the wall.

My mother sobs as a ranting madman justifies his actions and a frog's lips whisper softly into a child's ear, "You're just like Daddy."

"No. I'm not. I'll never hurt Mommy," I told Kermit. "But I did. I did! I did hurt Mommy!"

LEAVE ME ALONE!

"The farmer in the dell. The farmer in the dell.
Hi-ho the derry-o. The farmer in Dell City.
And the mouse takes the cheese
The mouse takes the cheese
Hi-ho, the derry-o
This mouse I took their cheese
And the cheese stands alone
The cheese stands alone
Hi-ho, the derry-o
The cheese stands alone
The cheese sits alone.
The cheese writes alone
The cheese is alone!
Alone.
Alone.
Alo—"

JOURNAL ENTRY:
FRIDAY, DECEMBER 10, 2010 - 8:45 A.M.

They kept me in that cell all night. I typed until the battery went dead on my laptop. Then I just tried to get through the night. Between the frightened screams, the sound of metal clanging, the bristling of the swirling air moving down an empty tunnel, and the water drops that pelted the steel girders in three-four time. It was a symphony of madness raining down on me all night. Every sound was magnified. Intensified.

My senses registered the beat of each sound, smell, sight, touch, and taste as the night slowly passed and the fluorescent lights dimmed into complete darkness. Even in pitch black, my eyes could see shifting shadows in patterns that moved in tune with the noises. My ears heard the occasional footsteps from something that marked distance in my mind and whispered the direction of suffering that accompanied the hollow screams from the person I believe is Annette Dobson.

Maybe I was close, and this was my opportunity to hide inside her skin, to feel the forces that kept her company in this dark place. Perhaps my other senses were finally aroused with the absence of light. Things that were indescribable suddenly had flavors and texture.

Lying on the cold, damp cot, the mustiness of the fabric penetrated my nostrils, but it was like sniffing a freshly made stew.

The flavors of rust, sulfur, and iron were seasoned into the stew, trying to overpower the dramatic presence of urine. A slight hint of vomit and blood seasoned throughout this bowl completed my dish.

What once had diminished my appetite and curled my stomach was now almost intoxicating as I could finally detect the scent of salt that covered those potato chips and the mustard that lined the molding bread of my long-forgotten ham sandwich.

I clawed across the damp black floor, feeling my surroundings like a blind man. Something darted across my fingers as I knocked against the paper plate and began ravishing my meal. I forgot I was in the cell, and the aroma of the mustard on my lips kept me concentrated on satisfying my hunger.

I must have been drugged because a little later I woke up in a cold sweat. I thought I had a heart attack, but it was a nightmare that had invaded my mind and imprinted a clear vision to me through the black air.

I was sitting in a big open field on this deep red blanket, watching the moon spin. It was a full moon that sort of danced in circles across the sky. From across the field, I saw this leopard moving toward me.

As the leopard moved dangerously close, I tried to get up, but I realized I was woven into the blanket. My legs and arms were intertwined like I was caught inside a spider's web, and I couldn't move as the leopard moved closer and closer.

I could see its face snarling at me as it took its claw and swiped through my chest and stomach. My skin peeled off like gift wrap, and my organs were exposed to the cold winter air. Its second swipe gouged through my rib cage, ripping into my heart and lungs. Pulling back its massive claw, it easily ripped my ribs open, and my organs dangled in front of me as the leopard began eating.

Its teeth would latch on to pieces of my muscle, and it pulled hard at them until they separated from my body like tenderly cooked meat. I looked down to catch its eye, and as it became aware of my glance, it pulled back so I could look deeply into it. The leopard's nose dripped with my blood, and its mouth was filled with my half chewed organs.

He gave me a moment to see my grizzled reflection in his eyes, then it sprang at me and sank its teeth into my skull, slowly breaking it open in its mouth.

I couldn't feel any pain. I had no emotion. I just quietly watched myself being devoured as if I was no longer in my body. I was no longer me.

And as I sat there motionless, reflecting on my departure from this world, one of the guards brought me back home to what was now a dry and brittle cell. As he unlocked the cell door, I could see a smattering of light that accompanied the sun, and the opened door revealed shades of color that brought feeling back to my body. He never said a word as we walked across the institution.

The brightness of the daylight painfully blinded my eyes, and it was hard to get a bearing on my location. My feet tried to memorize the patches of grass between the concrete, and the back of my mind counted steps as my mouth tried to make small talk and get information to my whereabouts, but it was all to no avail.

Now I'm waiting outside the office for Haworth and Billings to clear me. I'm exhausted, but thankful for an electrical outlet, so I can recall everything while it's fresh in my mind. Knowing that each piece of last night has a purpose to my investigation.

Here they come, walking down the hall together. I'm playing their game now. I'm on their home court.

This is the second recording in the first batch of recordings that Eddie sent me, arranged by time and date.

"This is Eddie Hansen with Dr. Alan Haworth and Rev. William Billings. It is Friday, December 10, at 9:00 a.m. I was forced to spend last night in a padded cell against my will. We are sitting in the assessment room, where I am told I need to get clearance to return to my room and my personal possessions. Is this true?"

The doctor responds forcefully, "Mr. Hansen, please note on your consent agreement, and in all our publications and contracts, that it is the policy of this center to detain any violent offender overnight for observation."

"Isolation?" Eddie yells. "In a black hole like a criminal?"

"The seclusion rooms are for your protection."

"You're full of shit!"

The minister says, "Eddie. We made specific mention to you about supernatural manifestations and instructed you for preparation, which you deemed unnecessary. You put yourself and others in danger by entering unauthorized."

"I'm sorry," Eddie says.

"You need to follow our rules."

"I need is sleep."

"You didn't sleep well?" asks the minister.

"With all the screaming, the drugs you slipped me?"

"You were not drugged, Mr. Hansen. There were no other patients in your ward," the Doctor tells Eddie.

"You love fucking with me, don't you?"

"Refrain from that language and tone of voice with me. You realize that your voluntary admission status at this facility is subject to change at my discretion."

"I know what's going on in here. People know I'm here, and they know why, so spare me the games."

The minister gently says, "This runs deeper than you imagine. We cannot risk your well-being."

"I'm fine. Timothy Nathan Tyler is not. You wanted me to see him. And Annette Dobson, she's here. What are you doing to them?"

"Rehabilitating," says the doctor.

"Bullshit! Tyler's a lifeless zombie."

"He was lobotomized for his safety and for others in this facility," the doctor explains.

"That explains the scars."

"However, Mr. Hansen," the doctor continues, "you will soon notice multiple personalities that transcend his mental condition."

The minister interrupts, "I believe Timothy is possessed by eight demons, but Achlys is not one of them. She came for you."

"What? You saying I'm possessed, Rev?"

"Not at this moment."

"Not at what?"

"I believe you are oppressed. Based on your MMPI, I believe you still maintain control over most of your behavior."

"Yeah. Most," Eddie replies.

The doctor intervenes, changing the subject. "Mr. Hansen, do you recall Timothy Tyler's murder trial?"

"The Vampire Killer? Of course. Tyler killed sixteen coeds over six years trying to make them his bride."

"Very good. If you had examined court records, you would have seen that I was the psychologist hired to determine if Mr. Tyler's plea of insanity was valid. My initial diagnosis was that he was suffering from a rare disorder known as Cotard's syndrome. He truly believed he was already dead and therefore not responsible for any actions in his present life."

The minister adds, "In spiritual counseling, it was discovered that Timothy Tyler was under the control of Ibwa, a demon from Philippines. Ibwa feeds off dead bodies and ordered the murders. Once possessed, Timothy claims he had no control or recollection of the events."

"How'd you come to this conclusion?" Eddie asks.

"Speaking with the demon directly, much as you witnessed yesterday."

"Don't expect me to believe your show. I'm not some pharmaceutical company who's gonna throw you millions to cure schizophrenia."

"You'll believe by experience, and that is why you are here, to record your story," the doctor tells Eddie.

"You do understand I can use this as your confession for holding Tyler?"

The doctor responds authoritatively, "Our research is protected. We are approaching a conclusion, and that is the only reason you were invited here, Mr. Hansen. This is your story, you're part of this experience."

There's silence.

"Tonight we'll review some case notes and tapes that will help you understand your participation in our research. You may go back to your room, Eddie," the minister tells him.

"I'm free to go? I can just walk out of here?"

"Yes, Mr. Hansen. You're not a prisoner," says the doctor.

"Great! I need to get my camera fixed, thanks to your staff. I'll be back tonight."

"Be cautious," the doctor warns. "The roads can be quite dangerous."

"Eddie," the minister adds. "Please review Matthew chapter twelve, verse forty-three, and Luke, chapter eleven, verse twenty-four in the Bible I left for you. I've highlighted them for your reference. You need to read this to prepare for our next meeting."

"Will do." Eddie tells them as he shuts off his recorder.

JOURNAL ENTRY:
FRIDAY, DECEMBER 10, 2010 - 10:03 A.M.

That was absurd. They had me and just let me go. I was helpless. They knew they held all the power. Why let me walk? I can go to El Paso right now and blow the whistle on Tyler. If Dobson is there too, it's a bonus.

How could they stop me from publishing my story? They know I can get this into the *Times*. As I long as I have proof to back my claims, this can be published.

Why aren't they afraid? Who's protecting them? The state of Texas? The US government? Some large pharmaceutical or medical company with billions to gain?

They're all possible suspects. What's the first thing you learn when investigating a crime.

Follow the money. Find the money, find the answer!

They want to feed me clues, because this is a twisted game to them. I may as well play, see what's relevant in this Bible that Billings wants me to see. He's pretty adamant about it.

Matthew Chapter 12, Verses 43–46

43 When an evil spirit comes out of a man, it goes through arid places seeking rest and does not find it. 44 Then it says, "I will return to the house I left." When it arrives, it finds the house unoccupied, swept clean and put in order. 45 Then it goes and takes with it seven other spirits more wicked than itself, and they go in and live there. And the final condition of that man is worse than the first. That is how it will be with this wicked generation.

The final condition of the man is worse than the first. If that isn't a mental hospital, I don't know what is.

Maybe Jesus was on to something. A rebel superhero standing up against the regime. Let's see what the other verse says.

Luke Chapter 11, Verses 24–26

24 When an evil spirit comes out of a man, it goes through arid places seeking rest and does not find it. Then it says, "I will return to the house I left." 25 When it arrives, it finds the house swept clean and put in order. 26 Then it goes and takes seven other spirits more wicked than itself, and they go in and live there. And the final condition of that man is worse than the first.

Damn. That's identical, except for the last line.

I read the whole chapter in both books to get a sense of the story. It's exactly the same but written over two thousand years ago. If Jesus said this and two different reporters wrote about it this precisely, is there any chance it could be true?

All the other information surrounding this event is from a different perspective, written completely different, except for this particular verse.

From my historical studies in the early part of the first century, if a scribe or historian wrote about a person or event, it was rare that you'd find two different reporters, in this case Matthew and Luke, record the exact same quote with the exact same words.

They didn't have tape recorders or video cameras to get a quote. People didn't carry parchment paper around like laptops, so this is interesting. Two guys, Matthew and Luke, hung on those words. It must have had a deep impact on them.

From reading the story, it looks like Jesus knocked demons out of some crazy people, then some people started talking smack. Jesus answered back like a press conference and gave this explanation.

When this evil spirit got pissed off, it went and found seven more demons tougher than itself to return and take over that person again. It makes sense. It's the law of the streets. If you get pushed off your turf, get reinforcements. Any schoolyard kid knows there's power in a gang.

Billings wanted me to see this, because he knows how reporters work. This means something. I'm going to circle this verse and call it: **SEVEN-X.**

Seven times the evil returns. Now that's a horror movie.

Know what else I find strange. Both reporters used the same word Billings used—*arid*, like that deodorant. Arid, Extra Dry. That air was extra dry in that room yesterday. I could feel it. Cold and dry.

When I woke up from that nightmare in the cell, it felt like that too. This brush of cold, dry air cut through me like a winter storm.

I felt something moving around me in the dark. I thought I was being paranoid, but could it have been a demon? I didn't see anything. Your mind runs wild when you're trapped alone in a room like that for so long. It plays tricks on you. I could have been drugged.

But for sake of the argument, let's play the devil's advocate and follow Billings' logic in this case. If demons are real, not fictitious characters like vampires or zombies or werewolves, then I got some research to do. I've got explore all possibilities.

For now, I better get on the road. I need to get a lot done before the big reveal tonight.

AUDIO LOG:
FRIDAY, DECEMBER 10, 2010 – 11:21 A.M.
ENTERED BY MELODY SWANN

This is my transcript of the first phone call I received from Eddie on December 10. He sent this with the first batch of recordings.

"It's Eddie Hansen, December 8. About 11:00 a.m. I'm in Dell City parked in front of the post office. I finally got clear cell phone reception so I'm going to call Melody to let her know I'm okay. I'm also sending my tapes to her… It's ringing… Mel. Hey, baby. It's me."

"God, Eddie. What took you so long to call? I was worried."

"I'm out in the boonies. There's no cell reception. You gotta see this place."

"Where are you?"

"Dell City. I'm sending you a thumb drive with my notes and recordings."

"You okay?"

"Yeah. Why?"

"Your voice sounds different."

"I think I'm catching a cold. It's freezing here."

"No, you sound disconnected."

"Maybe it's my cell. I'll step outside. Hear me now?"

"Better," I tell him.

"Guess what?"

"What?"

"Tyler is here!

"What? You're kidding me! Baby, that's huge."

"I know. It's bigger than we thought. I think Dobson is here too. But they got her under lock and key somewhere. This place is a freak fest."

"Be careful."

"Don't worry," he says. "And don't freak out about this stuff when you get it. Okay? You're gonna hear some whacked out shit. It's just a show. You got that? Just a show."

"What do you mean?" I ask, feeling worry crawl over me.

"Remember when we saw *The Last Exorcism*?"

"Yeah."

"Well it's like that. These guys put on a dog and pony show to get money from someone. Probably from the state or some medical company."

"Don't mess around with this."

"Baby, I'm fine."

"Eddie!"

"Mel, I'm okay… All right?"

"All right… I get worried," I tell him.

"Well don't."

"Okay," I say, not meaning a word.

"Mel, I need you to translate some stuff for me. There's this crazy old lady that speaks Greek. I need to know what she said. I don't trust them here. I think they tell me what they want me to hear."

"Okay."

"As fast as you can. And my notes, there's some writing. Figure out what it says and get back to me."

After a moment of silence, I tell Eddie, "I miss you."

"I miss you too, baby."

"I'm singing tonight. I'm gonna do Lonestar's 'Amazed,' for you."

"I love that one. Sing it for me now, babe. I could use a little cheer."

I couldn't resist, so I started.

"Every time our eyes meet,
This feeling inside me.
* Is almost more than I can take."*

As I'm singing, I hear something bang. Eddie yells, "Hey!"

"What? Eddie, what was that?"

"Some punk kid's at my car.".

"You okay?"

"Hey!" Eddie yells. "Get the fuck away from my car!"

He drops the phone. I hear him running off.

"Eddie? Eddie! Eddie, you there?"

JOURNAL ENTRY:
FRIDAY, DECEMBER 10, 2010 – 1:30 P.M.

Freak Fest continues. Some little punk kid threw a deer's heart on my windshield while I was at the post office in Dell City this morning. I chased him down and tackled him before he could get inside the diner next door.

He was about fifteen, sixteen, dressed all Goth with black eyeliner and streaked black and white hair. His hands were covered in deer blood, so naturally we made quite a scene outside with him screaming, "You're marked!" over and over as he swiped the blood on my face and jacket while I held him down.

Within a few minutes, the town sheriff arrived.

Officer Prick actually let the little punk go and warned me about coming into his town and causing trouble.

When I told him I was staying in Uphir as a guest of Dr. Haworth, he said he didn't want to see me "around these parts anymore" and wasn't "going to clean up another mess." Whatever that meant.

Now I'm the freak trying to cover up my bloodstained sweater as my jacket sits in the car and I sit in the lobby of Precision Camera, waiting for the technician Bobby to get my camera fixed.

You ever just have that feeling that you're caught in something that you can't get out of. I'm so close to getting this story and it's one thing after another, distracting me, pulling me down.

My nerves are frazzled right now. Maybe it's the repetitive cycle of corny Christmas music playing over and over. Or the fact I've been sitting here over an hour. Maybe it was spending the night in a padded cell. Or Dr. Haworth's calm, even voice echoing in my head all the bullshit he's been feeding me.

Or Tyler's scar-filled face, or Dobson's screams that kept me up all night. Or the way my childhood memories seem to swirl in the air before pouring out someone else's mouth.

Or is it this annoying kid in front of me, squealing while his stressed out mom is trying to figure out how to work a fucking camera?

Or Cowboy Jim here to my left who wants to know the difference between HD and HDV, like he's actually going to buy the camera and do something with it.

Or the sound of the bells on the door that jingle with each idiot who makes his way in and out of this place.

Or the squeaking of wet boots across the dirty tiled floor, and the rush of cold air that sweeps across me as the door jangles open and shut. Open and shut. Open and shut. Open and shut.

Maybe it's the sound of my own breathing and the clicking of keys on the keyboard, as I pound out these words in a flurry of strokes.

Or is it the smell of day-old coffee and bodily fluids that drip like a leaky faucet out of this old geezer next to me? If he sneezes on me one more time.

Maybe that's what's making me crazy! Maybe that's what makes me feel like I want to stand up and scream at the top of my lungs.

Or take this chair and smash it across the face of the next person who says, "Happy Holidays" with that fake "I don't want to work in this shit-hole" smile.

Maybe we're all holding back. Holding on, hoping that nothing happens this happy day to push us over the edge.

I know I'm not the only one with this look in his eye. I see it a thousand times a day in a thousand different ways, masquerading itself in fake smiles, exhausted eyes, slumped shoulders, and voices that crack before feigning that fake happy tone that says, "I'm fine and how are you?"

So you know what I'm going to do? I'm going to stand up, shut this computer off, take a deep breath of cold air outside, and wait patiently for this problem to get fixed.

Then I'll move on to my next problem and smile and joke like it's any other day.

This is the first recording in the second batch of tapes that Eddie sent me. There are lots of cameras and electronics around like it's a workshop, repair shop, something like that.

> "All right. Test. Test. You working now? Let's see…"

The camera spins to reveal some dorky kid, about twenty-five. He turns the camera around and walks out the door filming. I see Eddie. He's sitting in the waiting room. The kid's pointing the camera right at Eddie's face.

> "Yo! Eddie! Good as new, bro!"

Eddie's eyes are glazed over.

> "Thanks. What do I owe ya?" Eddie asks.
> "Three hundred forty-nine."
> "What?"
> "Check your face, bro," the kid tells him, pointing at the camera. "I had to put on a whole new plate. You're only paying for the part. That's a deal."
> "Thanks."
> "What'd you do? Pound a nail into this with a sledge hammer," the kid asks.
> "What? No!" Eddie tells him.

The kid shows Eddie the broken piece.

> "Something got a hold of this. Pushed the whole end in. Nobody's hand could do that. You'd need a dinosaur claw or something to do that shit. Put that much pressure on it! Transformers, Terminator, bro!"

"Let me see," Eddie replies as he picks up the broken piece and puts it in front of the camera.

"Dude. Maybe a bear stepped on it?"

"Maybe? Did you get the flash card out?"

"There was no card in there."

"You sure? I had one," Eddie replies, acting nervous.

"Positive, man. There's no way you could get it out unless you took off this plate... See," the kid says as he turns off the camera.

That mark on the plate is big. Some kind of animal had to do it. Could it be the same thing that bit the leg of that Spanish guy? He took Eddie's camera. Maybe he sent this flash card. Eddie just said that it's missing.

JOURNAL ENTRY:
FRIDAY, DECEMBER 10, 2010 – 7:30 P.M.

I'm sitting at a crossroads. Actually it's Denny's, just off Interstate 10. But I feel like it's my crossroad, because I'm looking east and west, and don't know which way to go. Eight hundred miles to my left is home safe home. I got some answers, and my gut feeling is telling me to leave now.

I peer to the right and see my future. I can't explain what's calling me to the right. It's a powerful force that I can't say no to. And I know it's not good for me.

Maybe it's my voracious appetite. Curiosity that killed the cat. Hidden danger. The excitement of pushing the boundaries. Riding the line of right and wrong, life and death.

My extreme nature calls. The bungee jumper. The party animal. The guy who hates speed limits and caution tape. He's here, and he wants satisfaction.

Ten years ago I thought I was invincible. But age has a way of gouging mortality, and the body has a way of saying you can't do this anymore. But I keep trying, feeding this youthful impulse for energy and attention.

Right now I'm starving for something. I can't get full.

I just ordered meatloaf after pounding out chicken strips and a mushroom-Swiss burger. I never eat like this, but I'm famished. I want to stuff myself. Drink until I fall, bang that hottie across from me until her eyes pop. I want to please every primal urge in my body. And I want it—NOW!

Why not test my luck?

I'll spend tonight in the twenty-first century. Indulge in the good life while I have it, and let tomorrow figure itself out.

AUDIO LOG/JOURNAL ENTRY
SATURDAY, DECEMBER 11, 2010 – 11:03
A.M.

I was about halfway through my meatloaf when I looked up and saw that angelic creature standing in front of me. She had long black hair and cat green eyes. She was about twenty-five, with a killer body, wearing these tight red pants and a low cut candy cane sweater that made me want to lick the peppermint off her.

For some reason I pulled out my recorder and tried to think of something clever, but before I could, she stunned me saying, "You ever find yourself drawn to someone?"

"Yeah," was all I could mutter, inhaling her like a deep breath of warm sunshine.

"Deeper than physical attraction," she said, moving closer.

"Sure?"

"Spiritual," she said, comforting me with her soft touch. "A connection."

"A rainbow connection," I joked.

By this time she nuzzled up in the seat next to me like we were old friends. "You're at a crossroads. You're looking for answers."

Then her eyes locked on to mine and a soft smile spread across her face as she moaned, touching my hand, looking into it.

"Mmmm. You feel you need to go back, because you have to know about her."

I tensed up, knowing she could feel something deeper inside me.

"Why'd you say that?"

"If she had the baby?" she continued, examining me.

"What?"

"It's not your baby?"

"Hold on," I said, pulling back. "How do you know this? How do you know about the baby?"

"She tried to kill him. But they tied her down. They keep her hidden. To keep her protected," she told me as she touched me again.

I could feel this magnificent pulse move through me. I told her, "Hold on. Hold on. You talked to Billings or Haworth, didn't you?"

"Who?"

"They sent you to follow me, right?"

"No," she assured me. "This is what I'm getting. There's a stream of energy, spirits all around you who are telling me things. You have to relax, so I can listen, and sort them out."

"You fucking with me?" I muttered, pulling back nervously to examine her more closely.

"No, Eddie."

"I didn't tell you my name," I said cautiously.

"It's on your card. Right here," she replied. "Relax, I'm Claire. I want to help you."

She could tell I wanted to run. But her beauty was mesmerizing, and her touch was calming. So I listened as she told me, "This is my gift. Or maybe it's a curse, because I know the other side of life. The angels and the demons. Sometimes the voices are confusing, because the path between life and death is narrow, and the road to God may go through hell, if you take the path Jesus took. But that's how He won the war for us."

"I have no idea what you are talking about," I said, mesmerized by her eyes.

"The voices, Eddie. All your voices in your head. One of them wants to bang me 'til my eyeballs pop, and one wants to listen and learn. Another one will distract you, and two will come and take you where you shouldn't go. Another takes all your frustration and throws it through a wall until your hands bleed, while the other comes to feed off your desire.

"One offers answers to your problems, but only one voice is the way, the truth, and the life. You choose who you listen to, but they have power, if you give it to them, and they can take control over you."

"Demons?" I asked, feeling her words resonating in my chest.

"Yes. We all fall short of the glory of God, but some use that to pull you into the pit. Be on guard, Eddie. The battle already started. And you can't see how you're getting hit."

At that moment I was hit. Run over by the love train. I knew I wasn't getting anywhere, but this was the most beautiful woman I've ever seen.

What's life if you don't give it a shot, so I asked her, "You want to get a drink? Party?"

"I don't drink, Eddie," she said, getting up.

"All right. You got a number. Can I call you?"

"No," she told me sincerely. "I'm just passing through here. I have to go. But be careful of Ose. He's the leader. The one strong enough to overtake you… God is stronger, if you give your life back to Him. Greater is He who is in you than he who is in the world."

As she finished saying that, she kissed my forehead. It was like warm rain, covering me in this moment of peace, forgetting the cold winter night.

By the time I snapped back to my senses, she was gone.

I was left with a half-eaten plate of meatloaf and my primal urges, desiring satisfaction. Claire was right. There was a lot of noise in my head. And I wanted it to quiet down.

All I could think of was getting drunk to silence the voices. The last few days are too weird. Too coincidental. Too contrived.

There's got to be really big money behind this, and they know I'm on to them. Goth boy, this hot chick, the parade of mental patients, and the Greek show. Somebody wants to break me down and get inside my head. Make me think these things may be true.

Suspension of disbelief.

That's the oldest Hollywood trick. You create a world that you believe in, then twist the truth, so no matter what you do, it always seems real. That's the power of believing in the story.

She wants me to believe her story. That every moment of my life is part of this grand plan, and everyone and everything have a reason for being. There's a war for my soul and a battle between good and evil, but I'm the one who will draw the boundary lines.

We all draw different lines. Sometimes they intersect. Sometimes they don't. We agree on forms of evil, but judge degrees of it, saying only the worst of humanity is truly bad. And everything along the gray lines is subject to opinion. These are the lines I constantly live on, crossing through intersections that lead down paths I barely remember.

And at certain times, for unknown reasons, the grim reality of consequence decides to rear its ugly head at me, and forces me to see what I've done. And I find myself staring at…

THE DEVIL.

It started innocently enough. After my meal at Denny's, I stopped at a corner market to pick up some beer. I planned to find a hotel nearby, kick back, watch some TV, do a little research and crash for the night. I wanted to check out those symbols I saw, translate the Greek on my recordings, and find out more about Uphir.

That was my plan. But as fate would have it, just as I got to the counter to purchase my beer, in stumbled Sandra and her friend Diana. I'm a sucker for a long wool coat with thigh-high boots. I got a thing for blondes, and a pair of drunken ones is a recipe for danger.

They came in giggling, and they put on a show dancing around, singing, sloshing change on the counter, then knocking the contents out of their purses like a piñata.

A helping hand was all it took to break the ice. Next thing I know I'm invited to their place around the corner to party. Who says no to that?

My scattered memory and this recording are my reminders of my night of triumph, mystery, and ecstasy.

"It's the *Legacy of the Divine Tarot* by Marchetti."

I remember Sandra saying that. I was sitting on a purple couch, in this trippy sixties apartment, full of pinks and purples and bright colors that danced with the psychedelic music, creating this shagadelic Austin Powers vibe.

I was feeling a bit "Randy" as Sandra stripped out of that wool coat, revealing a skin-tight black dress. She kicked off those thigh-high boots and started packing a bowl of sweet-smelling sativa.

That's when I noticed those cards spread across the table, glowing with mesmerizing images.

"That artwork's amazing. They seem lifelike," I told her.

"Because they are life," Sandra answered. "They hold the answers to life. Want me to do your reading?"

"Why not?" I told her.

I figured it was harmless enough. Sandra shuffled these beautiful tarot cards, and spread them face down on the table in front of me.

Diana scampered around the apartment setting the mood. First she turned on a black light above the table, then the lava lamp next to me, and finally, the pièce de résistance, *The Very Best of the Doors* began playing.

"Concentrate on the cards," she told me, as they came to life under the black light. The Egyptian face on the back of the cards looked hypnotic, with a thousand glowing eyes staring at me.

Sandra continued with her instruction. "When I ask you each question, you pick one card. Okay? My first question is, how do you feel about yourself now? Really think about that, then pick one card."

"Be right back," Diana said, as I tried to concentrate on the cards, while seeing her sultry body slip past me into the bedroom. Regaining my attention, I focused and chose a card.

"Don't turn it over. It goes right here," Sandra told me. "Now. What do you want most at this very moment?"

That was easy. I'm thinking *the two of you* as I ran my hand over the deck to her hand for a soft touch.

I'm not sure if she picked up my vibe. She seemed serious about doing this reading. I chose my card carefully, trying to match her intensity.

"What are your fears? Concentrate on the question," Sandra instructed me, as she moved her hands over the cards. "Let your intuition guide you. Which card speaks to you?"

"That one," I answered, trying to feel the energy she said would guide me.

"Okay. Next question. What is going against you?"

By this time the room was filled with smoke, and I hit off the pipe, staring at Sandra's long legs as she kicked them up on top of the table, getting comfortable and giving me a sneak peek at her hot, red panties.

"And finally, the last card. This determines your outcome," she whispered softly and sensuously.

"My future?" I asked.

"The inevitable sequence of your life's events," she exclaimed, guiding me with her eyes.

As "Riders on the Storm" surged through the room and the lava lamp warmed up with seductive smiles of molten heat, I passed my hand slowly over the cards, feeling the heat of the black light shine off my purple hand.

My fingers slowly crawled across the table, glowing with life and energy. It seemed like that card jumped out at me, sticking to my hand like two-sided tape on a Christmas present.

Looking down, my cards had formed the shape of a cross. They looked three dimensional, reaching out to me, calling my future.

Sandra flipped the first one over, saying, "The Tower."

What a wild image. It looked like something from the end of the world, a cosmic event from some sci-fi movie with a large glowing, round tower set on pillars above this golden, cataclysmic sky.

"What does it mean?" I asked.

"The Tower means that you feel disruption in your life, and you're afraid that the change you are about to go through will be catastrophic."

"Yes. Strange things have been happening lately. And I can't figure them out."

"This will force new directions you never dreamed possible, Eddie. Your solution isn't what you expect. Be open to new realms of possibility. Let's see what you want most," she said, turning the next card over.

"Oh! You chose The Lovers." Her timing couldn't have been any better. When she flipped that card, Diana entered, wearing a long, black silk robe, tied loose enough to reveal a black lace bra and panties underneath.

"Lovers," Diana groaned, as she slipped in next to me on the purple couch and took a long hit off the pipe. "She's good."

"I see," I replied, making the most of the opportunity by rubbing my hand along her leg, while dreaming of that cosmic intertwining of bodies that I saw on the card.

Diana moaned and began singing along to "Riders on the Storm," while Sandra continued my reading.

"It's not about sex, Eddie," Sandra told me. "The Lovers tell me what you really want right now is to know what choice to make. Stay where you are or take a risk?"

"Do you like taking risks, Eddie?" Diana whispered into my ear. "Dare to live."

Sandra crossed her legs back, knowingly revealing those red panties as she flipped the next card. Judgment.

"This is your fear. Judgment!"

"Am I being judged?" I asked.

"No," Sandra replied earnestly.

"Not by me," Diana chimed in, working her hand across my leg softly, and then down to the table to grab a beer.

Sandra continued, very focused. "What it means is that you're afraid the conclusion you want is being delayed. You fear big changes ahead of you. Things aren't turning out the way you expected, for some reason."

"Yeah. That's kind of true," I said.

"Well, we can change that," Diana moaned, kissing my ear, bringing my attention to her. "What are you expecting?"

I tried to focus on the cards, but my mind was swimming in the possibility of expectation.

What Sandra said made some sense.

She continued. "Your routine will be changed dramatically. Don't be afraid. The choice you make will change your life for the better."

"You sure?" I asked.

Something about Sandra seemed genuine. She had this innocent face. But I knew she wasn't innocent, so I probed, asking, "Did I tell you why I'm here? About my investigation in Uphir. At the secret mental institution. How they are testing missing death-row prisoners."

"No," Sandra replied.

"You know where Uphir is?" I asked.

"No. Never heard of it."

"You?" I asked Diana.

"Nope. Sounds cool," Diana responded. "Is it like Shutter Island?"

"I guess," I told her, noticing her hand on my thigh. "Some things happened there, and I don't know if it's safe to go back."

"Total Shutter Island," Diana laughed, taking another hit off the pipe, then blowing the smoke into my mouth sensuously. "You be careful."

"We can see what you have going for you, Eddie," Sandra told me. "This is your power card. Your intervention. The Emperor. That's good. It means you're self-assured. You're capable of influencing people or events to achieve what you want."

"What do you want?" Diana seductively asked.

"Other than you?" I joked.

"Yes," she replied, to which Sandra added, "Your real desire. In your heart, not your pants."

"To get this story. To succeed. To make things right in my life."

"Good," Sandra replied. "There's a man of significance you should draw guidance from. He could be the key."

"Who is it? Can you tell?"

"It might be a spiritual advisor or a teacher," Sandra said.

"Like you," Diana laughed, pointing to Sandra.

"No. This is a man. He might be a priest or a doctor?"

That aroused my interest more than the seductive touches of Diana. Could Sandra actually know something, or was she involved with Billings and Haworth? I needed to know.

"Which one is it?" I asked.

"I can't tell right now," Sandra said, moving toward the cards again. "We have to look at the next card. Maybe I'll get something from that."

"You worry too much," Diana added, kicking her legs up on my lap. "Relax. Party a little. What's the worst that can happen?"

"We'll see," Sandra said. She flipped the next card, instructing me, "This is what's against you. The force or power that wants to stop your progress."

The card turned over, slowly revealing a skull and an ax that seemed to cut right through me. I was speechless. Trapped inside that room. The lava lamp turned and made sinister faces at me, melting into my imagination. I felt like I was suffocating.

"You chose the Death Card, Eddie," Sandra said without emotion.

"What's it mean?" I asked, feeling my heart sink in my chest.

"You're so dead," groaned Diana.

I remember looking at that card thinking, *maybe I am going to die. What if it's my time?*

I got up feeling dizzy. That card felt so alive as I held it in my hand. It was like that skull was reflecting my own face. My mortality.

I felt like the horse could jump out any second, and the rider would cut off my head like Ichabod Crane in *Sleepy Hollow*.

I felt trapped. Like I could die right there. It was silent for what seemed like an eternity, before Diana started laughing wildly, blurting out, "I'm totally fucking with you!"

Sandra took the card from my hand and placed it back, saying, "It doesn't mean you have to die, Eddie. The Death Card means something is coming to an end, but that brings a brand-new beginning. It could be in your life. Or your career."

"Or love life," added Diana.

"Yes," Sandra replied. "It could be the end of one relationship and the beginning of another. You ain't married, are you?"

"No," I responded softly.

"But you got a girlfriend," Sandra said convincingly.

"You're the psychic; you tell me," I said, trying to gauge her knowledge.

"There's turmoil in your life, Eddie. Anxiety, depression, fear, distressing events that are about to happen. The Death Card says, 'It's time to show what you are made of.' You have to believe that life goes on, no matter what. Life is what you make of it."

I tried to read her deeper. She seemed to be pouring out her emotions as she went on.

"Believe that and you'll get through, to your dream. And that girl of yours. I wouldn't trust her. Should she really trust you?" Sandra finished.

"See, it ain't serious. He's ours," Diana said, as she slid her hands down my chest. "Aren't ya?"

"Sure," I groaned letting her kiss me. She pulled her robe open and pushed her body softly against mine.

"You want to see how it ends. Are you ready for your outcome?" Sandra inquired.

At this point, what did I have to lose? I nodded okay, and she flipped the last card, and there I was, staring at:

THE DEVIL

"Oh shit!" Diana yelled out.

"Shit what? Death and the devil. What's it mean? "What does it mean?"

"Relax, baby. You'll be okay," Diana consoled me, rubbing my thigh, before directing her voice to Sandra, saying, "Tell him, sweetie. Tell him what the cards mean."

"This is your final opportunity to change direction," Sandra said.

"You mean go home?" I asked.

Taking my hand and pulling me closer with every word, Sandra said, "No, you have the Emperor. You have the ability to get everything you ever wanted. But temptation and addiction will ruin you, if you let them overpower you. Don't doubt your ability. Be confident and take what you want. And you can have everything your heart desires."

By now, Sandra and I were face-to-face. Our lips only inches apart and our eyes locked together. Diana's hands moved down my back, and I could feel her breasts pressing against my back.

The music began to pulse in rhythms through me. Diana began to slide her body down me with each guitar note, making her way into my heart of darkness. I could feel her curves brush against me, slicing through my resistance.

Shaking with the tambourine, Sandra pulled me into her clutches. Her wet lips pushed into mine. Her tongue swirled in circles, beckoning my touch as the music spoke.

"This is the end, beautiful friend.
This is the end, my only friend, the end."

Jim Morrison's haunting voice came back from the dead to fill my senses. The music was our rhythm, slow curving bodies rounding together as one, in passionate embrace.

> *"Of our elaborate plans, the end.*
> *Of everything that stands, the end.*
> *No safety or surprise, the end.*
> *I'll never look into your eyes...again.*
> *Can you picture what will be,*
> *So limitless and free?"*

It was like a movie, so perfect. So playful. So artful and delectable. Moans of pleasure escaped into the air, breath that could be seen taking form in the smoke, like creatures moving through the air, intertwining forms of love, lust, and desire. My desire echoed in the music, penetrating the air with truth.

> *"Desperately in need...of some...stranger's hand,*
> *In a...desperate land."*

Colors flashed in the pounding of the drums, of newly naked bodies, turning from passionate to primitive. Guttural groans of the deepest pleasure emanated from me. I was the Emperor. I was the King. I was in control, in command. And I felt that power surging through me, like I was invincible. Incredible. Unstoppable!

> *"Lost in a Roman...wilderness of pain.*
> *And all the children are insane.*
> *All the children are insane!"*

Screams of pleasure burst out from my women. With each thrust, each taste, each touch! Louder and louder. Bigger and better.

Primal nature arose intensely in the smoky air, building through the echoes, the screams, and the music. Pounding with the drumbeats, we reached an unforgettable climax that I can still taste now.

It's on my lips with my morning coffee. It's part of me now. I can't explain it fully, but these women gave me power. They gave me strength. They gave me confidence.

Whatever it was, it's in me now. I felt it enter me like a rush of wind as I exploded with a primitive grunt that said I OWN YOU!

I'm going to carry that power back to Uphir and crack open this case. Nothing can stop me! I am THE EMPEROR!

AUDIO LOG:
DECEMBER 11 OR 12, 2010 - 3:00 P.M.

"This is Eddie Hansen, back at the Uphir Behavioral Center with Dr. Alan Haworth. It is Saturday, December 11, exactly 3:00 p.m. And we are discussing my re-admittance into—"

"It's the twelfth."

"Excuse me?"

"Today is Sunday, December 12."

"No, it's not."

"We expected you back Friday night."

"No. No. I was only gone one night."

"It appears two," Haworth replies confidently.

I feel my blood boiling. His voice is like nails on a chalkboard, screeching through me with an irritating tone.

"Is everything all right, Mr. Hansen?"

Mr. Hansen. He says that on purpose to feel intellectual, superior. He says it to piss me off. To make things formal and impersonal, so while he probes me, I'm supposed to feel indifferent.

> "Since you want to know how I feel," I answer, "I'm fine."

Could I have lost a whole day, slept twenty-four hours? Did I lose my memory? What happened? Or is Haworth messing with me? Trying my patience to see whether I lose control. For what seems like minutes, we stare at each other, before he gives in.

> "Would you like us to prepare your guest quarters?"
> "Please."

I watch him scribble notes on to the pad that is my developing file. Finally, he looks back up and calmly states:

> "Rev. Billings will be here at six for service in the chapel. You are welcome to join us. A special dinner will be served afterward."
> "Thank you," I reply.

I get up and move around the table to shake his hand and look at his computer monitor. As I peer over his shoulder, I can see:

SUNDAY, DECEMBER 12, 2010 3:03 P.M.

JOURNAL ENTRY:
SUNDAY, DECEMBER 12, 2010 – 3:33 P.M.

Sure enough, my computer and phone both say it's the twelfth. A day in my life is missing, and I can't remember a thing. I don't have a clue. I can't conjure up an image or a memory. Not even a dream. I'm trying hard to think of any clue.

The only thing that comes to my mind is a nagging voice that says, "I got you exactly where I want you. You're mine."

As if it were Haworth gloating over the fact that he's back in control.

Looking around, this room feels different. Everything looks the same crazy way, but it feels colder. I turned the heat on and feel the vent pushing hot air into the room, but nothing is changing.

It smells stale, musty in here. I think I've got a bit of a head cold or sinus infection, because no matter where I go, I smell that same smell inside my head. Like the inside of my head is rotting. I'm going to take some cold medicine, a hot shower, and a nap before service.

JOURNAL ENTRY:
SUNDAY, DECEMBER 12, 2010 – 5:40 P.M.

That shower felt like hot nails driving into my skin. Dry cracked skin that's been weathered by winter's chill. Each drop pierced through raw open skin. There's something that looks like a rash on my right shoulder, surrounding three long scratches running down my back. It's not four like a hand, but three close together.

I don't remember anything happening. It's amazing how the mind buries pain until your senses rediscover it, and then you can't stop focusing on it.

My leg is bruised outside my right thigh, and my arm has a tiny swelling around the inside of my elbow. Maybe from when the nurse took my blood.

My eyes have dark circles around them, and my skin looks a little pale. Looking into the mirror, I don't even feel like I'm looking at myself today. I don't recognize me.

I feel like I'm on the outside looking in. I feel older, tired. That surge of power I felt so strongly, faded.

Maybe it was the realization of lost time, or the nagging feeling that something is missing. Or the weariness of my mind telling me that I'm losing control, with an impending sense of doom crushing through my skull.

It feels like a vice grip crushing my bones. I sense this pressure, like cold steel, pushing in opposite directions in the same spot on my leg, like it is going to snap it into pieces.

I can't describe this fear any other way. It's like I'm locked in one of Jigsaw's traps, and time is running out. It's all I can think about lying on this bed after my shower.

These crazy ideas fly through my head. Crazy ideas like I should pull my fingers back until they break, or scratch though the marks on my back.

It's insane, my body's craving pain to feel alive. To wake up. I didn't want to give in, but my mind wouldn't let go. I couldn't stop staring at the leopard statue with its claws reaching out to swipe its prey. It drew me closer.

Leaning down, I just stared into the leopard's eyes, seeing crazy ideas of hurting myself fly through my head.

Finally I took my hand and pushed it hard into the jagged edge of the leopard's claw, feeling it pierce through my skin.

I can't describe it fully, but it felt like we connected. Like we were blood brothers, taking an oath. As I saw the first drops of blood trickle out of my hand, it brought me peace, a relief that let me rest, until now.

JOURNAL/AUDIO LOG:
SUNDAY, DECEMBER 12, 2010 – 11:08 P.M.

As I stepped into the arched cathedral, the dome engulfed me. The statues and paintings of the saints looked like a museum of Renaissance art. It took me back to the cathedral in my neighborhood when I was a kid. The beauty and magnificence of the work were only overshadowed by the angelic voice that echoed off its walls singing.

> *"Amazing Grace, how sweet the sound,*
> *That saved a wretch like me.*
> *I once was lost, but now am found,*
> *Was blind, but now I see."*

Her voice was beautiful, clear, warm, soothing, penetrating. It's the kind of voice that gives you goose bumps. My hair was standing up straight as I listened, but for some unknown reason, I felt irritated.

As I worked my way to the back row, I began to notice the freak show surrounding me.

I didn't see grace; I saw disgrace. I saw demented, mentally ill patients trying to find salvation in an empty manger, which stood on the altar.

But the most horrific sight to me now was the angelic voice singing.

As I looked closer, I recognized who she was, the monster she was. She stood there singing like an angel, pretending nothing happened.

This monster acted as if that pouch around her belly was not her next victim, but the child of Bethlehem about to be born. How could it be Annette Dobson?

I began to make my way closer, up the aisle, to make sure what I saw was real. She looked so transformed, so undeniably different and so at peace.

But that was her. I knew it.

My skin crawled, but I lifted my hands and smiled, joining the chorus as my eyes looked toward Rev. Billings, watching him as he did me.

He knew it wasn't the Christmas decorations on display; it was his show for me to witness. And his audience, captive to his words and the power of what he called "the Holy Spirit."

As the song ended, the demented choir took their seats and turned to the great Reverend who ceremoniously took the pulpit, saying:

"Suddenly a great company of the heavenly host appeared with the angel, praising God and saying, "Glory to God in the highest heaven, and on earth peace to those on whom his favor rests."

"This is what we say today. God's favor rests on us. We praise Him. He shall be called Emmanuel. God with us. Jesus is God with us, here right now, in the form of His Holy Spirit, our Counselor, our Comforter, our Friend. We welcome Him to bring us into this season of God's favor. For the next twelve days of Christmas, we will celebrate His life on earth, which gives us life in heaven."

Who are you fooling? I asked myself. God was not farther from any other place in this world. If God is truth, as Billings says, then He knows the evil that lives here. It was plausible deniability that any true joy could have rested inside the evil deeds of those in this room.

I laughed at the sight of these monsters pretending to have love. But as Annette came to me with a greeting, I could not help but feel genuine warmth pour out of her body.

She was indeed glowing as she introduced herself, "Hi, I'm Annie. God bless you."

"You too," I answered, pretending that I held innocence to her true identity. "You're due any day now,"

"Yes. My first. I think it's a boy," Annette said excitedly.

Her first? She couldn't possibly believe the words that spilled from her lips were any more true than Rev. Billings' words.

The sermon continued. Billings spoke about a new birth. About a man named Nicodemus who asked how a grown man could reenter his mother's womb to be born again.

"Jesus told him that no one can enter the kingdom of God unless he is born of water and the Spirit. Flesh gives birth to flesh, but the Spirit gives birth to spirit."

I was craving to speak with Dobson, but had to sit through the rest of *The Billings Show* first.

Soon I blended into the Christmas decorations, waiting for his sermon end, while I pondered the deeper meaning of dinner.

We finally got to eat. Surprisingly, it was like a Thanksgiving meal, complete with all the trimmings. All the happy little elves were gathered.

Billings, his wife Annabelle, Haworth, and I sat at the main table.

Annabelle Billings was an attractive woman, in her mid-forties, who seemed genuinely interested in my life, peppering me with questions about California and how she always dreamed of living there. I wasn't sure if Billings or Haworth put her up to this to get more information about me.

I told her basic facts and did a little probing of my own, finding out that they had a son at Texas A&M and a recently married daughter who moved to Phoenix.

It was actually refreshing to talk to her because it kept my focus off business for a moment and actually made dinner enjoyable. She had this joy, a contagious energy that brought life to the room. Even Haworth seemed at ease after a few glasses of wine.

He was more jovial and actually called me Eddie for the first time, even if by the mistake of intoxication.

As the dinner progressed, I could see Rev. Billings fading. It was as though he was coming down from a high, and the adrenaline that charged his batteries was diminishing by the minute.

His eyes would often retreat into a deep, meditative trance and this sense of remorse crept in, before he'd smile and bounce back into the conversation.

He also had a few scratches on his face and hands that I hadn't noticed before. There was something deep going on in the back of his mind, and his wife was acute to it. Her supportive touch and loving gaze always seemed to be enough to bring him back.

And as conversation took its normal breath of relief, a hushed lull inhabited the room. Maybe it was the peculiar sound of a phone ringing that seemed to stun the patients.

Haworth's cell phone rang, and he excused himself with a sense of urgency. He acted casual, but I read him for a change, and I knew that there was important information about to be relayed.

How was he getting cell phone reception when no one else can? My phone is useless out here. There's got to be a satellite or wireless service provider somewhere in this area.

I watched Haworth as he walked outside. I knew I couldn't get close enough to him to eavesdrop, but with the Billings' comforting each other, my golden opportunity arose. I could see it clearly across the room.

I excused myself to use the restroom, turned on my recorder, slipped it in my jacket pocket, then carefully made my way over to Annette Dobson for a few words. She seemed excited to see me.

"You were at the service. Are you the doctor who will be delivering my precious baby?"

"No, I'm just visiting," I told her, taking note of her bubbly new persona.

"Are you a friend of Rev. Billings?" she asked with an innocent smile.

"Yes."

"You're lying. But it's okay," Annette bluntly stated.

"What?"

"I can tell, when someone's not truthful. I just know."

"We're business associates," I said, watching this childlike confusion set into her.

"Then how come you weren't here yesterday? It was my birthday."

"I'm sorry. Happy Birthday!"

"Thank you. More people were here for the ceremony, but they're gone now."

"Ceremony? You mean party?"

"I don't know. I don't remember."

"What do you mean?" I asked, knowing she was being truthful in her answers, but hoping to strike a deeper chord into her persona.

"It's silly. I don't remember my own birthday party. But I was born again. That's what Reverend Billings told me. So Happy Birthday to me."

That made me laugh. She stunned me. For a moment I was asking myself, *"Is this the same person?"* There were physical similarities—height, hair color, eye color—but her persona was completely opposite from the murderer the media had crucified.

"Are you Annette Dobson?"

"I'm Annie." She smiled back.

"Where were you born?"

"Here," she said, completely convinced of her answer. "You ask a lot of questions… Isn't it beautiful?"

"What?"

"This," Annette said pointing around the room. "The lights. The tree. The chapel. Life. Isn't it beautiful?"

"Sure," I replied, and with that I felt a sudden tug.

"Mr. Hansen, we need to speak with you. Could you join us please?"

That was Dr. Haworth on cue to break up the conversation. He practically ripped my arm off trying to get me away from Annette Dobson.

"It was nice to meet you," Annie said as I was being dragged away.

Haworth held on tightly. His strength was greater than I imagined as he sternly exclaimed, "I should have informed you that Annette Dobson is in a very fragile state of mind. You cannot mention anything about her past. Is that clear?"

"That is her!" I smiled, knowing truth was at my door.

"We are not hiding anything from you, Mr. Hansen. Had you returned here as scheduled, you would have been briefed with the team."

"Briefed for what?" I asked.

"Her exorcism," Haworth said as he forced me back into my seat.

"What?"

"We were trying to prepare you. But you disappeared, and we needed to proceed as scheduled."

Billings and Haworth then informed me that they recruited a team to administer the exorcism, following strict procedures and confidentiality.

Haworth promised they would show me tapes of the exorcism at our meeting tomorrow morning, along with letting me observe Annette Dobson's post-exorcism psychotherapy sessions.

According to Billings the exorcism was very excruciating and Dobson had developed amnesia. After being delivered from her demon she had no memory of her past life.

They are not sure if it is temporary or permanent. I'm going to meet the medical doctor, Mark Preston, tomorrow. He's returning to observe Dobson and deliver her baby.

I'm exhausted right now, but I'm pretty sure I caught up with all my notes.

I don't feel like writing. I don't think I can. My body feels tense and cold. I feel like this room is watching me. That triangle window glows, and it's casting a strange aura throughout the room. When I stop focusing on writing and take in this atmosphere, it sends a chill through me. The hairs on my arms stand up, and this rush of anticipation hits me.

I want to knock myself out so I can sleep. I took one shot of NyQuil and I'm waiting for it to kick in.

I need to detach myself from this physical world around me. The objects in this room feel alive. When I touch things, like the bowl or statue, I feel energy surge through me. It's a dark pulse of energy. A haunting breath of life that feeds off this place. Even the eyes, the round shapes of stone and steel, which line the wooden furniture, seem to have something alive within them.

I checked them earlier to see if they were wireless cameras or glass mirrors built in to reflect my image back to some hidden camera. I don't think so, but it feels like these eyes are watching me, moving with me.

This energy steals my breath. It feels like I ran up a hill, and I'm struggling to catch my breath. Then the moment oxygen enters my body; it rushes out like it's afraid to stay inside me.

It feels like the air that comes into me in here is filled with some life force that my body rejects.

But I need to breathe to survive, so I take the good with the bad and let nature run its course through me, in the hope that I can adapt to this alien environment.

My mind tells me that this is a test, but my body tells me that there is a force here to be dealt with. Like that deer that senses when a predator is approaching, this is my defense mechanism, arising within me.

All I want to do is shut everything off and rest. Convince myself that there is no need to worry or fear. I wish I could just flip a switch in my mind and turn off the warning signals that won't let me sleep.

My last hope is that the drugs will take me there. Take me to the place of rest I so desperately need.

I think I OD'd on the NyQuil. I had trouble sleeping after I stopped writing, so I took another shot.

I couldn't get comfortable. It gets really cold in here, and when everything finally calmed down around me, all I could feel was pain.

Sleeping on my back hurt my shoulder, sleeping on my side hurt my leg, so I tossed and turned all night.

Around four in the morning, I flipped over and looked up at the ceiling. I noticed this thing hanging over me. Like a blob of smoke shaped like an octopus.

It just hovered over me with its tentacles spread across the room. I reached my hand out to touch it, but it moved with my hand, flowing with me as I sat up. There was no face or form to this thing, so I figured it was a reflection from the trees through the window, or cold air bouncing off warm objects in the room, causing smoke.

But the strange part was that I could see tiny dots of light moving inside it. And it seemed to follow me, looking at me with light.

When I addressed this form, it said nothing, so I turned over and tried to sleep. After a second, I could feel my blanket being tugged slightly, then I felt my shirt move, so I rolled back and looked up at this form surrounding me.

Pressure points of pain began throbbing on my back and my leg. I felt pressure on my stomach, then my heart. That gnawing on my chest was strong. It was hard to breathe, so I curled up in the fetal position, waiting for the drugs to kick in and knock me out.

As I lay there, curled up, I could hear thoughts speaking loudly, screaming inside my head.

"You're a loser."

"You're a liar."

"You've never done anything with your life."
"One failure after another."
"You're better off dead!"

That's the last thing I remember, before passing out.

I woke up starving. I'll have breakfast, then I'm off to my first meeting with Haworth and Billings, while I try to figure this all out.

AUDIO LOG/JOURNAL ENTRY:
MONDAY, DECEMBER 13, 2010 – 10:00 A.M.

Breakfast was interesting. I ran into that old Greek lady, Gloria. She seemed to be in a stable mind-set. She actually smiled and became quite talkative with me, rambling on about the weather and how she loves the snow. The purity, the comfort, the way every snowflake is different and how they can be shaped together to form so many different things.

She wanted me to take her outside so she could make a snow angel. They made her feel safe.

"Safe from what?" I asked.

"The devil," she said, solemnly. "He killed my mother. And he wants to kill me."

Here's what I gathered as she went on about her life story. Gloria's father was abusive. He constantly beat her as a child and when her mother tried to intervene, she was beaten worse. When Gloria was thirteen, her father came home in a drunken rage, discovering that her mother planned to leave him.

Gloria's father suspected that she was cheating and beat her badly before throwing her mother out the front door.

Gloria's mother fell awkwardly off the porch step, cracked her head open on a rock, and died on the spot.

Gloria buried herself in a snow bank for the night. The next morning she ran away, and she's been on her own ever since.

Dr. Haworth found her wandering the streets of Dell City about six years ago and brought her here to live.

When I asked Gloria how she learned to speak Greek, she answered, "Silly bastard! I'm a hundred percent Irish!"

After breakfast, I headed over to Haworth's office and was introduced to Dr. Mark Preston. He's a good-looking guy in his late forties with a strong medical background.

He gave me his credentials, which included work as a surgeon at the UCLA Medical Center and staff doctor at the Dallas VA Medical Center. We hit it off as former Bruins. He's an avid sports fan—UCLA basketball, of course—and an amateur musician.

I actually liked the guy. I felt comfortable being around him. It was nice to have a conversation where someone wasn't crazy or analyzing my every word and move.

He told me he met Rev. Billings in Dallas when they worked at the VA together. Apparently Billings was a psychiatrist before becoming an ordained minister.

In fact, all three of them had been digesting similar theories in various aspects of the medical field and decided to work together.

I had just about warmed Preston up to tell me how they all ended up in Uphir, when Rev. Billings entered.

Billings got right to business. He told us Dr. Haworth was with Annie, preparing her for our meeting. I needed to be prepped here. So I set up my recorder and got down to business.

"This is Eddie Hansen. It is Monday, December 13, correct?

"Yes," Preston replied.

"Monday, December 13, 10:00 a.m., and I am at the Uphir Behavioral Center with Dr. Mark Preston and Rev. William Billings. I have permission to record this meeting."

"Yes," they answered successively.

Dr. Preston exclaimed, "Eddie, we'd like to begin by showing you some video from Annie's exorcism yesterday."

Dr. Preston turned on the tape and there was Annette Dobson. This was the Annette I remembered. The murderer. Her eyes were black and glazed. She looked more evil than in her last television interview, before being sentenced to death.

Her lips were tightly closed, and her glare was venomous. Her face seemed taut and smooth.

She was restrained in a chair, but she did not struggle to move. To her, she was in the position of power.

I watched the video. Haworth was already in deep with Dobson. He looked intense and focused as he addressed her.

"Show yourself, Keron. Your lie has been exposed."

Dobson sat calmly, maintaining direct eye contact with the camera. Dr. Haworth then addressed her with a gentler voice, "Annette, I know he told you that your children would be like you. They'd hear the voice of hell take them home if you didn't help them get to heaven. You were afraid. But you don't have to be afraid anymore. Let go. Whatever is inside you, Annette? Let him speak. Keron Ken-Ken! I demand to speak with you!"

Dobson sneered, waving her head like a snake, humming in these pained, psychotic tones, half-laughing, half-snickering.

She's playing with him, and it showed in Haworth's voice as he yelled, "Speak to me, Keron! I know who you are. I called you out. You must address me."

She spit on him, and then screamed in a crazy voice, "Mind fucker! I drink her tears! Watch me drink her tears."

Billings paused the tape. The way Dobson venomously exhaled those last words, brought me face-to-face with a horror I've never seen captured. Her words were deliberate, poisonous, and spoken with a certainty of truth.

It was a horrible thought that some evil power inside Annette Dobson could devour her very tears. Suck them up from inside her. But that was exactly what I was looking at.

The sight of it drew me in. Looking closely at her face I noticed one of Dobson's eyes was bone dry, while the other eye seemed dark and wet.

It took Billings' tap on my shoulder to draw to get my attention as he said, "The expulsion of demons is not science or a routine ritual confined to Catholicism. Exorcism is spiritual warfare, Eddie. We are removing an unwanted predator from a host body. A demon is a parasite that takes hold inside the soul of a person."

"How?" I asked, unable to take my eyes off the frozen image of Dobson's deranged face.

Billings continued, "I believe, first through our thoughts. As thoughts become accepted as truth in the mind, they are allowed to take root inside a person's soul, much like a seed, which grows as we water it."

Dr. Preston then interjected with his assessment. "Cognitive behavioral modification was part of her therapy, but we still needed to define the source input for her thoughts, and eventual actions."

"Why a demon?" I asked. "That's iatrogenic. It's not science when you make the suggestion of a demonic presence to your patient, and they accept it as truth."

Dr. Preston responded, "We never suggest demonic influence to a patient; it's always revealed through psychotherapy. I'm glad you've done your research, Eddie. It will help you come to your own conclusion regarding our discoveries."

Billings continued, "A demon will lay dormant, using its power to become an ingrained part of the victim's personality. We call this part of its existence, 'a pretense.' In this stage, the demon or demons hide their true identity. Since they have assumed control of their victim and have a home, there is no need to identify themselves for fear that they might be sent back to their place of origin, or fail in their assignment. If you were assigned to an undercover investigation, would you reveal yourself to the source you were investigating?"

"Of course not," I blurted out, before suddenly coming to the stark realization that is exactly what I did to gain access to this facility.

Before the thought left my mind, Billings continued, "Our job at this stage is to break this pretense, find out who the demon is, then separate the demon from the victim."

Dr. Preston placed various pictures of Annette Dobson in front of me, stating, "This is the stage that Dr. Haworth is at here. It took a few weeks of psychotherapy and hypnosis for Annette to unveil his presence."

"Keron came out as Annette's childhood friend," Billings explained. "A make-believe friend Annette had long forgotten about. But his thoughts and intentions were consistently manifested in Annette's personality, even in her voice at times."

"How do you know it's a demon?" I asked, thumbing through the file of psychotic pictures.

"You sense its presence," Rev. Billings explained. "The same way you felt it in the room with me the other day. Eddie, it's undeniable."

"Okay, I felt something. Doesn't mean it's a demon. People can give you a vibe. They have an energy, aura, whatever you want to call it. You sense it. Some people are crazy."

"Exactly," Dr. Preston sided with me. "Which is why I conduct a series of medical tests to make sure that there are no abnormalities, lesions, or tumors in the brain that could cause behavioral problems. We also check for diseases, STDs, viruses, even unknown bacteria or a chemical reaction that may be responsible for the victim's behavior modification, emotional health, or identity disorder. This is followed by Dr. Haworth's thorough psychiatric evaluation and more testing. We want to absolutely rule out all mental illness as a root cause for these behavioral disturbances."

"How can you be sure that it's not?" I asked, with my eyes still locked onto these violent images of Annette Dobson and her dead infant children.

"Medical science is never perfect, Eddie. But victims of possession often transgress through boundaries of mental illness, with symptoms and behaviors that are not characteristic with their disease. They may even display supernatural signs that defy natural law, as well as our own logic."

"What if it's a strain of a virus?" I asked. "Aren't there strains of mental illness, strains of chemicals and biological disease that can cause brain damage? Even offsets of things we're still discovering that can affect mental health?"

"Excellent point, Eddie," Rev. Billings said. "The success of science always comes from asking ourselves, 'What if?' So I asked myself, 'What if demonic influence is a root in mental disorder? What if demons can cause biological and physical changes in the human body?' Please watch and give us your honest opinion."

Rev. Billings proceeded to show me another clip of Dr. Haworth's pre-exorcism psychotherapy session with Dobson.

"It's not your fault, Annie. Right? Someone helped you? That's why you're still alive. That's why you weren't executed. Because you are innocent. It's why you're here with us. So we can find the real killer. Do you want to find the real killer?"

"Yes," Dobson said sobbing. She looked completely drained, not restrained like before. That's freaky! Tears keep coming down one side of her face. I clearly see it now. Her left eye is dry as a bone. It looks like the liquid is evaporating inside her eye as Dr. Haworth probes her deeper, asking, "Was it Kevin?"

"No," Dobson muttered, sounding like a little girl in trouble.

"Was it someone you know?" Haworth pressed in.

"Yes. Yes." Dobson cried.

"It's okay," Haworth said, holding her hand. "You can be honest with me here, Annie. No one can hurt you. I promise."

"Promise?" she begged, looking for relief from her torment.

Dobson then shifted in her seat, shrugging as if she were a horse, trying to shoo off a fly that was molesting her. You could tell something was deeply affecting her, but the animal was unable to express words. She tried to regain control over her bodily functions. It took a moment before Dobson could respond again.

"Okay. I want to tell you," she said in her childish, high-pitched voice.

"You can tell me," assured Haworth. "Was it a friend?"

"Yes," she groaned, forcing out her words, as if some force within her were trying to hold her down. "He taught me how to do it," she cried.

"Who did?"

Dobson paused, needing to summon the energy within her to force her answer through. With a childlike moan she uttered, "Keron," before falling back in her chair with force.

"Who's Keron?" Haworth inquired.

"My friend. Keron Ken-Ken."

"How long have you known Keron?"

The fight within Dobson gained strength. Tears welled up in only her right eye, leaving her left eye dry and red, almost bloody. Her left eye fluttered. She rubbed it as if it were causing her great pain.

Dark tears poured out from one eye, while the other looked as though it was cracking from dryness.

Dr. Haworth handed Annie a tissue, saying, "We can stop here. If this is too much, let me know, Annie."

"No! No!" she cried, with childlike innocence. "I need to tell. I have to!" She forced herself up, saying, "When I was little, we had tea. He came when I was sad. We played hide-and-seek. Now he's hiding."

"Where?" asked Haworth. "Where is Keron hiding?"

"I can't tell," Dobson moaned, changing rapidly into her adult voice, fully aware of her surroundings and sensing grave danger inside her. She squirmed uncomfortably in her seat, digging her nails into the armrest.

"He's here?" Haworth inquired.

Annette's eyes shifted again, her left eye pulsating as she shrank deeper into her chair, like a child, before squealing with pain, "Umm…hmmm."

Haworth leaned in to her confrontationally asking, "Why doesn't Keron want me to see him?"

"I can't say," Dobson cried, clutching the chair tighter.

"Are you afraid?"

She shook her head yes, taking solace in her childish persona. "You can't tattletale on your friends. It's a no-no."

"You're not tattling honey," Haworth told her, reaching out cautiously toward Annette's arm. "You're letting me help Keron. Don't you want to help him?"

"Yes," she cowered.

"Good, Annie," said Haworth, moving closer. "Can you tell me where Keron is?"

She was afraid to speak. She pointed to her chest. Haworth tried to touch her, but Dobson was afraid. He said, "Okay. It's okay. I'd like to speak with Keron."

"Keron Ken-Ken!" Annette screamed in a voice that was neither hers nor her alter ego of that innocent child. She lunged to Haworth. The restraints held her down as she screamed, "Address me by my proper name, mind fucker!"

This was the vicious Annette Dobson I remembered. The ruthless, savage killer. The one who took the stand in court and confessed to her crimes. Her face showed no innocence, no remorse. It was ice-cold. Her eyes beamed with disgust and hate as she bellowed, "Want to know what she did, ask mind fucker!"

"Okay, Keron," said Haworth, proceeding with a warranted caution.

"Keron Ken-Ken!" screamed Dobson, vomiting out words in another language as she spit on Haworth. *"Quieres saber como se hace, amigo. Mente hijo de puta!"*

"Forgive me, Keron Ken-Ken," Haworth told her. "I would like you to tell me what you taught Annie."

"Poner al bebe a dormir," the voice vomited.

Haworth leaned in, watching Dobson's eyes carefully as he probed. "Let Annie speak, Keron Ken-Ken."

She moaned as if about to orgasm before plainly stating, "We put the baby to sleep."

"How did you do that?"

Dobson began laughing sadistically, toying with Haworth as he continued prying her psyche. "How did you put the baby to sleep? Tell me! How did you put the baby to sleep?"

Dobson rolled her eyes back, taking a deep breath. She let out a deep guttural groan. When her eyes opened again, the blackness of her pupils expanded into a large dark hole. Dobson's voice was hidden somewhere inside this creature as she began to sing in a calm, chilling tone.

> *"Bye, baby, Mama's here,*
> *Rocking her little baby so dear,*
> *Angels guard you while you sleep,*
> *Hush now, baby, do not peep.*
> *Oh! Bye, little baby, bye oh,*
> *Bye, little baby, bye oh."*

Billings shut off the tape and slowly walked toward me, carefully examining my body language. He didn't say a word. He was waiting for me to speak. He wanted my honest opinion. Here it is.

"That's one sick bitch! You want me to believe that monster is a little girl again. You cleaned her up, like magic. Now she's singing *Hallelujah*. Innocent as a dove and she can't remember a damn thing! That's what I'm supposed to believe? How do I know Little Miss Sunshine is Annette Dobson? Not some look-a-like you want me to pawn off to the *Times*, so you can get your grant money or stock offering, or whatever you're trying to sell me!"

I figured my response would shake some feathers and now it was my turn to observe their reaction.

Billings smiled and turned his head, deferring to Dr. Preston, who calmly replied, "It's okay, Eddie. You have every reason to doubt us. We will conduct DNA tests; get you fingerprints to match the state's file. Anything you need to confirm her identity."

Billings added, "The only thing we ask, Eddie, is that you make no mention of her past to Annie. You are here to observe our work as an independent reporter. You may not interfere with or suggest anything to Annie that would make her remember any of the previous events in her life. You may record this session but no modification will be tolerated, and the punishment for interference will be severe. Are you clear with these terms?"

The way Billings said that, I knew he meant business. He was dead serious, so I agreed. I needed their trust as much as they needed mine, and this was a golden opportunity to break my case wide open.

Dr. Preston smiled, tapping me on the shoulder like a friend, "We'll reconvene in thirty minutes. Ward C on the third floor."

"Sounds good," I told him. "I'll get my camera."

"Thank you for being honest, Eddie. We appreciate your input," Preston told me, as he gathered his personal belongings and headed toward the door.

Damn that guy has got a way of making people like him. He puts you at ease and lulls you into buying whatever he's selling. Now I'm off to meet the new Annie.

VIDEO LOG/JOURNAL ENTRY:
MONDAY, DECEMBER 13, 2010 – 11:30 A.M.

The third floor of Ward B is made up like a fairy tale for Annie. There's lots of kids' stuff, bright colors. It's very clean and comfortable. She's in her room with Billings. I'm waiting outside for permission to enter.

There's the signal. I'm all clear to enter *Snow White's Adventures*.

Dobson is on her bed, wearing pajamas with her Bible in hand. What a paradox of humanity. I'll introduce myself and set up my camera.

"Hey, sweetheart, are you ready to film today," I say.

"Yes. Praise God, I'm so excited. I'm going to be a mommy tomorrow. I can't believe it."

Billings sits next to her, touching her hand gently, "That's right. How do you feel, Annie?"

"I feel strong. God is so alive in me. I feel the Holy Spirit bringing me peace. And joy. I have so much joy!"

Smiling like a child, Billings continues, "Dr. Preston says your contractions are almost twenty minutes apart, Annie. Do you feel any pain?"

"No. Just pressure in my belly. I feel him in there. God's gift to me. I can't wait to see his face. When his eyes open and he looks at me, it will be like seeing the baby Jesus."

Are you kidding me? I think to myself as I finish setting up the camera. I turn on the microphone before beginning.

"This is Eddie Hansen, and I'm with Annie in her home. She's going to talk to us about her new life and the baby on the way. It's okay to record you, right, Annie?"

"Okay," she replies.

Billings continues with his playful banter as if he were talking to a child. "What would you like to talk about, Annie? Do you want to say something?"

She looks at me funny, then says, "You don't believe I'm truly happy, do you, Eddie?"

"Sure I do. You look beautiful, Annie," I tell her.

She smiles. "I told you; I can tell when people are lying. You don't even believe what you say because there's a shield over you. Like a cover, it's dark, and it won't let you see light. It blocks light from your eyes, so they're dark. Your eyes are the windows to your soul. But they're dark."

"All right," I say, not knowing where she is headed, but I keep recording as she asks, "Do you feel love, Eddie?"

"Sure," I say.

"For who?"

It takes me a second, but the answer comes naturally. "My daughter, Kennedy."

"You said that with so much pain, Eddie. But when you said it, the cover of your shield cracked a little."

She took my hand gently and guided me down to the bed next to her.

'Love is patient, love is kind. It does not envy, it does not boast, it is not proud. It does not dishonor others, it is not self-seeking, it is not easily angered, it keeps no record of wrongs. Love does not delight in evil but rejoices with the truth. It always protects, always trusts, always hopes, always perseveres. Love never fails. But where there are prophecies, they will cease; where there are tongues, they will be stilled; where there is knowledge, it will pass away. For we know in part and we prophesy in part but when completeness comes, what is in part disappears. For now we see only a reflection as in a mirror; then we shall see face to face. Now I know in part; then I shall know fully, even as I am fully known. And now these three remain: faith, hope and love. But the greatest of these is love."

I don't know what it was but those words punctured my heart and I sat there silent, reflecting.

      "Do you understand?" Annette asks me.

      "Some."

      "The love of a father, Eddie. You understand a father's love."

      "Yes."

      "You would do anything for your little girl, wouldn't you?"

      "Yes."

      "It's the same with your Father in heaven. He does not want to see you perish. *My people perish for lack of knowledge. The devil roars about like a lion seeking those he may devour.* Only love can crack that shield so that you know the truth. That shield will not protect you, Eddie, it will devour you."

      I don't know whether it is what she says or the glow that seems to emanate from her, but her words were powerful.

      I want to see Kennedy badly, it chokes me up.

All of the sudden it feels like I can't breathe. I have to leave the room.

I get back to my guesthouse and break down. I'm having a difficult time describing what I'm feeling.

In Annette's words I could see the part of her that Kevin fell in love with. And yet I still saw the devil she kept hidden, and it got me angry.

Jaime was the same heartless bitch, but she was killing me instead of our daughter. I was never good enough for her. I could never do enough. I never had enough to earn her love. Why did I have to earn it?

If love was kind and patient and kept no record of wrongs, why was I always wrong? Why was this love denied from me? Why could I never feel it? The kind of love Annette described, does it even exist?

If it does, am I capable of it?

Maybe I was too busy trying to please myself, instead of being a husband and a father.

The way Annette said everything was so effortless. The words flowed out of her mouth as if she wasn't even thinking about them. There was genuineness, passion, conviction like I've never heard before.

I keep watching her on this tape and her words echo someplace deep inside me.

> *"For now we see only a reflection as in a mirror; then we shall see face to face. Now I know in part; then I shall know fully, even as I am fully known."*

What does that mean? I'm looking in the mirror, and I see myself. My eyes are dark. I look empty. I stare into the mirror, into my eyes, and it feels like I am looking into eternity. There's this world out there beyond me, inviting me to explore. But the mirror stares back with an evil grin, laughing at my efforts to understand.

My face mocks me, laughing at my failure. Both my eyes melt into one as I stare at myself.

I feel I'm on the outside of my body looking through me. I see the lost years and ravages of time drawing lines on my face, scars to remind me what I've lost.

The years of wearing down and breaking apart cover my skin. And the longer I stare at myself, the blurrier I become.

Soon my body begins to fade into nothingness, and the mirror looks back at the blank wall.

Memories and words are my only reminder of the man who once stood here. And sadness covers me like plastic around the infant who barely realizes that his life is slowly disappearing into the black night.

AUDIO LOG/JOURNAL ENTRY:
MONDAY, DECEMBER 13, 2010 – 2:00 P.M.

For our post lunch briefing, we gathered in the conference room. A video deck was set up with a small stack of tapes and case files spread across the table.

Dr. Haworth opened the folder pulling out a picture of the demented Dobson on death row. "We've never had a case like this," he told me. "It defies all our statistical data."

Billings continued, "No exorcism is alike. Tactically each one presents unique challenges with varied results."

"How many have you done?" I asked.

"In my career, six full-fledged exorcisms, hundreds of deliverances," Billings stated.

"What the hell's the difference?" I asked.

Billings laughed, "Hell is the difference."

Even Haworth got a chuckle out of that as Billings continued. "An exorcism involves complete or perfect possession. The victims have lost all of their own power and are completely ruled by the demon or demons. An exorcism can last a few days, whereas deliverance may take a few minutes to a few hours. The victim is usually tormented or partially possessed, but they still have some control over their life. The victim is usually involved in some ritualistic sin or evil they cannot control themselves from participating in."

Dr. Haworth pulled a post-exorcism photo of Annette. It was completely opposite. If it weren't for the scar above her right eye in both photos, I would have trouble identifying her.

"What's unique about Annette's case," Haworth said, "is that she's been in this euphoric state over two days. The longest we've previously encountered was approximately twelve hours."

"Euphoric. You mean the hyper-religious happy meal she's chomping on?" I retorted.

With that, Dr. Preston displayed charts of Dobson's medical test results, adding, "It's more than that, Eddie. Physically she's stronger than she's been. We've done conditioning tests and her body has drastically improved, even with her pregnancy. Her heart is stronger. Her hormone levels have increased. Her red blood cell count is elevated. There's even increased brain activity—higher electrical charges mostly in her right temporal lobe."

"The area responsible for hallucination or paranormal activity," I responded.

"Yes. But the right temporal lobe can also activate spiritual awareness as evidenced in case studies on prayer and praise," commented Rev. Billings.

Dr. Preston then displayed Dobson's brain scans saying, "See this, Eddie? These colors. The blue is the repressed area without activity. The yellow to red areas measure activity in the brain, with red being the highest recorded activity. In our memory testing, this area spiked higher than she's ever recorded."

"Which you heard from her Scripture memorization," Billings replied.

"Is that what she was quoting me?" I said.

"First Corinthians, chapter thirteen. Love. It was her morning Bible study," Billings added.

"So it didn't mean anything," I replied. "She was just parroting what she read earlier."

"Everything means something. That Scripture was on my heart as I prayed this morning, so we studied the chapter," Billings commented. "But her exact recitation, after reading this passage once, is astounding."

Dr. Preston continued showing me more charts.

"What's also perplexing is her pain threshold. Annette is not reacting negatively, not feeling pain, which is in contradiction to the increased awareness of her body in labor and her brain function. To have that much brain activity and no remembrance of her former life is supernatural in and of itself."

"Why don't you remind her? Show her what she did?" I asked.

"That might have catastrophic effects, especially before childbirth," Billings warned. "It would be dangerous, not only for the baby, but for Annie as well. If she can deliver a baby in this state, it would be unprecedented."

"That's what you really want, isn't it?" I told them, already knowing the answer to my question.

"What if a baby were born like Jesus, from a completely pure vessel in a controlled environment? What would that child be capable of?" Billings excitedly stated.

"A pure vessel?" I replied. "Are you listening to yourself?"

Doc Preston could tell I was working to knock Billings off his religious pedestal.

"We wanted to deliver her baby immediately after the exorcism," Preston said. "But the risk of inducing labor was too great with her elevated heart rate. We have not given her any drugs since. All signs point to Annette having a natural childbirth tomorrow."

"Are you going to keep brainwashing her with religious impetus until she delivers?" I asked.

Dr. Haworth finally commented. He had been curiously absent from most of our previous discussion, keeping his eye on me for my reactions.

He stated informally, "We're simply keeping her from negative stimulus. It's why we don't have television, Internet, or phone service here, Eddie. Psychological testing in a controlled environment produces the most accurate results."

"Yeah, but what are you controlling?" I asked.

Billings walked over to the monitor and popped in a tape, saying, "We are very excited about what is unveiling here, Eddie. A consistent pattern of truth."

Haworth stated, "We're going to show you part of Timothy Tyler's post-exorcism therapy. This was taken two hours after the exorcism. For the record, Timothy Tyler was not introduced to any other stimulus nor given any medication."

Billings played the tape. I couldn't believe what I saw. The man resembled Tyler, but if it weren't for the neck tattoo extending from the collar of his suit, I would not have believed it.

"How are you feeling, Mr. Tyler?" asked Haworth,

"Amazing, Doc. I got me some energy. You know, when I walked over from my room, there was this baby bluebird out there. Imagine the odds. He flew in front of me. I mean, right in front of me. I had to stop. This little baby birdie, on the ground in front of me. He looks up at me and starts chirping. Like he was singing. Singing just for me. You know what? Know what came to mind?"

"What?" Haworth asked him.

"Mister Bluebird's on my shoulder. It's the truth, it's actual, everything is satisfactual…. Zip-a-dee-doo-dah, zip-a-dee-ay. My, oh my, what a wonderful day. Plenty of sunshine headin' my way. Zip-a-dee-doo-dah, zip-a-dee-ay."

They were both laughing. How could you not? The look on Tyler's face singing was priceless.

"Hey kids, it's time for the sing-along serial killer, featuring Timmy Tyler and the brides of death. I can't wait to see him cover *Pinocchio* and *Snow White*." I joked.

But that album wouldn't come anytime soon.

According to Billings and Haworth, Tyler said he never felt better. He danced about in a jovial mood as they put him through a series of tests. He enjoyed dinner, even played poker with Donald and a few members of the ward. Then he headed to bed.

Tyler went to sleep and that's when they showed me the surveillance video from inside his room.

Tyler woke up in a maddening rage around 3:00 a.m., as if in a nightmare. And then, the unthinkable! Tyler began to chew on his own arm. It was sickening watching him rip through his own skin.

Gnawing into his arm, Tyler tore right through his own muscles, his mouth filling with blood, eating himself down to the bone before two guards entered to restrain him.

He threw them against the wall like rag dolls. The force was incredible.

According to Haworth, one guard broke three ribs. The other guard was Santiago. He received a broken nose and concussion.

A third guard entered and fired a tranquilizer dart into Tyler's leg. The guard took a few shots to the head before escaping and running out of the room.

Tyler chased down the hall after him, before finally collapsing. It was surreal to watch. Tyler looked like a rabid dog. His eyes were glazed over. He foamed at the mouth.

His language was a series of gibberish rants and animal noises. Growls, hisses, barks, and groans. It seemed he was no longer human. When Tyler awoke, he had to be constantly restrained. Billings stated that he manifested eight different personalities over the next three days of examination.

They were categorized as eight different demons that took possession of Tyler. It was as Billings explained:

"THE SEVEN-X PHENOMENA."

This is the same theory I read about days earlier in that Bible story. It was why I had been given that highlighted passage.

To these men, SEVEN-X was not just a theory, it was a fact.

"It's a constant, immutable spiritual law," Billings told me.

In all six of his previous exorcisms, the demon brought back seven more demons to torment the victim, until they could reclaim possession of the body. And the final condition of that victim was much worse, or as Billings would comment, "Precisely what Jesus told His followers."

Only two of his exorcisms remained successful for an extended period. The other patients, Billings claimed, wore down over time. They let their old ways of thinking resume. Patterns of thought would begin to consume them again. They became aware of their past, and something inside them began to crave the comfort of their former life.

Billings told me that although the voices they heard were no longer a part of them, as was evidenced through post-exorcism therapy; the demons were consistently around the victim, offering suggestions and insight.

As the victim began to associate and act out on these demonic suggestions, the demons would resume their occupation of the body.

This is what Rev. Billings explained as we walked over to meet Tyler. Now I'm about to see in person what they are talking about, and unlike Annette Dobson's interview, I have permission to ask or say anything I want.

AUDIO LOG/JOURNAL ENTRY:
MONDAY, DECEMBER 13, 2010 – 4:15 P.M.

I believe this is the ward I was confined in overnight. As I walked with Billings, a strong feeling came over me. My mind clenched to the patterns of my footsteps, recalling the earlier progression of grass and concrete. Grass then concrete. Without the glare of the sun, I could see my surroundings and take note of the path we traveled.

Ward D was for the dangerous patients; the ones who needed restraint and isolation. It was an unspoken place. Upon its mention, patients tensed up, bodies cringed, and mouths sealed shut.

There was genuine fear about Wards D and E. Fear that could be cut with a knife, as rumors of the whispering kind settled in.

No one wanted to see them or talk about them, much less go there. A sentence to Ward E was a death sentence. No one ever returned.

Ward D, Crazy Donald coined "the cutting room." The place where they drilled into your head to find answers. Where ice picks slid through eyeballs, plunging into the depths of the brain, killing independence, and slaughtering personality. Cold steel gouged through your head from the hands of those the patients say are truly the madmen.

Rev. Billings and I proceeded down the stairs through a dark tunneled area that could only be entered with a set of keys and keypad combinations. I listened closely as we entered, trying to hear the dripping water or the echoes of screams, but it was unruly silent. Too silent. As if everything here were dead or abandoned long ago.

The only sound I could hear was the constant rhythm of our shoes clicking on the cold pavement, and the occasional interjection of Rev. Billings.

"Remember, Eddie, it's not Timothy speaking, but the demons speaking through him. Identify each one, so you'll understand how they attack."

"Alrighty," I said as he led me to the end of the hallway where a security guard opened the door. This guy was big. He looked like a UFC fighter. I've never seen him before, so I introduced myself. You want to be on this guy's good side.

"How ya doing, man? I'm Eddie."

"Curtis," he answered. "You can go in. Tyler's restrained."

Billings nodded with approval then asked, "You sure you want to go in alone?"

"I'm fine."

Curtis opened the cast-iron door, and I slipped inside. The entire ward was empty, except for the last cell. There was no glass separating us like *Silence of the Lambs*, just bars. And I certainly didn't feel like Clarice when I entered the cell area.

For the record, Tyler was worse than Hannibal Lecter. Hannibal was civilized. Tyler was pure monster. And yet, there he was sitting quietly, draped in his straitjacket.

As I approached, he gleefully yelled, "Alrighty! I got myself some company."

I pulled up a seat and placed it about three feet from the cell's bars. Timothy Nathan Tyler stuck his head between the steel bars asking, "What's your name, buddy boy?"

"You don't remember me?" I asked him.

"I don't get out often, my friend. Got this castle to myself. My own private Idaho."

"I see," I said, examining him cautiously.

"So what brings you 'round?" he asked, scratching himself up against the steel.

"I need someone regular to talk to. I'm sick of all the psychobabble," I told him.

"Hell yeah!" Tyler said enthusiastically, pushing his head further between the bars before noticing my recorder, "That's pretty. You know you gots to have permission for these sorts of pursuits. Can't just be taping things."

"Yeah. I know."

"Lest ye be punished."

"So I hear," I told him.

"Well you got?"

"Yeah."

"Not from me," Tyler grumbled, shuffling with excitement. "Nobody asked ole' Timmy if they could be running tapes of his golden vocals."

"May I?" I asked, holding the recorder close to the cell door.

"You may not."

"No problem. I'll turn it off. I just wanted to chat anyway."

After a little negotiation, we came to an agreement. I got to turn my recorder on, if I loosened his straitjacket and let his arms out. Tyler said his shoulder was hurting, and the sadistic bastards took joy in seeing him suffer.

I couldn't just sit idly by and watch him suffer. I'm not that kind of animal. So I moved in close to him when I started feeling that presence again.

It's hard to describe, but the closer I got, the more my heart raced. I wasn't scared. It wasn't fear. It was just this queasy, uneasy feeling, like something was crawling on me.

Maybe it was the smell. His stench was putrid, like decay. Like something was dead inside him. Maybe he was suffering from Cotard's syndrome. Maybe he was already dead inside.

His breath smelled like rotten garbage. Were they afraid to let him bathe or brush his teeth? Would he stab himself or someone else with the toothbrush, or ram it down his own throat, choking himself to death?

I don't know. I held my breath as I stuck my fingers inside the small metal opening and loosened the straps that held his arms in.

Part of me felt like he was going to spin around and stab me with something, or bite my fingers off, but he stood there perfectly calm. Maybe that's what felt the most disturbing. That dreadful silence of anticipation.

But Tyler never moved or spoke. He acted perfectly normal, not psychotic. I almost felt sorry for him, strapped up, isolated, not cared for. I know what one night in these conditions did to me. I couldn't imagine what six years in this place could do to a man.

He seemed genuinely grateful for the company and a chance to move his arms.

"Feel better?" I asked.

"Whooo Hooo! Hallelujah. Free at last," he said stretching against the iron bars.

"So, Timothy, what do you remember about your exorcism?"

Suddenly his demeanor changed, and he pressed his face as far as he could through the bars, groaning, "Exorcism? Is that what they told you?"

"Yeah. They rid you of your demons."

"Liars! They're the crazy ones."

"How?" I asked, watching him carefully to see if there was any way he could break free, now that he was unrestrained.

"They told me I'd get to see Mama before she died. You know, at least let her visit me. Just so she knew I was all right. But no, man. They lied! I called 'em on their bullshit. Know what they did?"

I shook my head.

"Sons of bitches took the knife to my head. Cut me up. See!" Tyler said, pushing his scars toward me.

"That's wrong."

"Fuck right, it's wrong! Know what else?"

"What?"

"They put acid on my arm. Chemicals. Something. Burned so bad, I had to bite it out. Suck that shit out, before it chewed up my whole arm."

"That's messed up," I said, remembering the video.

Tyler continued, "They're going to get to you too. You're staying in crazy house. Out by the gate."

"How'd you know?"

"I see you. I got my eyes on the prize. This is the big business, baby."

"What do you mean?"

"Turn it off, man!" Tyler scowled, making his way back to the metal bars and pressing his face through them. "They know you know…" He paused and looked me straight in the eyes, saying, "You're here forever."

Then he smashed his face even harder between the bars and whispered, "Turn it off. This is for your ears only. If you want out, put the ear in."

I did what Tyler asked. I shut off my recorder, and moved toward the bars, pressing my ear to the metal. I felt a chill go through me as he pressed his face even deeper into the metal, inches from my ear. Close enough to bite it off. But instead, he whispered with his foul breath that turned my stomach.

He told me the government was in on this experiment. They were forking over millions to develop mind control techniques and create drugs to put fear into people, so they could take over. If they could keep people passive, poor, and fearful, they could control them, Tyler said.

He told me his whole murder trial was a setup. They drugged him and tortured him. They made him tell everyone he was the vampire killer, so people wouldn't believe his story.

He said the pharmaceutical company he worked for was putting the drugs into foods. He was about to blow the whistle when they made their move and set up the murders.

I wasn't sure if he was crazy or not, but I wanted to know more. There was something about his story that intrigued me. Just then, with perfect timing, Billings returned, telling me time was up. That's when Tyler said something that really shook me.

"Hey, Eddie. Them two blondes in El Paso. You be careful! When your outcome's death and the devil. No turning back from those cards, ya hear!"

I spun around quick, but that security guard Curtis blocked me and escorted me out.

Tyler continued ranting, "Come back and see me. You want to know what happened that night with those witches? Or should I say two nights. I was there."

His voice got fainter as I was forced out the door, which sealed shut behind me.

Tyler kept ranting in muffled tones, trapped behind iron walls, while Billings acted innocent about the subject. He seemed convinced it was a demon speaking through Tyler. I couldn't get a straight answer.

According to Rev. Billings, I had met "Ipos," a cunning but powerful demon who has special insight into the past and future. His possession turns a man proud and gives him charismatic appeal.

I must be shopping in the Costco demon section, because they got one for everything. Mix and match personality traits, pop them into the "Demonatic," and presto! You've got your custom-made, demonic possession. Order in the next ten minutes and we'll throw in the voice modulation kit absolutely free! How much would you pay for this?

Idiots! Nobody manipulates me. I have to get my battle plan ready.

First I'm dumping my media on a hard drive and shipping it out. All my video, audio, and notes up to today. I need to get to the post office in Dell City before it closes.

I'll call Mel. Let her know what I got.

Then it's off to the nearest food supply to stock up. Maybe in El Paso. I can't take any chances eating the food here. If I am being drugged, my time may be limited.

I'll let you know my next move when I get there.

AUDIO LOG/JOURNAL ENTRY:
MONDAY, DECEMBER 13, 2010 – 6:22 P.M.

I hate that it gets dark so damn early. I had to drive down those unlit, back-ass country roads with no streetlights. I finally got reception.

I'm back at the diner, logging in with my favorite waitress, Aida Mae. Now that I'm in civilization and my food is ordered, I'm giving Mel a call.

"Hey."

"Hey what?" Mel replies harshly. "Didn't you get my messages?"

"No. I didn't check anything. My voice mail's full."

"Really. I've been trying to reach you for days. I'm worried, Eddie."

I can sense it in her voice. "Relax, babe. I'm out of cell range. I was gonna—"

"You're in some deep shit!" she interrupts.

"Hmm?"

"You're in deep shit. Come home."

"What?"

"Eddie. Get in your car and drive home. Now!"

"I can't."

"You have to."

"Mel. Relax. I got it under control."

"No, you don't," she snaps. "No, you don't! No, you don't! I did what you asked, okay? That writing. It's not Greek. It's Latin. I went to that lingual school in Beverly Hills where you wanted me to go. You know what it says? You wanna know?"

"Yeah, sure."

"You really wanna know?"

"Yeah."

"Really?"

"Mel?"

"You really want to know, Eddie. Here goes! It says 'Your soul is mine!' You hear that? YOUR SOUL IS MINE!"

"Relax!"

"No. No, Eddie, no! I'm not. I'm not relaxed. That shit is fucked up. That tape said, 'I will inhabit your soul like I inhabit this recording.' When I listened, I felt something in the room with me. It touched me! I swear! It kept saying the same thing over and over. The translator even freaked out. I'm having bad dreams, Eddie. Really bad."

"Sweetie. Calm down. Don't let your imagination get to you… I'm sorry. Hear me out… Mel, can you do that?"

"What?"

"Hear me out, baby, just listen. Can you do that?"

"Okay."

"Good. These guys are the ones in deep shit. I got the goods on them. This is big, and when we break this case you and I are going to be rich and famous. Can you handle that?"

"Okay."

"Good. Then we'll finish that album of yours."

"Really?"

"Yeah, baby, of course. We can do this. You can't let them get to you. They know who you are and know you're helping me. So stay tough!"

"All right."

"Here's the best part. Annette Dobson's here. I got her on tape."

"Really?"

"In the flesh! I'll send you the tapes first thing tomorrow… Mel, Dobson's pregnant. They're going to deliver her baby."

"Oh my God."

"Yeah. Check this out. They told me she had an exorcism. She's a freak. That bitch is acting like the Virgin Mary. You wouldn't believe it. They got Tyler in here too."

"You saw them?"

"Yeah. Get this. Tyler claims he was framed for ratting on the pharmaceutical company he worked for. You remember anything about that?"

She pauses for a second. "He worked for Dow Lantra way back, before his trial. I remember. You saved the story. It's here with your notes."

"Exactly. See if you can find anything about Dow developing new food preservatives. Tyler said they were making preservatives and additives with drugs to induce fear. I think they conducted some experiments here."

"You serious?" she asks. I could sense the panic coming back into her voice.

"Yeah. They're big players. Someone at the FDA had to let this pass through. Check FDA records. Get a list of all the new FDA-approved drugs, food additives, preservatives. Whatever you can dig up. Got it?"

It's silent for a moment before I hear. "I'm scared, Eddie."

"Don't be. People prey on fear. That's how they get power. Don't give in. We're on to something. I need you to follow through."

She pauses again. I know that silence. Finally she whimpers, "Eddie?"

"What, babe?" I say, knowing something is wrong.

"The minister wasn't lying. She was speaking Greek."

"Okay. I know."

"Everything's true. Was that whole translation true?" She pauses. After a moment, she comes out with it. "Jamie, at the hotel. Did that happen?"

"Don't worry about that."

"Did it happen?"

"Mel!"

"Answer me, damn it. Eddie, be honest for once. If we're ever going to have anything, you have to be honest with me."

That's when it hits me. She's gonna find out about El Paso and the girls. What do I do? I mean, it's not like we're married. Should I tell her?

"Eddie? Eddie, you there?" she asks.

"Yeah," I'm at a loss for words.

"Tell me! Did it happen?"

"Yeah. I'm sorry. I never told you the whole story. I went there to kill Scott. But I didn't… Okay?"

"How would that lady know, Eddie? In fucking Greek! What if these demons are real?

I can feel her pulling back tears.

"I don't know," she says. "I don't know if I can do this!"

I feel it in her voice. She's scared. What am I going to tell her?

"Mel… Mel! C'mon," I plead. "Ain't no such thing as demons. When billions are at stake, people make shit up. Break shit up! Fake shit up! You know that. We covered an election."

Just then, who should appear out back, but Aida Mae, peeping her head around the corner.

"Your meatloaf is getting cold. Want me to put it back in the oven, honey?"

"No," I answer. "I'll be in, in a sec."

Now back to Mel.

"Baby, I got to head inside. I'll mail the hard drive tomorrow. Take that video of Dobson to Carl. Tease him with it. Tell him we need my next advance and all our expenses paid now. Got it?"

"Yeah. Call me tomorrow," Mel begs. "Please, don't let a week go by, Eddie. It scares me. I'm worried."

"Don't. I gotta run," I tell her.

"I love you, Eddie." I know she means it. And the next words are hard for me to say.

"Love you too. I got to go."

"Bye," she says and hangs up.

My brain's off. I can't think now. I need to rest. And I'm not getting it at the Mad Villa. Now Mel's got me thinking about everything. Damn it!

I better head inside, finish my food, and concentrate on what I need to do.

Here comes Aida Mae on cue, bobbing her head like Daisy Mae Duke, with a flick of her hair or wig or whatever that is.

"You all right?" she asks.

"I'm great, thanks," I tell her. "I'm addicted to your meatloaf."

"Thanks," she smiles. "I made it with love. If you make everything with love, it just comes out better."

"I guess so… Aida, what do you know about Rev. Billings?"

"He seems nice. He comes in sometimes on Sundays after church. But I never go there. I'm not the religious type."

"Me neither," I add. "You believe in demons, right?"

"I guess," she answers. "People do bad things. Just God-awful stuff. I don't even watch the news anymore. They just all shoot each other like animals and carve them up like a chicken and not even think one was the other. People and animals, I mean. Not chickens."

"Believe me, you don't want to be a reporter."

"No. I'm happy here. Real happy," she says, as she cleans up around me. "I mean everyone here's pretty nice. Except Geoffrey. Now if anyone's got a demon, it's that boy. I'm sorry 'bout that blood he rubbed on you. He's not all there. And his mama, she drinks all night. And she's mean. Ornery little bitch. I hate to say it, but she is."

"It's all right," I tell her. "Geoffrey. He's that Goth kid with the eyeliner?"

"Evil little child. I'm convinced he killed Rhonda Daniels' cat. No animal did that. It was that boy. I know it."

"You know anyone in town named Ose."

"Not off hand, hon," she says, casually moving between the tables.

"You mentioned that name to me. Last time I was here. You said Ose was calling me."

"I'm sorry," Aida tells me, looking confused. "I don't remember that. And I'd remember a name like Ose. That's a very unusual name. Ose."

"Yeah, it is," I say. "You said you thought Uphir was demon possessed. You called it the heartbeat of hell."

"I did? I'm genuinely sorry I said that," she replies, moving over to the next table to wipe it down. "My memory is not good. Sometimes I say stuff, I guess. I don't even know what I say. I think I just hear things and say them out loud. Say my thoughts, maybe. Is that weird? Am I weird?"

"You're fine," I assure her.

"I did it again. Said my thoughts. 'Cuz I was talking about that with you. But I heard him talk again. That voice. I heard him say it. Should I say it? Say what he told me."

"Please."

"You won't stiff me on my tip?"

"No. Of course, not. I promise."

"Okay. Here goes. I'm just saying what I heard," Aida closes her eyes and lets out a rush of breath.

"It's your last chance to turn around. Whatever that means. That's just what I heard. I'm sorry," she says, scurrying away from my table.

"It's all right. How'd you hear it?"

She stops and looks back. "Promise you won't laugh?"

"Yeah," I nod.

She gets quiet for a second, and then in this girlish, shy little voice she tells me, almost embarrassed, "Like a friend talking to me. Been like that since I was little. We played games and made cookies. I know it's just my thoughts, but they run wild. It's kind of how I am. I just always heard things."

"That's fine. If you hear anything else, let me know."

"Will do," she says, walking toward the kitchen." You want some coffee, dear?"

"I'm good. I need to get going, but thank you for everything," I tell her, getting up and leaving money on the counter. "Keep the change."

"Thank you. Have a nice night," she replies, placing the money in the register.

I get about halfway to the door when Aida Mae yells, "It just came again. I heard it. 'It's in the cards.' How do you like that? That's what I heard. 'It's in the cards.' I just get the funniest stuff. 'In the cards.' That doesn't even make sense, but I thought you may…need to know that. Maybe?"

Then she turns and walks into the kitchen.

That was strange. Aida Mae is no Rhodes scholar, but this made sense to me. There's no way she could know about my tarot reading, or how Sandra told me to turn back.

Am I just swimming in the pool of coincidence?

It's maddening and I don't want to figure it all out this minute. I need to escape, to ease my mind.

I should hit that liquor store on the road to El Paso. Load up on some goodies, hit the Post Office early tomorrow then drive back to Uphir.

I just have to…

Son of a bitch! How could I be so stupid?
I grabbed my laptop and forgot the hard drive. I swear I grabbed it, now it's not here.

Where the hell is it? Did I lose it? Did I bring it? Fuck! I'm so tired. I don't even know. I'm going to rip everything apart and look for it. If I don't find it, I have to go back.

JOURNAL ENTRY:
MONDAY, DECEMBER 13, 2010 – 10:37 P.M.

I hate driving here at night! God forbid you get lost on the way and wind up in Jason's cabin from *Friday the 13th*.

It took an extra hour to get back from the Route 160 junction. There are no signs, no lights, no GPS out here. This godforsaken place isn't even on a map. I felt like I was driving in circles half the night. Spinning my wheels through slosh, hitting dead ends, and winding through the trees that stalked the path back here.

Roads split, then curve, then circle back to the same place. There's a constant fear that you'll hit a low hanging branch, or a deer, or just slide off the mountain and crash to the ground a thousand feet below.

The madness of impending disaster constantly pounds your nerves, while the sound of churning tires spitting wet snow guides you like a theme park ride.

I kept thinking if I get stuck in this slush, I'm dead. I'll freeze to death out here. No one would find me for days, maybe weeks, or longer.

Every time I heard the tires spin, my nerves would lock, my heart would race, and I'd look out into the blackness hoping I'd see that old water tower looming ahead. It marked the last mile stretch before reaching the asylum.

These roads are archaic. That's my new word. I want to use that word. *ARCHAIC!*

If you can't see it on Google, it's archaic. If it's made of dirt, it's archaic. If there are no streetlights, it's archaic. If there's only one lane for driving both ways, guess what? That's archaic!

The only guidepost I had was that hand-sketched map Renaldo Gonzalez made. He led the way to Uphir and without him, I'd never have discovered this place. Hence, I dedicate this road to him.

I dub thee, *Renaldo Gonzalez Drive*, named after the soon to be famous prison guard who watched Timothy Nathan Tyler and Annette Dobson get shipped secretly into this "Heartbeat of Hell."

If I was weak, I'd be terrified of all this. But I'm a reporter, and I've seen crazier shit. Infiltrate a drug gang. Get that story without getting killed. That's scary.

You don't get real money without taking real risks, and this, boys and girls, is not a risk. Fake crazy for money is a pharmaceutical company's wet dream.

A whole colony of prisoners are held here, ripe for experimentation.

What if they are not just death-row inmates? What if there's also people with nothing to lose, who can't do another day in the pen, or someone who's marked for murder, going down inside a state prison?

Or maybe it's some victim of the mafia or gang who was in the wrong place at the wrong time, so they get an all expense paid trip to Club Dread to be experimented on.

Who knows what warrants a visit to the Uphir Behavioral Health Center. Hundreds, maybe thousands of prisoners have passed through these gates. And there could be places like this all over the country.

No one knows, except the unlucky souls sent here or the sadistic minions in charge.

There's so much left to this story, so much to be figured out, so much for my imagination to unravel.

I have to go to Ward E, bring my camera, and get some proof of the real madness. One more shot of Jägermeister and I'm good to go.

VIDEO LOG:
MONDAY, DECEMBER 13, 2010 – 11:45 P.M.
ENTERED BY MELODY SWANN

This is the second part of the second batch of recordings from Eddie. I'll add my notes as I watch.

Eddie points the camera at himself. Mr. TV Host. He's drunk. I can tell by the look in his eye. I've seen it enough times. His brass balls pop out, and he's the life of the party. That's why I love you, Eddie. You're a trip.

> "Hey! It's the one and only Eddie Hansen, in the flesh. Look around! Are you scared? Come join me for the ride of your life."

It looks like some horror movie, but it's strangely beautiful. This Gothic architecture is amazing. They don't make buildings like this anymore.

I remember Eddie said before he left, this was undiscovered history, swept under a rug of misinformation. We're rediscovering a piece of American insanity.

"That's Ward E, my friends. The patients, or should I say the hostages here call it 'the cutting room.' Because inside these insidious walls, skulls are burrowed into.

"Soon you'll meet two death-row inmates reported dead by the state of Texas. And only I, Eddie Hansen, can bring them back from the dead, straight to you!

"Annette Dobson and Timothy Nathan Tyler were evil people who committed atrocious crimes. But is what's happening to them karma or torture?

"Tyler had a lobotomy. They jammed an ice pick through his eyeball into his frontal lobe. Is it payback for his crimes? Or is this heinous torture for attempting to rat out the dirty secrets of the drug company he once worked for?

"You may be involuntarily ingesting their chemicals right now.

"You wonder why you don't feel so good. Why you can't shake that headache? Why you feel agitated, uncomfortable, terrified watching me walk across the grounds of this mental institution alone at night?

"Well, we're going to get to the bottom of it right now. The stairwell around this corner leads to the dungeon where evil lives. Let's go take a—

"Hey! What the fuck?"

Someone shines a flashlight into Eddie's eyes. That guy's huge. He looks like a pro wrestler wearing a security uniform.

"You can't go in there. Turn around."

"Hey, Curtis. Remember me, bro? It's Eddie."

"Yeah. Turn around."

"I need to see Timmy Tyler."

"You don't have permission," the guard says, stepping in front of Eddie.

"Doc said it's cool. Ask him."

"Don't matter. Turn around."

"C'mon man. It'll just take a minute."

Eddie tries to walk past him but the guard knocks him down like a rag doll.

"Don't make me hurt you."

"Let me go in," Eddie pleads.

The guard pulls out his club. "Turn around."

"You wouldn't," Eddie says, pointing the camera at him.

"Turn that off!" the guard warns Eddie, pulling his club back to strike.

"Step back! It's off. It's off," Eddie screams, setting the camera down.

The camera shuts off. But Eddie must have had his recorder turned on. This audio file is from the same event; created December 13, 2010 at 11:28 p.m. Everything is the same up to this point.

"It's off. It's off. See? You can hold it. Just don't break it like Santiago did. That idiot pounded a nail in. Cost me three hundred bucks to fix."

"No, he didn't."

"What do you mean, 'No, he didn't'?"

"It wasn't a nail. Something ripped apart his leg," the guard tells Eddie. "Skinned him to the bone."

"You serious?"

"Dead," replies the guard. "He's laid up in Ward A. Freaked out of his mind."

"That's why I haven't seen him?"

"Stay away from E. I'm warning you."

Eddie broke the silence.

"Hey, Curtis. I got a nice bottle of Jäg here. Want it?"

"Give me that."

"So, you go down there?" Eddie asks.

"Inside. Hell no. You need a code, fingerprints. Only Dr. Haworth has access. Farthest you get is the tunnel entrance at Ward D."

"What's down there?"

"Don't want to know," the guard tells Eddie.

"How long you been here, bro?"

"Too long."

"Ever want to leave?"

"Can't."

"What do you mean, you can't?" Eddie asks.

"Make the best of it, Eddie. Obey and you can get promoted to guard or cook, maybe maintenance. Then it ain't so bad here. Just follow the rules."

"Let's go down. You and me."

"No," the guard insists.

"Curtis, c'mon. I'll give you five hundred bucks... Cash!"

"What am I going to do with money, Eddie?"

"What do you want?" Eddie asks.

"Got any more of that?"

"A couple bottles. Case of Bud. What do you want?" Eddie tells him.

"All of it!"

"What? Come on man."

"You heard me," the guard orders. "All of it! I'll get you a key for the tunnel to D. Go wherever you want at night. When I want more, you get it. Deal?"

"Deal," Eddie agrees.

"I ain't going down for you. You get your leg ripped off, your heart pulled out of your chest, don't call me. Got it? You die, it ain't on me."

"No problem, bro. I'll hook you up," Eddie tells him.

"Go! Before anyone sees us!"

"I need my camera."

"No."

"What?"

"If they find you filming out here. That's on me," the guard explains. "I ain't going to the hole for you. Bring my booze."

I hear the guard walk away. Eddie's still talking.

"That was interesting," Eddie says. "I hope you heard that, my friends, because we're going to take a little detour. Who wants to hear the gruesome sounds of Ward E? It's around the next building. Let's have a look."

"I hear something," Eddie continues as he makes his way down the steps. "Listen."

I hear a loud humming sound like a generator. Wait, there's something else.

"Someone's screaming. I hear them through the walls. I need to get closer. There it is."

I hear it now. That's disturbing. It sounds like torture. Like that scene in the movie *Hostel*. I don't know why, but that's what I see in my mind, listening to this. The scene where that torturer burns out the Asian girl's eyeball, and it's just hanging off her face. Why am I even thinking of that?

"Damn it! Son of a bitch!"

Something happened to Eddie. He's gagging. I hear him running up stairs. He falls. I think he's vomiting. He sounds sick. He's choking, rolling around, gagging for air.

That's it. His recorder shut off.

JOURNAL ENTRY:
TUESDAY, DECEMBER 14, 2010 – 3:03 A.M.

It's three minutes after three in the morning. Something shook my bed so hard, it woke me. I think a water pipe burst, or the generator blew, because I have no water or electricity. It's freezing.

I'm using my phone to see through the blackness.

It's too long a hike to get to the guard's gate. I called, but no one answered. Maybe he's investigating the explosion. I should wait here and see if someone comes. It's too dangerous to hike the trail without a weapon.

My nerves are fried. That trip to Ward E wore me out. I can't even listen to the recording.

When I hear it, I think of that smell and want to vomit. I can't even describe it. Burning flesh, sulfur, decomposing animals, rotted fish, piss, shit, bile, infected skin—all come to mind. That river of sewage punctured my nose.

I looked down and realized the soft, wet ground I was kneeling in was filled with maggots devouring what looked like a torn-up animal carcass.

My hand was buried in guts, and I could feel the maggots squirming up my arm. But the foul smell wasn't from the animal. It was from inside the dimly lit confines of Ward E.

Something moved over my head. I felt it. There's a dark, black shadow moving across the ceiling. It looks like it's watching me.

Maybe it's my shadow reflected. I'm closing my laptop to see if I can still see it up there. Hold on.

I'm going to record this.

VIDEO LOG:
TUESDAY, DECEMBER 14, 2010 – 3:10 A.M.
ENTERED BY MELODY SWANN

"It's Eddie Hansen. It's three ten in the morning, December 14. I'm inside my cottage, at the asylum in Uphir, Texas. I'm on the bed, recording this with my phone.

"See the shades of black, that thing on the ceiling? Look at the two specs of light. They're almost like eyeballs, looking right at me, hovering.

"It's getting closer. Floating down toward me. It's not like the tentacles I saw the other night. This thing is more like a bat, or maybe a vampire, because the body is long.

"Look, that's about six feet. It resembles a human body, but there are no arms or legs.

"Hey! What are you? Eddie says.

There's something up there. It's hard to tell what it is on that phone camera, but there is something moving on the ceiling. It's pulsating. Eddie, stay away. He's standing on the bed, trying to poke it. Oh my God, it opened.

"Shit! It's got wings. They spread across the room. There's another one. See the other one inside."

I have no idea what he is messing with. If there's some kind of animal hanging off the ceiling… It's so dark in there, it's hard to tell.

> "It's a little one, like a baby in the opposite corner. It's got the same shape. Look at the shadows open and close. They go wide, then narrow, hovering over me. It's getting closer."

I hear something like wings or feathers flapping. Get out Eddie! What are you doing?

> "Get the fuck out!" Eddie yells.

He swipes at it.

> "It won't move. They just keep hovering over me. I can't see what it is. I need to get the lights on. I'll freeze to death if I don't find the circuit breaker. I'm going outside to look… Shit, it's cold!"

Everything is pitch black. He's holding on to the house as he feels his way around the back. There it is. He finds the light switch.

> "It's dead. Damn it. I've got to figure—"

Something just ran past Eddie quickly.

> "What the fuck was that?"

It looked like an animal. A wolf or bear or something. It was big and fast. I hear tree branches crack in front of Eddie.

> "Something's out here. Maybe wild animals. I can't go anywhere without a gun. You need a gun here. I need to go in. It's my best chance to try to stay warm and ride this out 'til morning."

That place is wicked. Everything about it looks evil. Every time I see the video, it makes the hair on my arms jump. I'd never stay there. Eddie's crazy. He's shining his phone around the room. It's creepy. I hate that place. Those tables with the eyeballs popping out make my skin crawl.

> "Nobody is in here. But something is still hanging off the ceiling. Is it some kind of bat? Look, my light wraps around that dark, black shadow. What the fuck is it?"

Oh my God, the shadow is pulsating, like it's breathing. I've never seen anything like it.

> "What do you want? Come on! Say something!"

Nothing moves, but it looks like something is alive on the ceiling.

> "Maybe I'm seeing things. Maybe they drugged the water, or the heater's pumping chemicals in the air. I'm lying on my bed, and these things hover over me. Go! Go! Get out!"

Eddie jumps up on the bed and swipes his hand through the shadow.

> "I swiped at the little one, but my hand went through it. Now he merged with the big one, hiding like a kangaroo in its mother's pouch."

Eddie crashes down on the bed again. He turns the phone to himself.

> "My chest is pounding. I don't feel good. I feel like I'm going to have a heart attack. I just want to sleep. I need sleep. I want to sleep. Please! Let me sleep. I just want to sleep. I need to sleep. Everyone, just leave me alone. I don't feel good. It hurts. My chest, it hurts. It really hurts."

That's it. His phone went dead. I can't take this anymore. Not knowing what is going on. Hearing and seeing these things. My mind runs wild. I can't imagine what you are going through, the pain you feel. Eddie come home.

JOURNAL ENTRY:
TUESDAY, DECEMBER 14, 2010 – 9:23 A.M.

The knock on the door scared the hell out of me. I was out cold. I scratched my left hand. It's swollen and sore. I didn't want to get out of bed because of the pain.

But the daytime security guard woke me up, with his constant pounding. Where do they get these guys?

I got up to find Simon, a lanky Englishman with the same nervous jitter as Santiago. Watching him twitch made me realize my paranoia may have substance to it, or at least chemicals.

Something tells me my gut is right and "Birdman of Alcatraz" is another prison refugee who couldn't do another day in the pen, so he took the Club Dread vacation package.

I opened the door and the idiot just stood there, holding my camera nervously in his hand, waiting.

I don't get this whole "permission" scenario with these guards. Are they like vampires?

"Come on in," I told him. "I grant you permission." But he wouldn't step inside.

He set the camera down at the door in front of me and told me Annette Dobson went into labor. I need to report to Dr. Haworth's office immediately. Then he left.

"This is bullshit! Now I have to wait for permission to see if they are going to let me inside for Dobson's delivery.

"They love messing with me. They give me just enough to keep me needing more, but never enough to get my whole story.

"Apparently, Preston and Billings are already inside with Dobson, and she's about to pop. Haworth is at the medical center checking my status now. So it is up to Billings to decide my fate.

"Meanwhile, Haworth left me alone in his office. So I'm going to see what's in his computer while he's gone! It's my turn to get answers I'm going to copy his files.

"Come on… Come on. How many files are in here?

"I hear something. Footsteps! Haworth's coming!

"C'mon, copy… No. No! C'mon…Got it!

"Now I'll just walk around like nothing happened. Here he is.

"Mr. Hansen."

"Hey, Doc! What's the good word?"

"Sit down."

Haworth makes his way back to his desk and examines his computer. He observes me for what seems like minutes before I interjected:

"So she's having the baby?"

He checks around his desk, like something is missing. It seems like an eternity before he finally digs up a pen from under the keyboard. He opens his desk drawer and pulls out a file, then begins jotting something down on a notepad while he tells me:

"Rev. Billings and Dr. Preston were very specific with their method and instructions for this birth. Only Nurse Evans will accompany them. You and I will not participate."

"What?"

"I'm allowing them to use discernment. For the sake of this experiment."

"How do *I* skew the result?"

"That's not my decision."

"Great!"

I start thinking of a solution to get my story. Then, it hits me.

"Is anyone taping this? Are there cameras in there?"

"Yes."

"Can you feed me the signal? Please?"

"I'll consider that."

"Thank you."

Haworth looks at me for a moment with concern. I try to play innocent of any accusations his eyes might be making. Then I see it. My death sentence hanging from the upper corner of the room. A video camera hangs on the wall above Haworth's desk. It's blinking, staring down at me, convicting me of my crime. I look up, trying not to let Haworth notice me as he states firmly:

"You may not bring any recording materials inside with you. Is that clear? You may only observe if Rev. Billings approves."

"That's fine."

I feel momentary relief, but the back of my mind keeps wondering what that security camera recorded. I stand there, dwelling on my guilt as Haworth looks up and says:

"We'll reconvene at ten thirty in front of Ward A. You are dismissed."

"Thank you. I appreciate it."

"You're welcome, Mr. Hansen," Haworth replies coldly, never looking up as I leave.

JOURNAL ENTRY:
TUESDAY, DECEMBER 14, 2010 – 10:12 A.M.

I got those files by the skin of my teeth. I was so close to Haworth walking in on me while I was at his computer. But I'm worried about that camera in the corner above his desk. If it recorded me, I'm going down!

It got me thinking. With all the cameras planted all around this place, there has to be a control room somewhere. A storage facility. A database for all the video and case files acquired through the ages. That archive is a goldmine. I can only imagine the treatments, torture, mutilation, exorcisms, and demonic activity that has been recorded.

If I could access that control room and secure those files, I'd recover a hidden piece of history. I'd get a Nobel Prize, something. This would be enough to make a whole series of films, TV shows, documentaries.

The Smithsonian, museums, private collectors, public events—they'd all pay. Everyone would want this. I can't even begin to count the wealth it would bring.

There's no way they'd ever let me see the control room or know its whereabouts. That information is probably as classified as a government test site.

So for now, I play their game. I've taken enough risks today. I'm not going to push it, but I've got to get proof of this birth. I need concrete evidence that this baby is alive. That Annette Dobson delivered him and did not abort her pregnancy. I need that evidence!

JOURNAL ENTRY:
TUESDAY, DECEMBER 14, 2010 – 11:06 A.M.

Here's our compromise. I'm sitting in the doctors' lounge in Ward A, watching the video feed from one of the cameras in the birthing room.

I get to witness this spectacle. What's odd is that Dr. Haworth doesn't seem remotely interested in what's going on. Maybe there's more pressing events elsewhere, but this is a sight to see.

Let me describe this carnival under the big top, because I don't think anyone has ever seen a birth like this. Never underestimate the sheer paradox of watching a reportedly dead serial killer sitting in a warm tub of waist-high water, birthing her presumed dead victim.

Annette Dobson is wearing this white gown like she's getting married. Her arms are raised and she's smiling in complete bliss. She breathes in and out rhythmically. They've been singing and laughing like they're on drugs since I've been watching.

Rev. Billings is praying over Annette, putting his hands on her stomach and head most of the time.

He started shooing demons away, saying that their rights were broken, that they had no legal ground to be there or to affect the birth of this child.

No one will believe what's happening here. This is history. The kind of history that people won't dare talk about!

And like a circle, it repeats itself, asking the same questions about who we really are under the surface.

Speaking of which, Preston just reached his hands into the water and instructed Dobson to push. It looks like the head of the baby may be coming soon. I wish you could see this. Dobson's face is glowing.

It's weird. She doesn't look like she's in pain.

She's actually singing. They're not words coming out of her mouth, just beautiful tones echoing through the room. This unspoken language of her song is pretty powerful. It's almost like a chant or opera. It's very emotional. She's in another dimension, connected to her child or connected to something out there. It's actually beautiful, different!

With Jamie, all I remember was a lot of cursing. She squeezed my hand so hard, it turned blue, and she yelled at me for being an irresponsible jerk.

But here I am, listening to a serial killer sing her child into the world. Her voice is so pure. There's no strain in it at all. It's like this fountain pouring out life.

I really wish you could see this. It's so bizarre. Oh wait! Wait! You can! I got it. Why didn't I think of this before? I can turn on the camera on my laptop and record the monitor feed.

Watch this my friends, serial killer Annette Dobson's singing birth.

As insane as this looks, there is a magnificent beauty to it. I can't comprehend how such a beautiful voice can come from within this woman. It pierces through me. It actually brings a tear to my eye. Maybe I'm getting soft.

Part of me wants to see that monster for who she is, but she looks beautiful. She's giving birth to a child, and there is something so organically pure and beautiful about this moment. The miracle of a child being born.

It feels like it was yesterday. That was me in there, with Jamie. I saw Kennedy take her first breath in this world.

My little girl was so beautiful. I was the first one to hold her. The doctor handed her to me, and she looked into my eyes as if looking through my soul. I melted. I felt pure joy. I was so happy, so grateful for everything.

I don't know if I've felt that way since.

Right now, Annette Dobson is engulfed in pure bliss. This woman, a serial killer, looks like an angel. She's laughing as Preston delivers her baby.

Oh my God. Here it comes. Here it comes.

Wow! It's a boy. A baby boy! He's beautiful. He's not even crying. The little guy's laughing like someone is tickling him. I don't know why, I feel like I'm a daddy again.

That's so stupid, but looking at him makes me forget everything else in the world. I'm looking at her holding him now, watching her cry with joy.

I know those tears. They are the most beautiful tears you will ever cry. The tears of a brand-new parent.

JOURNAL ENTRY:
TUESDAY, DECEMBER 14, 2010 – 3:00 P.M.

I was a blubbering idiot. A visual reminder of Kennedy's birth combined with the fact that I just had what might be the greatest success of my career—it broke me a little.

Serial killer Annette Dobson, pronounced dead by the state of Texas, gave birth to a baby boy, and I have it.

This video's worth at least fifty thousand. Between this journal, my recordings, and Haworth's files, I just about have a million-dollar story. Just a few more questions to be answered and I can unlock the gold.

Who's really behind this?
What's their real motive?

If figure that out, the sky is the limit. If I uncover that video vault, the world is mine for the taking! But first things first, I must concentrate on my present assets and use them to the fullest capacity.

Annette Dobson is now under constant surveillance. I'm hoping to get permission for another interview, to get that kid clearly on camera.

Get this—she named him, Kevin. She has no idea why, but she said, and I quote, "I feel like I'm missing a Kevin in my life. Now I have him."

No sweetheart. Kevin is your husband. You were childhood sweethearts, and you married him when you were seventeen and pregnant with your first child. Maybe Kevin should come visit. He'd love to reminisce. But he thinks you're dead. And your baby might stir the hornet's nest.

This makes me think. If somehow in her unconscious mind she feels this need for a "Kevin," what else is lurking in there? What else is about to unravel within her? How can I be there when it happens?

It's time to organize my plan. I'm copying everything over to my external drive including Haworth's files. I can't have them on my computer. I can't risk it.

When this finishes, I've got to move fast. If anyone saw video of me in Haworth's office, I'm on borrowed time.

I need to get to Dell City before dark and get this done! It's time to make history.

JOURNAL/VIDEO LOG:
TUESDAY, DECEMBER 14, 2010 – 4:55 P.M.

I made it to the post office, just before closing. I wanted to film this historic event of me sending my story to Mel.

I approached the post office guy with my camera in one hand, and the mailing box in the other, and asked, "Want to be part of my history, my friend?"

"No thank you. Sheriff has rules about that and if he catches you filming 'round town without permission, he'll lock you up," he said casually, accepting my package and placing it on the scale.

"Am I back in Los Angeles? I need a permit?"

He looked back at me blankly. I could tell he'd seen some bad things in his life and just wanted to be left in peace. I've spent enough time in prison and with war vets to know.

He was a big boy. He had this scar across his right eye, and another long one down his arm, partially covered by a tattoo of an eagle with some writing beneath. I think it said Isaiah 40:31.

Maybe Isaiah was his name or his squadron. I didn't bother to ask. He just stared at me, with the package sitting on the scale, before groaning, "It's best you shut that off, son. Head back home."

"No problem, pops."

I didn't mention what I was sending or what my documentary was about, but I got a feeling that word travels fast around this little town.

That old guy seemed nervous about something. He just kept staring at me, like he was trying to figure it out. I wondered what he was hiding.

He wasn't real chatty, until he looked down at the box I was mailing. He calmly picked it up and examined it. Then he paused for a second, looked me deep in the eye and said, "God must be smiling on you."

"Why?" I asked.

"You made it back here," he replied simply.

Then he set the package down and paused again. This time he closed his eyes and squinted like he was trying to avoid something or get rid of a pain.

He looked like a heavy weight was bearing down on him. Finally, he let out a long groan and with what was left of his breath, he asked, "Is this what you want Melody to remember you by?"

"What're you talking about?" I said.

"Last night, I dreamed I saw this name on a package, Melody Swann. I remembered her name so clear, because my dream was vivid. I saw you too, trapped inside a giant web. I knew you'd come here today."

Here's where it got strange. His eyes welled up. I thought he was going to cry as he told me. "I don't know how to say this, but here goes. Pick up your camera. Tape this so you remember. You need to remember! Do it before the sheriff sees!"

I picked my camera off the counter and turned it on. I can't explain, but my body was shaking as he rapidly and passionately began speaking.

"'This day I call the heavens and the earth as witnesses against you, that I have set before you life and death, blessings and curses. Now choose life, so that you and your children may live.' Deuteronomy 30:19."

As I recorded, he continued, looking directly into the camera.

"Until this day, this very hour, you have chosen death. And if it is death you want, then death you shall see. In my dream, I saw you ripped apart by a leopard. He sank his teeth into your skull and devoured you, until you were no longer human. Until you were no longer you, as you yourself have written."

Now it was me trembling as I held the camera.

"In the last days," he said. "'I will pour out my Spirit on all people. Your sons and daughters will prophesy, your old men will dream dreams, your young men will see visions.

"Joel 2:28," He said moving closer to my camera.

"This is how I know these things. If they are untrue, may I be the one devoured by my God in heaven. But if my words are true, then may God have mercy on your soul!"

His next words pierced through me like a sword cutting into my heart.

"Repent! Turn away from the lust of your heart. You're not strong enough to battle Ose on your own, and you refuse the service of your savior. Go! Go home!"

Then he looked away from the camera and yelled, "Sheriff's coming! Turn it off. He's pulling in now. Walk out slow."

As I exited, he continued. "I'll get this package out promise. Go!"

There he was, right on cue. Sheriff Bud Mason, the last word in Dell City, and the prick that had it out for me. His squad car pulled up next to my car, and he watched me intently as I slowly walked out the door and got into my car.

Neither of us said a word as I took the camera hidden in my jacket and jammed it in the back seat.
I grabbed my laptop and entered the diner. He followed me inside. My heart was in my throat the whole time. Not just because of him, but something was gnawing at me.

So here I am now picking at my food for almost an hour, feeling like any minute could be my last.

Hunters surround my table, devouring their meals, making small talk. But there's something beneath the surface that makes my skin crawl.

I'm the odd man out again. I feel their eyes on me, trying to decipher my place in this hunt.

Outside, I see their shotguns strapped to their cars like flags, as they proudly display their kills on the roof or stretched across the flatbed.

Blood drips down slowly, forming puddles under the tires, and the frozen earth reflects these dark lakes as I watch the sun fade into the horizon.

The sheriff strolls through the diner again, scoping me like a vulture looking at road kill.

I don't know why I say it; maybe it was to get rid of him, but I tell him I finished my work in Uphir and am heading home.

Maybe I should heed my own prophecy for once, take my kill and head back to the safe zone. When all the freaks in Los Angeles start looking normal you know you're in trouble.

Why risk it? I'll call Mel and let her know I'm on my way. I got enough for my story, don't I?

"You all right? You haven't touched your food, hon. You don't look so good," Aida Mae says, as she sneaks up on me again.

She's always on cue, always at a comfortable distance, then bam. She pounces on me with conversation.

"I'm fine, my stomach's off," I finally confess.

"I'll make you a nice hot tea and warm this plate up for ya. I made ginger-apple pie. Just what the doctor ordered."

"Thanks," I tell her.

As she returns to the kitchen, I get up. All those words of of warning start running through the back of my head, percolating in this part of my brain I can't ignore.

Some things in life become ingrained in your psyche. You can't shake them no matter how hard you try. They're tattooed inside your skull, lying dormant, 'til the moment you need to draw from them to survive.

I need to clear my head. I'm heading outside to get some air.

The odor's strong out here. Putrid. Rotting. Decay. Looking around, I see animal carcasses propped up on the trucks that surround me. Even in death their eyes penetrate me, as if looking into my soul, saying, *'be careful where you tread.'*

Drops of blood splash into the dirt. It's rhythmic, a dirge for the dead, beating softly like rain.

Night falls quickly here. Soon, the black skies will inhale the howls of the living, while cold dirt drinks the blood of the innocent.

So that you know I'm among the living, I will let my voice echo through these airwaves as I call Melody."

AUDIO LOG,
TUESDAY, DECEMBER 14, 2010 – 7:22 P.M.
ENTERED BY MELODY SWANN

This is the first recording in the third batch of material I received. The phone rings and I hear Eddie's voice.

> "Mel. Hey"
> "Baby. Thank God you called! You okay?"
> "Yeah, I'm still here."
> "Where?"
> "Same place."

He sounds solemn; I can tell something's different with him.

> "You were right. About all this," I tell him.
> "I know," he muttered.

I figure I'll give him good news to perk him up.

> "I took all the stuff you sent me to Carl this morning. He says it's great. He can sell it. He said if you got authentic video of Annette Dobson, he'd reimburse your expenses, plus ten thousand upfront against a book deal. That's what he told me to tell—"
> "What?" Eddie screams.
> "That's great. Ain't it?"
> "Asshole!"
> "What? What'd I do?" I ask Eddie.
> "Not you. Carl. He told me fifty before I left."

"Fifty what?"

"Fifty thousand, Mel. He said fifty thousand if I proved Dobson was in Uphir. A hundred for the book!"

"What? Why didn't you tell me?"

"Damn it! What else? What else? What'd he tell you?"

"Why you mad at me?"

"Forget it! Fuck it. I'll call him myself."

"Don't be mad at me, Eddie."

I hear his breathing swell within our awkward silence. Then he finally breaks the moment.

"What happened?"

"When?"

"Jesus, Mel! At the meeting! Did you give Carl my journal?"

"Uh?"

"Did you transcribe the tapes the way I asked and give him the book teaser?"

"I… gave him… We…"

"We what? Did you do what I asked? Simple question, Mel."

"Why are you so mad?"

"Because I'm risking my fucking life, and I'm not doing it for ten thousand measly dollars. I told you, spell it out! He pays for results. I got results! I got results, Mel! I got results!"

"Why are you talking to me like this?"

"Do I need to spell it out?"

"You sound crazy, Eddie. Stop. You're scaring me."

I hear him shuffling in the dirt, getting erratic, groaning, and panting.

"Scaring you! Scaring you! You freaked out listening to one tape. Come here! Live this shit! You wouldn't last one night here. Padded cells! Shaking beds! Drugged up food! No sleep! Disturbing shit all the time. All the time! Set up to rattle me! I got crazy mother fuckers in my face, telling me how I'll die, or what I did! How God says the days are against me and the devil's going to kill me! You want that? Huh? You want that?"

"No," I answer softly, trying to calm him.

"Damn fucking right you don't! Focus! Get everything together so I can close this deal."

"I'm busting my ass all night, Eddie!"

"Singing karaoke. Really?"

"Fuck you! I got dreams too, you know."

He's silent again. I don't know what to say. I knew I said the wrong thing. I hear him pacing, breathing loudly, before he calms down and asks.

"What did you show him?"

"When?"

"At the meeting, Mel. At the fucking meeting!" Eddie explodes.

"He listened to the tape."

"What tape?"

"The Greek one. I played him that. He said he felt it too."

"Felt what?"

"Whatever it was, Eddie. The weird chill that runs down your spine when you listen. That was fucked-up, and he liked it. Okay?"

Eddie pauses. I anxiously wait for a response.

"Ten grand. He's nuts! That tape alone is ten. Dobson is fifty, got it! I want fifty! Fifty! Hear me, fifty!"

"Calm down! I don't like you like this."

"Like what?"

"Like a madman. I'll take care of it."

"Then take care of it. I mailed proof, living proof. I'm not crazy! I got Annette Dobson giving birth to the baby Jesus, and I want my money!"

"Your money…or our money?"

"What's it matter? You spend it all anyway!"

"Asshole!"

I guess I got to him, because Eddie calms down.

"I'm sorry. I'm wound up. I don't feel good. Just listen, okay?"

"Okay."

"Okay," Eddie says softly, before continuing. "Everything is on the hard drive I mailed to you. My audio, my video recordings, my journals. Some files from the institution. Take them to Carl as soon as you get them. I'll brief him. Whatever you do, don't let him copy these files."

"What?"

"The files, Mel. Please. Don't let him take anything, copy anything, until you get a check from him. Got it?"

"Yes,"

"Good. Only copy the files I marked green. The name of the file on the drive is highlighted green when you look at it. It's green. Green for go! Red means stop. Don't copy that. Got it. Like a traffic light. Remember. Green go! Red stop. Green go. Red—"

"I'm not an idiot!"

"I need to be clear, baby," Eddie says sternly. "Only the green files! The rest you put together the way I showed you, in our book. Can you do that?"

"Yes," I say, sensing some relief at the other end of the line.

"Thank you."

"I love you, Eddie... I do."

"I love you too."

I felt it was true this time. Something in his voice, cracked a little when he said that.

"When are you coming home?"

"Soon...maybe."

"Maybe? Eddie, what's wrong?"

"I don't know. Something's gnawing at me to come now."

"Then come. Come now!" I beg.

"I got to call Carl and straighten this shit out. I'll talk to you later, okay?"

"Come home."

"Okay. Bye."

"Bye. Love you," I tell him, to make sure he feels it.

"Me too baby."

That was it. I know I have work to do. Eddie is on to something. All I can do is follow his instructions, and pray that he makes it back alive.

I'm back inside the diner, awaiting fate, devising a plan as night falls. Hunters have been heading out while I was on the phone, leaving trails of blood and dirt as they screeched out to the ever-darkening roads.

I'm sure I might see them in front of their cabins tonight, under the moonlight with flashlights or by campfires with knives sharpened and the axes ground, waiting to crush through bones and gut out the innocent deer who thought he'd take a stroll and enjoy his day. Little did he know it would be his last! How ironic! With death set before me, what am I walking into?

If the mouths of babes and the crazed ring true, then demons are hunting me down, systematically using people as weapons to fire words into my psyche, opening doors into my soul to use as an entrance.

Like an alien army, they assume their positions and organize their takeover of me.

To Rev. Billings this is a unique spiritual species, highly evolved and organized in function and cause, slowly stripping me of self-control, then using me as a host to commit their crimes against humanity.

Every face I now look at beckons me to ponder how much control the demons have. The slaughtering mob around me, could they kill humans as easily as they split open deer? Is their conscience unknowingly seared by the mind of an alien race hell bent on destruction?

And how can Annette Dobson, the worst of humanity, be free from her tormentors and no longer fathom this evil?

Billings claims she's filled with a spiritual enlightenment so powerful that her mind and soul are now purified and protected against invasion.

And her baby, Kevin, born free into a wild, untamed world. What is he carrying or burying within his soul? Or as Rev. Billings told me, his bloodline!

Billings' words rise to the surface of my brain. He said the importance of Dobson's exorcism was to purify her family bloodline with the blood of Christ.

This is Billings' take, not mine. He believes that curses, even demons, can pass through the bloodlines to infect up to four generations of a person's lineage. "This is biblical fact," he emphatically stated to me. Something Jesus said and Billings quoted.

Like I said, I'm no Jesus groupie. I'm a reporter. My job is to put together facts, hear all sides of the issue, and go deeper to find motive, truth, and method.

Which brings me back to blood. Staring at bloody boots and stained camouflage pants, I can't help but think of blood. I ask myself, could a demon invade my blood?

Microorganisms live in blood. Viruses. Bacteria, fungi, even parasites. They can all survive in blood.

So what is a demon?
What's it made of?
Can it really infect my blood?

Is this why they wanted blood tests from me? They took my blood. Could they have injected something into my blood to infect me? All those vaccinations. What was in those needles?

Fuck! I took that heart test too. I had an IV in me. They shot me up with some shit in a blue container that burned right through me.

The nurse said it was nuclear medicine, so they could see my heart with the camera. What if she lied?

That stuff burned inside me. Maybe that was why Tyler ate his arm off. Who knows?

I could be a guinea pig. Infected with something while they sit and quietly observe my fate. The late-night chills, upset stomach, headaches, my nerves!

What's happening to me? Even my phone ringing runs through my body like a freight train!

Every noise sends vibrations through me, keeping me on edge, like an animal alerted by its senses to the coming storm. The storm that's now ringing is Carl. I'm stepping out to take this call. This time, I'm going to tape him, so he can't swindle me out of my money.

AUDIO LOG:
TUESDAY, DECEMBER 14, 2010 – 8:06 P.M.

"Hey, Carl."

"Hey, partner."

"You get my message?"

"Yeah. Let's talk."

"Yeah, let's," I told Carl. "You said fifty grand if I proved Dobson was here. Why'd you tell Mel ten?"

"I didn't."

"What? You didn't say ten?"

"Yeah, I said ten. Ten for what you got."

"You mean, what she showed you or what I got?"

"What do you have, Eddie?"

"Proof that Annette Dobson's here, just like I said. I got a video interview and footage of her giving birth."

"You're kidding me!" Carl excitedly answered.

"I kid you not. I sent it to Mel today, along with case files I took from the mad doctor running this loony bin."

"Beautiful. What else?" Carl asked.

"What else?" I said, in shock. "What do you mean, what else? That ain't enough? You want more? I got more! This is everything I said it was, plus they got Timothy Nathan Tyler here to boot."

"Don't lie!"

"Oh, I'm not. I'm dead serious. He was the one on that tape Mel played for you."

"That shit spooked me. What the hell was it?"

"Some kind of hypnotherapy session. Mind games. Demon control. I don't know. Crazy shit goes on here. They experiment on inmates. My guess is for pharmaceutical companies or some kind of bio-drug they want to test. Maybe bio-weapons to induce fear."

"Keep going. Anything substantiated?"

"Tyler told me he was framed for trying to rat out Dow Lantra about some fear drug, hallucinogen. Something they were going to be put in our food supply. They keep him locked up tight and say he's possessed by eight demons."

"What?"

"For all intents and purposes, I'm on demon farm," I told him. "People see demons, act possessed, exhibit multiple personalities. Talk in fucked-up languages. It's a dog and pony show for some serious players. I'm thinking the FDA may be letting something slide through as a preservative or additive, with the 'side effects may include' tag."

"You can't just make these claims, Eddie!" Carl warned. "You'll drive into a pile of shit we'll never crawl out of."

"Something big is going down, Carl. They're faking deaths and shipping people here. That's huge, right?"

"Yeah. Who's pulling the strings?"

"They told me their research is protected."

"By whom?"

"I don't know."

I looked around my surroundings to make sure the sheriff or some other intruder wasn't listening in on us as I continued.

"That's what I'm trying to find out. The state. The Feds. Private equity investors. The pharms. Could be all of them."

"Can you substantiate any of your claims?" Carl asked.

"I sent files from Dr. Alan Haworth, the boss man running this freak show. I don't know what's on them, so look through. You tell me… I'm risking my life, Carl."

"You trying to jack up my price?" he laughed.

"No," I said with a dead serious tone. "But what's it worth if I'm right?"

There was a moment of silence, and I knew that Carl was running numbers in his head, so I got quiet and let my words work their way into the equation. He finally came out with it.

"Two fifty up, against a fifty-fifty split."

"All right," I told him. "Fair enough."

"You have a best seller, Eddie. I think I can get us at least a million for movie rights. But I need the whole story. Substantiated."

"Fifty tomorrow. And Mel turns over my files."

"I only got ten, Eddie."

I knew he had more.

"Fifty!" I added sternly.

"If it's what you say, all I can do now is twenty tops. You'll get another twenty next month. I'm strapped. We're in a recession."

"Don't give me the party line, bud. I know you. I want it in writing. And so you know, I'm recording. So listen carefully. Do you agree to pay me forty thousand dollars for my files up to December 14, 2010? Two hundred and fifty thousand up front for substantiated findings that back the claims that I spoke about in this conversation, and a fifty-fifty split of any movie rights or deal we make, with me holding my authorship rights to my story?"

"I agree, it's a deal."

"Shit!"

"What? What?" Carl asked.

"That sheriff. He's coming back here again. This guy's been up my ass since I got here. I'm telling you, Carl, it's dangerous. I'm risking my life."

"Nothing you haven't done before, Eddie. You always come out with the story. Be smart. Git 'er done!"

"Twenty tomorrow. Git 'er done," I said. "Carl. One last thing. Check Dow Lantra and the FDA. See if anything's moving through. Dr. Alan Haworth, he testified in Tyler's trial. See what you can find on him. The other main guys are Dr. Mark Prescott and Rev. William H. Billings. Dig in. See if there's anything I missed. I got to run."

"Will do! Get me that story," Carl said just as the sheriff approached.

"Up against the car," were the next words I heard staring down the sheriff's gun barrel. "Give me your phone."

JOURNAL ENTRY:
WEDNESDAY, DECEMBER 15, 2010 – 1:41 A.M.

Dell City is no longer a safe zone. And much like every other lesson I've learned in life, I found out the hard way.

Uphir is a very strategic location, handpicked to avoid people like me, and dispose of them if necessary. My biggest mistake was not planning an emergency exit strategy, in case I ran into trouble in Dell City.

The next closest city is Sierra Blanca, Texas, a literal sewage dump of about five hundred people, seventy miles south of here.

Then it's over a hundred miles to either El Paso or Carlsbad, New Mexico, depending if I trail east or west when I get back to Route 180. Everything on the road to Carlsbad is National Forest. And with most of these dirt roads off the grid, I've never been able to fully track my bearings.

All I know is that Uphir is tucked in somewhere near the Guadalupe Mountains. I'm not even sure if I'm in New Mexico or Texas.

The satellite maps show about a hundred fifty crop circles around the dell, and once you get past the farms and go off road, it's no-man's-land with Dell City's four hundred residents being the last vestige of humanity.

I figured Dell City was safe, but now I'm convinced they played a big part in Uphir's development, and all that money bought off the town and provided privacy, water, and food routes.

I never talked to the food truck guy, but I saw him bring in a load on Friday. At the time, I didn't think much of it.

But now that I think about it, only he, Billings, and Prescott have ever left and returned, other than me.

Maybe God is smiling on me.

Tonight was another shining example, and I dodged another warning shot. I'll recap these events while they are fresh in my head, like the seven stitches I just had sewn in.

How'd my head split open? I'll answer that too.

After I got off the phone, Sheriff Mason arrived like he was checking out a crime scene. He jumped me like a rabid dog, took my phone, frisked me, and then confiscated my camera from the trunk.

Luckily I swapped out the cards. He's too much of a back-ass hick to understand digital video, so I gladly cooperated to prove that I did not film anything without permission.

I led him through the camera menus and showed him how to check everything. I only had some personal photos from LA, of Melody, and a few pictures of Uphir with Dr. Haworth and Rev. Billings on that card.

It's a thousand-dollar fine payable in cash, or ten days in jail, he warned me, as he cuffed me and dragged me to the police station. He proceeded to rifle through my belongings.

My computer was clean of any evidence I gathered. I only let them see what I wanted them to see. That was my plan. It's worked so far. I sat in my cell, getting a taste of what it felt like on the inside.

My life hung on a 64-gigabyte thumb drive, cleverly designed to look like a credit card. Luckily, the sheriff had no idea what it was when he glanced through my wallet. That drive has everything backed up on it. All my journals, video and audio recordings.

I have another backup in the glove compartment of my car, shaped like a key, in case of emergency.

After checking through my things, the sheriff left and returned about ten minutes later, saying that Dr. Haworth requested I return to Uphir.

That got me thinking, there must be an emergency phone line out of Uphir, and the sheriff must have access and communication with Haworth.

I wonder now if my package was even mailed out to Melody. Is Dell City a part of this whole setup? How much is really at stake?

Everything that's happened to me might be planned, coordinated, and calculated down to the minute detail.

I was escorted out of the station and back to my car. The sheriff trailed me all the way back, following a few car lengths behind. He seemed to know the roads well, if not better than I did.

As I weaved down the trails, he'd flash his high beams giving me direction by turning on a blinker to guide me. We were pretty deep into the woods when I heard a gunshot. The first one was deafening and ripped through the silence with a thundering *crack!*

I froze for a second on the narrow road in the pitch-black forest and looked around, only seeing the light of a flickering campfire in the distance.

The blast of the sheriff's horn shook me, and I kept driving deeper into the woods toward Uphir, but slower and more cautious.

My headlights were cutting through the blackness when I saw something dart across the road. I thought it was a deer but it moved too quickly, and the color was light, almost white, and it looked more like a leopard, now that I think of it.

It moved fast and I barely saw what was out there, but that thing was big. Real big.

Maybe someone was after it, or after me.

A moment later, another gunshot roared through the air, but this time, within a second, I heard it rip through the metal of my car and wedge into something. The next bullet went through the hood! Then one shattered my rear window, and my nerves shot into high alert!

The hairs on my arms were standing on edge, and my hands were shaking, gripping tightly to the wheel as I peered into the rearview mirror. I saw the sheriff in front of his car, firing shot back into the forest.

Another bullet whisked through the back window. I lost control, and the next thing I know, I swerved into a tree.

It hit me really hard. I got knocked back by the airbag. A tree limb snapped through the driver's window, ripping into the side of my forehead.

I was dazed. I got out of my car, yelling.

The sheriff drove up and tried to get me to ride with him, but I wasn't leaving my car in the woods, alone with my camera, computer, and thumb drives and no way back.

I jumped back into my car and locked myself in. I couldn't hear any more gunshots, and I think that freaked me out even more.

Trying to start the car in dead silence was terrifying. I kept thinking about death, and how I chose it. How any second the next shot could come ripping through the window and take me out.

I could feel the warm blood dripping down the left side of my face, and all I wanted was for that car to start.

"God, help me! I don't want to die," I yelled as I kept turning the ignition, but nothing happened.

Then just as the sheriff pulled alongside of me,
Bang!

The car started, and I backed away fast, leaving scraps of metal wedged in the tree. I backed out onto the road and sputtered through the woods, praying all the way that I'd make it back alive.

The drive was excruciating, mentally, physically, and emotionally. I could taste my blood hitting my lips. It ran down my face, blinding my eyes, while the headlights kept flickering, making the nebulous woods seem like they were strobing in front of me.

It felt surreal, winding through silent black roads, shadows reflecting off trees, the sound of my engine sputtering and tires spinning, anticipating another crack of a shotgun any second that could usher in my last breath.

Somehow I made it to the threshold and could see the pale lights of the asylum welcoming me home.

As we pulled up to the gate, smoke began pouring out of my hood.

The night security guard arrived to greet me, but it wasn't Curtis. It was a new guy, Reggie, this dark mountain of a man who I guess did some serious time judging by that menacing look in his eye and ice-cold stare that seemed to ward me off.

When I asked him where Curtis was, he finally perked up with a salacious grin and said, "You don't want to know, brother."

"What?" I asked.

"You don't want to see him," Reggie told me, grinning. "But he'd love to see you!"

And then with a stern look, he told me, "Report to Ward A. Dr. Haworth is waiting for you."

I drove off. The sheriff followed me into Ward A, where the night nurse met me and cleaned up my wounds, sewing seven stitches into my forehead.

She removed a few chunks of glass from my skull, then bandaged up my wrist and ankle for support.

Dr. Haworth and Sheriff Mason had a quiet conversation in the hallway. I couldn't make out what they were saying, but I don't think it was good, because two more security guards came up within minutes and positioned themselves outside my door.

The looks they threw me were not inviting as I tried to make conversation. When the nurse finally finished, they forcefully escorted me down the hall to my room.

Making matters worse, I passed Santiago on my way. I heard someone crying and looked inside the room as I was dragged past.

It was Santiago propped up on the bed, motionless, with his head bandaged and his leg strapped up high in a harness.

He looked as if he were being tormented by something. His eyes were wide open, and tears ran down his frozen face. His skin was ghostly pale and his body frail.

His face was locked in this expression of terror, like he was trapped in a constant nightmare he could not escape.

He was disturbing to look at, and although it was a brief second, it seemed like an eternity.

Time froze like the midnight air, and my body tightened to the fact that I was alone in this fight. My search for allies was narrowing by the minute. I was greeted by icy stares and silent answers.

Now trapped inside the recovery room, my options for finding the truth of this story and getting it back to the outside world are significantly diminishing.

I have a sinking feeling that I am no longer a visitor, but a patient, judging by my wristband, new patient identification number, and hospital gown.

I'm probably staying here under observation until the morning, but this place is far better than sitting in that seclusion room.

I've been stripped of all my things, except for my laptop, so I'm being careful with what I write for now.

This is the one freedom that allows my mind to focus on the task at hand and take it off Santiago's desperate crying.

His moans are a constant, dulling background noise, like the space heater, fluorescent bulbs, and medical machines that accompany the tapping of my keyboard, the footsteps of the guards, and the occasional gust of wind that taps on the window behind me, beckoning me to see the world outside.

That won't come until tomorrow, when I'm scheduled to meet with Dr. Haworth for my evaluation.

Here I was again, face-to-face with Haworth. The dulling silence was killing me, so I decided to turn on my recorder and get the party started.

"This is Eddie Hansen, Wednesday, December 15, and I am at the Uphir Behavioral Center in Uphir, Texas. May I have permission to tape this interview, Dr. Haworth?"

"You may. May I have permission to examine your computer?"

"Excuse me?"

"I'd like to see your files, Mr. Hansen," he told me, getting up from his desk. "I'm sure you know what I'm talking about."

"I don't," I told him, playing innocent.

"Would you like me to play a video to refresh your memory?"

"That's okay," I said, watching him circle me like a vulture.

"Mr. Hansen, I hoped our relationship would be built on trust. But you seem to keep violating that trust and creating your own rules for this assignment."

"Investigation," I corrected.

"Certainly, investigation," smiled Haworth, peering over my shoulder. "Call it what you wish. But let me ask you, what are you trying to find that I haven't already shared with you?"

"Why did you let me in here?"

"You let yourself. I have nothing to hide," he told me, squaring off.

"Really? Then may I see your video control room, the tape archive, Ward E. I want to see what you've done here."

Dr. Haworth sighed. "Oh you will," he stated, returning to his desk. "You'll experience it all, firsthand. But first we must address our rules."

He pulled my file from his desk and slid the contract in front of me.

"You knowingly violated article seven of your consent agreement, which states, explicitly, that no alcohol or drugs may be brought on to this premises during your visit. Not only did you violate this rule, you provided excessive amounts of alcohol to our staff security, who became negligent in their duties, and allowed a fatality on our property."

"I'm sorry. I didn't know."

My surprise was genuine. This wasn't what I expected. Haworth stood up and confronted me.

"You didn't know or you didn't care? The first is ignorance, the second is foolishness, and foolishness is not tolerated. Foolishness is why Curtis Anderson is being held in Ward D, awaiting his sentence, why Simon Manning is dead, and why Santiago Ortiz is in a coma. Foolishness!"

"What?" I said, trying to defend myself and comprehend the charges against me.

"Foolishness, Mr. Hansen," Haworth stated. "A blatant disregard for authority. A brash sense of entitlement. A complete lack of respect."

"I apologize."

"Don't patronize me with impersonal appeals because of the sudden realization that you lost control."

I stood up to meet him eye to eye.

"I haven't lost anything."

"You've lost everything!" Haworth retorted.

"Enlighten me."

Haworth turned and walked away. "I'm sure you are intelligent enough to figure it out. You are a very predictable creature, Mr. Hansen."

"Don't patronize me with arrogant assessments of your perceived authority over my life."

"What's left of it." Haworth casually stated, rubbing his hand over the leopard statue on his desk.

"Is that a threat?"

"It's a fact," Haworth responded. "Based on the cycle of your behavior and the nature of this situation. You're not the first person to travel down this road."

"Nor the last," I told him, moving closer to gain advantage. "You're not off the grid anymore. People know where I am, and if they don't hear from me— *bang!*—the cavalry rushes in."

"Delusions of grandeur will not help you survive here, Mr. Hansen. You need psychological and medical attention before you become a threat to yourself and others. I'm ordering you to be held in Ward D pending further observation."

With that, two guards rushed into the room to detain me.

"You can't do that!" I yelled.

As they grabbed me, Haworth added, "You tried to commit suicide last night, you drove your car into a tree."

"That's a lie! That Sheriff forced me off the road."

"That's not what's in my report." Haworth replied as he instructed the guards, "Please take Mr. Hansen to Ward D."

JOURNAL ENTRY:
MONDAY, DECEMBER 20, 2010 - 9:16 A.M.

That was it. Haworth shut off my recorder, and that was the last I've seen of it. I should have listened to my gut and gone home when I could. Taken the small victory I had and got the reinforcements needed to knock these walls down later.

But I got greedy, and this is my punishment. My equipment is locked away. I've been sitting in this disgusting cage for who knows how long.

I finally received my laptop back, after begging for it every time anyone came in here to feed us.

Any confidence I had was shattered when I turned my laptop on and saw today's date.

It's Monday morning, December 20.

Five days whisked past me without a trace, leaving no trail except scattered memories and severely depressing thoughts, most of which are concentrated around my death.

I'm a dead man. I've been forced into compliance, and I can't figure out how to escape my fate. If I had indeed chosen death, then this is the place for me to reflect on that decision and prepare my defense for any hope I had to return to the land of the living.

The smell that induced my vomiting, the screams that drew my curiosity, and the pain and terror that haunted my sleepless nights, all belong to Ward E.

Ward E is a death sentence; no one had ever gone into that ward and returned to the facility.

It was a hopeless place for the condemned to feed off each other, and incite the very essence of hell. There was no supervision. No rules. No restraint. It was merely survival, according to the voices that accompany me here in this pit.

I am confined in Ward D, one step from that grave.

Blocked from the sight of others, voices are the only tangible evidence of existence and means of communication in here. Isolation is supposed to provide a suitable arena for contemplation, self-examination, and repentance, but I choose this place to be my vessel of information.

I want to understand the bowels of Uphir, and the stories that harden even the toughest criminals here.

My fellow prisoners fear talking about these things will incite further punishment, but one voice barks authoritatively at me. It's Curtis. He's made it evidently clear that if Ward E doesn't devour me, he will.

"Eddie, I'm going to kill you!" is the most repetitive phrase I've heard over the last five days. I've tried to reason with him, but to no avail. Curtis is convinced that he is a three-strike offender and he will soon be sentenced to Ward E as his final resting place. Of course, I am solely to blame for his predicament.

I think that Timothy Tyler may be in here too, but it's hard to communicate with all the screaming, growling, and banging going on.

I scream back with the rest of the animals, howling to the moon and raging with the forsaken. It's hard to contain your emotions in this environment.

A backed up toilet, rusty sink, uncomfortable cot with molded sheets, and a crusty, stained blanket are not enough to stay warm and sane.

I'm afraid to eat the food, but starving to death is my only other option. Every time after eating, I can't help but wonder if it's the food that's making us crazy.

My thoughts are spinning out of control. The abundance of voices I hear, whether imaginary or imprisoned, keep speaking clearly to me that my time is near.

They want to kill me, or watch me do it to myself. Bash my head into the steel bars until it cracks, or rip out the pipe from beneath the sink and jam it into my eyes or through my chest.

Or should I wrap the blanket around my neck and choke myself, suffocate, or drown in the sink.

All these ideas hover over me, trying to find their way inside me and force me to press the button in my mind that says, "Yes! Do it!"

My inquisitive mind reexamines my wasted life, trying to add reason to my existence. Am I worthy of my next breath, or impending death? The inquisitor wants to know why I invite danger. Why do I constantly put my head in the leopard's mouth? Why do I avoid my feelings and build up walls inside to repress the torment? Why do I invite pain and misery to accompany me?

I was never like this before. I was the life of the party. I was the class clown. The joker. The guy everybody wanted to party with.

And now, this metaphysical change is happening. It's like there's a monster growing inside this cocoon of a body, evolving and feeding off my blood.

I'm transitioning, losing control of my power to remain positive.

My laughs are engulfed in tears, and my smile has to be forced open through the pain. I feel the scratches on my back tingling. It's like my skin is bubbling up.

The deep scratch from Gloria hasn't healed, and the constant itching and burning makes me want to sink my teeth into it and suck the poison out.

Maybe that's why Tyler did it. Maybe that's all he could recall. The feeling of contamination, frayed nerve endings, and irrational impulse.

The toxins are building inside me. A chemical imbalance and wave of defensive response from within my body to heal itself.

My feet are cracked, dry, and cold, and when I stand, it feels like needles inserted into my heels.

My eyeballs are pressed into the back of my head, crushed against my brain, so I can't see, think, or process information accurately.

Everything is constricting inside me, tightening in pain, closing up like a cocoon.

Maybe I am just like that vampire bat, with wings that retract around my body, locking in pain, squeezing the breath out, so I can see it form clouds in front on me that shape themselves into the demons that hunt me.

My fingers feel the frigid touch of cold aluminum, as I pound on the keyboard. But the bottom of the laptop feels warm. I press it against my chest to feel life. Even the light of the monitor brings me some hope, a form of expression to focus my thoughts into.

Another gust of cold air swept through here, and I hear the main door open. Footsteps echo on the concrete, getting closer. I look up to see my first visitor, the Reverend Billings.

JOURNAL ENTRY/AUDIO LOG:
MONDAY, DECEMBER 20, 2010 – 9:49 A.M.

Rev. Billings was a sight for sore eyes. His smile relaxed me as he stood outside my cell and handed me my audio recorder.

"Follow the rules," he said.

I was grateful for his trust and thanked him as I turned it on.

"I appreciate this, Rev," I told him.

"You're welcome. I want to talk to you about a few things, Eddie," he said as he pulled up a chair.

"When am I getting out of here?" I asked, feeling Curtis getting riled up in his cell, slamming his body around.

Rev. Billings glanced over at him before addressing me. "Soon. I don't have the authority to make that decision."

Then Curtis exploded! "I'm going to kill you, Eddie! Hear me? I'm going to stomp on your skull, and split your face open! I won't stop until I hear the last breath ooze out of your body. You hear me? Tell him, priest! I'm going to kill him!"

"Shut the fuck up Curtis!" I yelled.

"You're dead, Hansen!"

Rev. Billings calmly stated, "Curtis, I'm working on getting you out too. But you have to cooperate."

"I didn't do anything!" Curtis yelled. "Simon was at first post. Something ripped him open, not me! I didn't kill him. It was his fault! All his fault! He left that gate open!"

Billings answered Curtis. "Dr. Haworth will hear your side of the story soon. But you must stay quiet and let me talk to Eddie."

"He's a dead man, Rev!"

"Eddie," the Reverend continued, now focusing on me. "I can't help you if you continue to violate your agreement here. Do you understand?"

"Yes," I told him.

"I fear for you. I do. You are letting things build up inside you that are unhealthy, in fact, demonic in nature."

"DEAD MAN!" Curtis exploded again, banging himself into the cell bars. I tried to control my feelings and bit down on my lip, containing my urge to scream back.

I calmly replied to Billings, "What do you want me to do?"

"Repent. Allow God's forgiveness to cleanse you. Create a place for Him in your heart."

"Are you blackmailing me with God?" I asked Billings. "Is this my only way out?"

"No," he told me politely. "I can't force you to do anything. I can only give you my perspective and tell you what Christ did for me."

"I don't mean to be rude, Rev. But please. Let's talk about something else. I'm not bringing religion into a legal investigation. I'm not skewing my perspective based on intangible evidence."

"That's fine, Eddie," Billings answered. "Understand, I may be your only ally in here. I'm on your side. I'm here to help you and guard your spiritual welfare."

"All right," I said, sensing his sincerity.

"That's why I was hired," Billings continued. "I promised God I'd do it. And I'm going to."

The stomping started again. "Hear that, Hansen. Hear it! It's your skull."

"Curtis. You're not helping yourself," the Reverend warned.

"I need to get out of here," I begged. "You know that there's something wrong with this whole setup. What goes on in Ward E?"

Billings hesitated for a moment and adjusted his seat, thinking of how to frame his next words. "When a person loses complete control over themselves and cannot be redeemed, they are sent to Ward E. It is where the perfect possessed are kept."

"Perfect possessed?" I said, trying to comprehend.

"When demons gain complete control and power over a person, we have no other choice," Billings continued. "The exorcism of one ruling demon is excruciating, eight is nearly impossible, and fifty-six can be lethal for an exorcist."

"Seven-X, right?" I asked. "They each bring seven back."

"Seven demons more powerful than themselves, and the final condition of the person, is—"

"…worse than the first." we said together

"You really believe that?" I asked Billings.

"Believe it. I've lived it," he responded confidently.

"Really?"

"Eddie, do you honestly think anyone chooses to be an exorcist? Would you want my job?"

"Not my first choice," I told him honestly.

"Mine either," Billings responded. "My dream was to play in the NFL. Did you know I was the Big 12 Defensive Player of the Year in 1977? A First Team All-American Linebacker at the University of Texas?"

"A Longhorn, you?" I said. "You know I'm a Bruin at heart."

"I won't hold it against you." Billings smiled. "I was going to be a first-round draft pick. I had that money spent. My life planned out. Then—*bang!*—I ruptured my ACL in the first quarter of the Cotton Bowl."

"Damn," I moaned.

"I sat in the locker room, iced up, watching our undefeated season, National Championship, and my career vanish, all at once."

"That hurts."

"It killed me inside," Billings said. And I could almost feel the pain well up in him as he continued. "Notre Dame 38, Texas 10. The last game I ever played in."

"That sucks. That was it, huh?"

"I prayed to God," Billings said. "Prayed so hard that I'd heal up and get drafted. I prayed someone would give me a chance. All I wanted was a chance. One chance. That's all. You ever feel that way?"

"Too often," I told him, and judging by the look in his eye, I think he felt my pain too.

"Exactly," Billings answered as his raw emotion began to flow for the first time in our conversations. He seemed hurt as he continued.

"I worked so hard to get healthy again. I kept working out every day for hours and hours, hoping for that call. Then, one day, my buddy Earl Campbell put in a word for me with the Houston Oilers, and they gave me a tryout."

"Did you go?"

"Of course I went," Billings said, perking up. "This was my chance to prove myself. I put my heart and soul into every second out there. Every play. Every practice. I was the first one on the field and the last to leave. There was no way I was going to lose this opportunity. And when I made it past the first two cuts, I thought, I'm back. I'm going to make it to the NFL! I was feeling great, playing great… Then…"

He stopped for a moment of reflection.

"Then, what?" I asked.

"Then… I let my guard down. Just once, during practice. One time. I lost focus on a reverse and doubled back in pursuit, not seeing the guard pulling. He chopped me, I stepped back hard, and put all my weight in the wrong direction. My Achilles tendon snapped."

"Shit!" I responded.

Billings somberly continued, "That was it. It was all over. And I just kept thinking, how could I be so stupid? I saw that play a million times before. I studied it on film, over and over, reacted and made that tackle. I did it a thousand times. But this time, this one time, I was a split second behind. Just a split second! That's all! I was trying so hard to catch up that I lost focus of everything around me. I never saw it coming. That's what did me in. Follow me?"

"Yeah," I answered. "You think I lost my edge."

"I think you're blindly chasing something you want so bad, that you lost sight of your surroundings," Billings warned.

"At least you knew what color jersey your opponent was wearing," I told him bluntly. "I'm not sure who the bad guy is here."

"You need wisdom. God says if you ask for wisdom, He'll give it to you."

"You love throwing the God thing in my face, don't ya? Little jabs whenever you see the opening. My hands are up, Rev. Give me a break."

Billings got up and said, "I'll check with Dr. Haworth. See if we can get you out of here today."

"Thanks," I told him.

"Don't forget me, Rev. I was quiet!" yelled Curtis as Billings made his way out."

Then another somewhat familiar voice barked out. "Ready. Set. Blue 42. Blue 42. Red 3. Yellow 6. BHA. Yopa dopa! Hike!"

I could hear him scampering around the cell, banging, "I'm fading back, looking for someone to take this and run with it. Run Eddie, run!"

"Is that you Tyler?"

He stopped shuffling. "Tyler's dead. But we keep him around to play."

"Who's that?" I asked.

"A friend, Eddie. We're going to help you sort out this conundrum."

"What are you talking about?" I asked, trying to gauge who was talking.

Curtis pounded the bars, yelling, "We're talking about killing you!"

The other voice laughed sadistically; "Don't you worry, ET. We all get it in the end. This place gives it to you one way or the other. *Acacia karroo. Anadenanthera peregrina*," he laughed, singing those words out like an insane nursery rhyme.

"What the hell you saying?" I asked, peering through the bars.

"Yopo. Mopo. Nopo," echoed through the cell walls.
"What?"

"Yopo, mopo, nopo, jopo, cohoba, parica," he sang out again.

"You're babbling nonsense!" I told him.

"Am I?" I heard clanging through the bars. "Or are the less intelligent, less informed of your species unable to comprehend scientific data and the chemical properties of the things they are induced with. Mopo. Nopo. Yopo snuff. Get it?"

"No!"

"No," he laughed. "That's because it's inside you! Yopo, jopo, cohoba, mopo, nopo, parica. All names for *Anadenanthera peregrina* fool. Hallucinogenic plants harvested at the greenhouse a mile outside this property. Who's crazy now! You are a contaminated vessel. Now you get it!"

"You saying I'm drugged?" I asked, feeling some truth to his insane ramblings.

"Your blood is contaminated. Tryptamine, methylone, DPT. The levels are building up. You're seeing things. Feeling nauseous. Agitated. You don't feel like yourself anymore, do you?" he groaned.

"No," I replied, sinking back in my cell.

"It's only the beginning of the game, Eddie. Mere days for you. After weeks, years, then what do you do? What do you do when your senses deceive you, your mind plays tricks, and your soul is left bare to figure out what is really happening here?"

"That's when—"

JOURNAL ENTRY:
MONDAY, DECEMBER 20, 2010 – 12:12 P.M.

...you realize the battery died. I finally had my audio recorder back, and the battery goes dead. I have no replacement. Great!

Somebody knows what they are doing because the microphone and camera on my laptop have been removed. Nothing works. With no Internet, no software, no backup, I'm exactly where they want me. Dependent on everything they give me to investigate and survive.

My friends in Ward D believe we're lab rats, subject to chemical testing by genetic engineers growing bio-foods and plants at a nearby greenhouse.

Apparently, the greenhouse is about a mile east, hidden away in the mountains.

A small river leads to it, and there is a reservoir at the mouth where the greenhouse and lab rest. This guy, this voice, said he was the toxicologist hired to examine cadavers and provide reports on various test subjects.

The tests were conducted to decipher the absorption rates of various non-regulated chemicals and medicines, ingested from our food and water supply here.

As he was ranting about the greenhouse, two security guards entered and cuffed me, then escorted me to a waiting room back in Ward C.

As I was leaving, I could hear this man scream in pain. Maybe the guards beat him senseless. I was just glad to be out.

About ninety minutes later, Dr. Haworth entered. His assessment was brief and to the point.

I could stay in Ward C supervised under observation, or return to my cell in Ward D.

I will be given access only to my computer, and may write privately and without examination by any third party.

I will be allowed outside with an escort at appointed times during the day. I no longer have my keys, my clothes, my personal possessions, or my car. I've been fitted with a tracking bracelet like the other patients here.

I was given an Uphir patient number and ID. This officially makes me a prisoner. There was no way to argue this with Dr. Haworth.

He knew he had me. I was helpless. I want to kick myself in the head for not seeing it coming. I pushed too hard to get information.

I lost focus of the warning signs and drifted into the hunting zone, ripe for the kill. The only advantage from my perspective is that I'm in position to get the real story from the inside.

I'm no longer on the outside looking in. I need to figure out how to use this to get information, resources, and hard evidence of what is happening here, then find a way home.

JOURNAL ENTRY:
MONDAY, DECEMBER 20, 2010 – 8:26 P.M.

I'm having trouble focusing. Every time I sit down to write, this wave of exhaustion hits me really hard. I go completely blank and stare at the screen, slowly losing control of my motor skills.

Then my head falls back, and my eyes roll into my skull. I can't see anything, and I get light-headed.

I just roll my head in circles, groaning and squinting to clear the pain.

The next thing I know I'm out. When I wake up it's a few hours later. This happened at least four times, and I can't remember anything that happened. Now it's dark and I feel that wave coming over me once again.

I slept about eighteen hours total. I must have needed it badly. All those sleepless nights added up. My body broke down. I don't remember dreaming or feeling anything last night. I was out cold.

But that was rudely interrupted when Ward C managing Nurse Regan poked me awake and immediately began my orientation.

This was one stone-cold bitch. She laid it out straight, with an attitude that matched her size 16 scrubs. She's a bit sadistic. We didn't hit it off. My jokes bounced off her like flubber.

I must strictly adhere to her schedule and attend all my therapy sessions.

Meal times are scheduled at 8:00 a.m., noon, and 6:00 p.m. We are escorted to the cafeteria in groups and must arrive at the front desk five minutes before leaving. Bed check is at 10:00 p.m. and wake-up call is 7:00 a.m.

Remember the four *S*'s.

No smoking, swearing, spitting, or sex.

Break one and you are going to the fifth *S,* seclusion.

All scheduled activities are mandatory, and I must be cooperative with staff and accommodate any requests for testing, whether verbal, written, or physical.

Violation of these rules would subject me to an undetermined time of seclusion, or permanent residence in Ward D. Violation of Ward D protocol is subject to administrative action; which may include, but is not limited to, permanent seclusion or direct admittance into Ward E.

I should stamp that bitch with a "side effects may include" tag!

JOURNAL ENTRY:
TUESDAY, DECEMBER 21, 2010 – 10:35 A.M.

There is no doubt Dr. Haworth is committed to breaking me down, in every sense of the word. He's testing me, pushing my boundaries, seeing how far he can push me before I snap!

I reported to the nurses' station for my escort to breakfast, but instead of eating, I was escorted to the lab for more blood work, another physical, and CAT scan.

They want to look inside my head, read my mind, or at least the activity in it.

Nurse Evans, clumsily prepared my arm with a tourniquet and prepared to draw blood. This time her ditsy act was gone. She seemed serious, not flirtatious like before. Every answer was a straight yes or no.

"Please hold out your arm," was the closest thing we had to a conversation. She acted like a puppet of this hierarchy, under instruction. I can't help but wonder what she did to earn her stay here.

Something in her eyes pointed to a deep-seated despair, a sense of loss. Her sexy smiles and cute bends were replaced with robotic, non-emotional gestures, focused on the task at hand. As the needle inched toward my vein, I tensed up and wanted to knock it out of her hand. I don't trust them.

What are they doing to me?
Why do they want my blood again?

The puncture through my skin was like a shot of adrenaline to my nerves, and a rush of fury swept through me.

I needed to remain in control. I took a deep breath, closed my eyes, and tried to think about something positive, as the needle found its way into my vein.

I could feel the blood draining from my body, and my head felt light, but I kept concentrating on Kennedy, remembering her birth like it was yesterday.

Then something happened to bring me back and disrupt my happy place. My senses heightened again. I was on alert. My ears focused sharply on people talking outside the door. They were nervous as they picked up supplies from the next room. I heard one woman say they needed to protect the baby. The baby was in danger.

Then I heard, "Get prayer warriors up there."

I had no idea what she meant, but something major was going down. Their footsteps were rough, and the door closed hard as they left.

The needle slid out of my skin and Nurse Evans taped a cotton ball over the hole.

"Press hard," she told me, finally breaking a smile. "Follow me. We're going to take a CAT scan."

As we walked through the lab, I thought about Melody, I hope she got my videos and notes. I hope she made it to Carl and got my check. Money would help. Take some stress off us. Then it hit me. Curtis turned down my bribe with a frown that spoke volumes of truth.

"What am I going to do with money, Eddie?" he said. He wanted my liquor. Something he could touch, taste, and use to forget this experience. That's a frightening reality.

Those thoughts clung to me as I slid into the CAT scan machine. Soon the thumping sounds began. The knocks, the rhythmic clicks of a machine peered through me, as I lay motionless.

Tap. Tap. Tap. Tap. Tap
Tap. Tap. Tap. Tap. Tap.
Tap. Tap. Tap. Tap. Tap.

The sound transported me back into the seclusion room; hearing drops of water pound into my nerves. I was trapped in this cocoon, and the developing monster inside me kicked like a fetus inside a pregnant woman.

I could feel my stomach burst in waves of pain, bubbling with indigestion, poison, or something worse.

My fingers began to tremble, and I could hear the nurse asking me to hold still.

My heart rate spiked, and I started panting. I was fighting to maintain control, but all I could see was this beige tomb of fiberglass engulf me.

The tomb wrapped around me, moving as if I were being swallowed by a serpent. My head was inside its mouth, slowly melting as the acidic toxins of the snake's belly burned into my skin, liquefying me so I could be completely digested into its body to nourish him.

Tap. Tap. Tap. Tap. Tap.
Tap. Tap. Tap. Tap. Tap.

That tapping is crucifying me inside the serpent's belly. My legs began kicking, and I could feel hands grip them and voices telling me to stay still.

I see mounds of intestine engulfing me. Holes beginning to form on my skin as the acid burns through.

Tap. Tap. Tap. Tap. Tap.

Each vibration opens deeper holes, drawing out my heart, soul, and mind. It was all leaving me as I disappeared into blackness. Everything became dark and quiet, and a distant fire burned flesh that I could smell.

Maybe the scent from Ward E never left me, or maybe it was growing inside me. Maybe I smelled my own rotting corpse expanding within me.

This was the smell of Timothy Tyler, the walking dead. Was Cotard's syndrome spreading through my body too?

What if it were contagious? What if it were harvested? Genetically engineered. What if it were created in a lab to destroy an enemy? What if that enemy was me?

Tap. Tap.
Tap. Tap.

My pulse is slowing down.

Tap. Tap.

My eyes close from the weight of my thoughts.

Tap.
Tap.

I'm fading into nothing. A new journey begins as I depart from my body and drift into this dark sky. I'm floating inside a vast empty space, without sound or light.

There is absolutely nothing here. No clouds or skies. No stars. No sun. No moon. No grass or trees or water or plants or animals or people.

I am terrified by lack of any substance: the absence of noise. There is no time here. I feel no sense of my past, present, or future.

There's no memory of life.

But I'm still here. Still alive.

I still exist in some form, which I can neither see nor feel.

I can't touch my limbs or smell anymore.

I am absent from my body, and there is neither pleasure nor pain to be felt. Or for that matter, reason. There is no reason for this existence. There is no creation. No thought of mass or substance or density.

There's no design for life. Yet my cognitive process remains active. I can receive and process thought, but cannot put it into action.

If I think of a tree or water, it does not appear in my thoughts or reality. I can't concentrate or remember events of my life, where I was, where I am now, or where I am going.

It's just this repetitious cycle of reasoning without matter. A vast and endless region of emptiness.

And it goes on and on and on. And I am here, trapped! Help me...

Please... Help! Somebody help me...

At the very moment my mind spoke, the darkness began to divide and in the distance was an incredible light straight ahead of me burning bright. Straight behind me was the piercing blackness.

As I moved toward the light, I could see shapes inside. The shapes were my life. My happiest moments were there in flashes of substance, suspended in time.

I see myself as a baby in my father's hands. And in my hand, I see my daughter Kennedy at birth. And in her tiny hand, I see her daughter. I don't know why, but I knew that was my granddaughter.

I just innately knew as I glimpsed into this window of eternity. And a feeling of contentment and wonder covered me. I was filled with pure love.

Then suddenly I began to drift away and everything spun 180 degrees as I was pulled toward the blackness.

As my girls disappeared, I slid through that empty cavern again, knowing and feeling nothing.

And then, another light appeared in the distance. As I got closer, I could see it was a fire burning.

Flames engulfed this region, and my senses were tricked by the fact that I had feeling, but it was getting colder as I drew closer.

Ice-cold fire was not even fathomable to me, but it appeared as reality as I journeyed inside.

Inside the fire, I could see a different me. I was old and battered. Bruises covered my body and lesions crowned my skin. I was festering with blisters and in tremendous pain. But I was writing. Writing about things I hated to think of. My fingers typed so fast that my fingernails wore off. The tips were bloody and calloused, but I could not stop writing.

I was screaming and writhing in pain, shouting with words someone needed to hear. But it was silent. I was alone. My pain was for nothing.

So I stopped typing and looked down at the keyboard, realizing it was made of broken glass wedged deep into me.

I cried out for help and in an instant this large hand pulled me out. My eyes snapped open, realizing I was back inside the lab, out of the serpent's belly, staring at the warm face of Nurse Evans.

It took me a moment to adjust to the light of the room. I stepped down on the cold, hard floor. My bare feet absorbed the chill through my body and I was back to this reality and on to the next test.

JOURNAL ENTRY:
TUESDAY, DECEMBER 21, 2010 – 11:15 A.M.

Rev. Billings gave me time to write down my thoughts to begin this session. We are having an open forum to express ourselves on paper first. We begin with nonverbal communication, then share what we had written.

I didn't write anything about my vision, or the five days I spent in Ward D. I just expressed what I was feeling inside at the moment. Rules were broken on both sides, yet I'm the one who was punished.

I feel betrayed. You are cheating me out of information. I'm the one whose rights have been violated and whose freedom has been taken away.

I gave up those rights to get this story on the condition that I would have unlimited access to this facility and privileges to record information and interviews as needed.

I'm infuriated this policy changed and with the way I've been treated.

Billings simply wrote, "I will ask the Father, and he will give you another advocate to help you and be with you forever—the Spirit of truth."

We just looked at each other's writing for a moment, before I began.

"Truth, now we're getting somewhere. A spirit of truth. Please share," I said.

"Ask me anything you want," Billings said calmly.

"What happened to Annette Dobson's baby, Kevin?"

Instead of a straight answer, Billings excused himself, leaving me with my laptop and suspicions. I've been sitting here five minutes waiting patiently, knowing that cameras are recording me, but I can't record what I need.

The paradox of it all infuriates me, but I need to play it cool. Here he comes. Let's see what his answer is.

To my shock, the Reverend brought me batteries for my recorder, and he's allowing me to tape our discussion.

AUDIO LOG:
TUESDAY, DECEMBER 21, 2010 – 11:32 A.M.

I finally have my recorder back, and a sense of hope. Billings waits patiently for me to put the batteries in and turn it on. Now it's time to get answers.

"I'm a man of my word, Eddie. I'll do everything I can to help you. But please, record only when authorized by Dr. Haworth. Am I clear? I'm putting myself on the line for you."

"Thanks."

"You wanted to know about Kevin?"

"I do."

"Kevin slept through the night, every night, since his birth. He hasn't cried. He's been perfectly healthy. We've kept him with Annie. There had been no incidents until last night. Around 3:00 a.m., Kevin woke up, crying loudly. A few moments later, he was gasping for air; his face turned purple. He stopped breathing. Annette was sleeping so deeply, she didn't hear anything. The monitor went off alerting Nurse Regan who immediately entered and performed CPR on Kevin. As she was resuscitating him, Annie rushed out of bed screaming, thinking Nurse Regan was trying to hurt her baby. Annie hit her several times. Security had to restrain her. When they returned to check the room, one of our guards discovered a sheet of plastic wrap in the baby's bed. Annie says she knew nothing about it."

"Did she try to kill him?"

"I don't think so. Annie knows nothing about her past. But she confessed to me in therapy that she had a nightmare where she strangled Kevin. She was so distraught by it, she had to be taken to the infirmary for an IV."

"Where's Kevin now?"

"With Annie. We can't let her feel that she's done anything wrong, but she's under observation."

"Prayer warriors. What's that?"

"They're part of our prayer team at church. They are trained and have a specific job to intercede for others in prayer.

"Praaayyyyer Warriors, come out and praaaaayyyy!"

I'm humoring myself. I just want to see his reaction so I say it again.

"Praaayyyyer Warriors, come out and praaaaayyyy!"

"Eddie," Billings warns.

"You really think a bunch of people praying is going to stop a serial murderer from repeating her crimes?"

"I do."

Billings says it sincerely. Then he gets up and moves toward me.

"I'd like to pray for you now, if you want."

"I'm good."

"Eddie, are you all right?"

"Yeah."

"Are you in pain?"

"I'm fine."

I feel a weird energy hit me as he moves closer.

"I haven't eaten. I got my blood sucked out, and I'm trying to comprehend how a bunch of church groupies think they can pray away the inevitable actions of a psychotic serial killer who thinks she's the Virgin fucking Mary."

Billings places his hand on my head.

"Let me show you... Father God, I ask in the name of Jesus that you bring Eddie—"

"Stop!"

"—peace. May your blessed Holy Spirit fill his mind—"

"Stop!"

I feel pressure build behind my eyeballs, but he continues.

"Fill his heart with your love, Lord Jesus."

"Don't mention that fucking name!"

I scream as I lunge in rage. I don't know why, but my body explodes with energy. Billings backs off carefully, saying:

"I'm sorry."

"I got a serious migraine! My head feels like it is going to explode."

The lights in the room sear into my skull. I curl up on the floor with my head under my hands.

"Would you like me to get you aspirin?"

"No... No aspirin. Or yopo snuff. Anderthera, whatever that plant is."

I begin awakening back to the facts of my investigation.

"What do you mean?" Billings asks.

"The drugs from the greenhouse."

I try to muster the energy to get up.

"What greenhouse?"

"What do you mean, what greenhouse?"

I snap at him, feeling a surge of energy return to my body. I get up and make sure to look him in the eye, even though the pain is nauseating.

"A mile east, at the end of the river. At the edge of the mountain, there's the greenhouse."

"Not that I know of," Billings says innocently.

"Don't bullshit me! I heard the whole thing in Ward D. I spent days listening to the toxicologist ramble about hallucinogenic plants grown at that greenhouse. They put them in our food and water."

"I've never heard this."

"Don't patronize me! I'm being filled with increasing amounts of Tryptamine, Methylone, and other trace hallucinogens in my bloodstream. That's why I'm seeing things!"

"You never mentioned this, Eddie," Billings said, concerned. "What are you seeing?

"What the fuck does it matter what I'm seeing? What matters is we're being poisoned against our will. You need to do something!"

"If anything illegal is going on, I'll report it."

"Will you?" I retorted, squeezing close to him.

"I'm on your side. Trust me."

"Can I?" I said, holding back a piercing pain from my eyes.

"My word is my bond."

"How can I trust you?"

"The Spirit of truth. Ask and you shall receive."

"Ask? All I have to do is ask?"

"Yes."

If I am ever going to get the truth, now is the time.

"Why'd they take my daughter? I want to see her."

> "Who took your daughter?" Billings answered
ignorantly.
> "You did. You all took her."
> "No one took your daughter, Eddie."
> "I want to see Kennedy. Let me see her. Why
won't anyone let me see her? I just want to see my
daughter. She's my child too. I know my rights!"

I'm not going to take it. He can't look at me with that confused
tone. People can't just come and steal someone's child. I know
my rights.

The pain intensifies. It is crippling me. My eyes are
ready to explode out of my head. My teeth tingle. My jaw feels
like it is being crushed. It is all building up inside. Crushing
me from the inside out.

> "I'm sorry, Eddie," Billings says, feigning
sincerity. "Your daughter is not here."
> I scream, letting the steam out. "Stop lying.
Everyone's lying. Everyone's lying to me."

I start pacing. I have to release this energy. I have to release
this energy on something.

My body is convulsing. The pain is writhing through
me. I feel my insides contorting. I can't take any more of their
condescending tones, the arrogance, the lies, the manipulation,
the greed, the callousness. It is all circulating through my
blood.

Now Billings is on the defense. I can see him circle me
like a hawk, as I begin constricting on the floor. The poison is
taking affect, and he just observes, waiting to make his move.

I want to strike, but my body grows increasingly weak
on the outside while my insides rage with a consuming fire.

What the fuck is he doing? Is he praying over me?

I feel blinded by the pain. I can only see shadows hovering over me, but I hear Billings mumbling in some foreign language. The gibberish is stirring my stomach, and I am ready to vomit out this rage.

I curl up on the floor and cover my eyes. The words keep pounding me in the gut until I puke out this river of bile and blood.

JOURNAL ENTRY:
TUESDAY, DECEMBER 21, 2010 – 5:15 P.M.

So much for any badly needed rest! Before I could make it back to my room, I was accosted by Nurse Regan and brought into the lab to undergo a series of tests.

After drawing more blood, they gave me some sort of serum to help me relax, take away the headache, help me think. Then came a series of mental tests.

First there was this Myers-Briggs personality test, then a Rorschach Inkblot, then screening tests for depression, mania, bipolar, OCD, PTSD. Then finally, an IQ Test. It was exhausting. Every stupid question was skewed to provoke a reaction from me, to determine my mental illness.

How unstable am I? Am I a threat to myself? To others? I'm a threat to Dr. Haworth because I have information that is detrimental to his health.

Maybe you should take the test, Doc. You're the sadistic madman playing God with death-row murderers.

I barely read the questions. I used my time to absorb my surroundings, get information, and see what resources were here at my disposal in case of emergency, or in the case of my inevitable escape from here.

As fate would have it, my primary source of information came directly to me. Annette Dobson was brought to the infirmary around three in the afternoon.

At the time, I was in the psych lab reviewing inkblots. I glanced up and saw her escorted in. I tried to excuse myself to use the bathroom, but Nurse Regan was all over that, making sure I wasn't going anywhere.

The blots were a joke. They all looked like things I saw in the cottage. Winged bats, snakes, leopards attacking, ghosts, demon-like characters. I could tell the way Regan was eyeballing me, with her puffy black eye that everything was designed to illicit a reaction from me.

But I acted casual, making shit up, saying what the stupid blots looked like. It was a joke to see how they'd react to me, not me to them. I'm the one in control.

I focused on Annette Dobson and any information I could obtain regarding her status.

Here's what I discovered. Baby Kevin has been crying since last night, nonstop. Twice he stopped breathing and his neck is bruised. Bruises were found on his left leg and right arm.

The nurse's report stated tears came out of his left eye only. His body temperature dropped to ninety-five degrees.

This prompted Rev. Billings into action. His diagnosis is that the demon Keron Ken-Ken returned with seven of his friends to wreak havoc and take back his home.

Hence, Billings ordered in the prayer warriors, who arrived like a swat team to fight the demons off baby Kevin and Annette.

The warriors have Kevin in the chapel, while Annette undergoes testing. She no longer looks ditsy and bubbly with that religious giddiness tattooed on her face. She's worn out.

Speaking of worn out, I returned to the serenity of my room only to find that I've been assigned a roommate. The bed on the other side of my room now officially belongs to Rudy Martin, my impish breakfast companion from a few weeks back.

My reflective thoughts became deflective grunts, as I tried to concentrate on writing before dinner.

The last thing I need is a sidekick nipping at my heels, buzzing around with questions and comments every two seconds. His only value to me is information. I needed to find a way to put him to use, keep him occupied, away from me.

After assessing his ability to provide and retain information, I invented this game we call "Quest."

I send Rudy on missions, and he reports back to me, winning points and prizes for completing successful quests. I told him the missions are top secret, so he can't mention them to anyone or he is immediately disqualified and has to report directly to Ward E for admittance. This freaked him out, so I definitely have his silence and cooperation.

I just sent him on mission one. A trip to the nurses' station to report anything he hears about code names *baby*, *Kevin*, *Annie*, or *Dobson*.

He gets two points for every piece of information he brings me. Ten points earns a special prize. But he can't report back to base camp until after dinner or after completing his mission.

Dinner brings me to my next quest. I need to make befriend the kitchen staff, perhaps volunteer. I need to see the food prep and processing areas.

I need a precise layout of this entire compound and an accurate account of all security locations and personnel, as well as weapons and ammunition counts.

I need to monitor the food truck schedule. I have to find a way to establish trust and obtain concrete evidence of human rights violations committed here at Uphir Behavioral Health Center.

There's another one of Billings church services tonight, of which I am officially invited. The attendants are mostly from Ward B—where Dobson is being held—or staff members.

Ward C patients like myself are only allowed to service by invitation. We are escorted to and from the Ward. We are always supervised when leaving.

Ward B patients are awarded unsupervised outdoor activity within restricted areas.

Obviously Ward D and E patients have no escorted privileges or rights.

Ward A is the recovery ward, lab, and infirmary. It is also the building that houses the offices.

Then there are Dr. Haworth's living quarters in the penthouse. They can only be accessed through Ward A.

What I've observed here is a hierarchy of patient privileges based on mental condition and religious belief. It seems those cooperating with Billings' program are given more freedom.

A migraine is closing in on me again. My eyes feel like ten-pound weights falling into the back of my head.

I have to get what little rest and peace I can while I have it. I'll report back later.

JOURNAL ENTRY:
TUESDAY, DECEMBER 21, 2010 – 9:15 P.M.

I resigned myself to the fact there's absolutely no way I'm going to get my new roomie to shut up. He's wired like a six-year-old kid in a fifty-year-old body, nonstop yakking about baby Jesus, wise men, and angels.

I swear Rudy acts like it's the first time he's ever heard that story. To me, that's all Christmas is, a story, like Santa Claus and the elves.

I'm trying to tune him out by agreeing to whatever he says to shut him up.

Yes, church was great. Christmas is fun. I love the songs too. No, I don't want to sing them now.

My head is rolling in circles, and I can't shake that agitated adrenaline rushing through my body.

I clench my fists, and my hands shake like they want to punch through the walls. Or I want to smash my head into the floor as I nod and smile at this lunatic, who unwittingly stands in the path of my destruction if he doesn't shut the fuck up.

This bomb has been ticking inside me all day. I wanted to scream the whole time I was in church.

Every word that came out of Billings' mouth was like a razor. I could feel this deep groan building in my gut, ready to explode watching this euphoric carnival of emotion.

It swung like a pendulum of extremes. The room erupted singing "Joy to the World."

Patients danced, sang, and celebrated like their team just won the Super Bowl. I merely observed as the patients clung to Billings' every word between songs with child-like awe.

The elation of "Joy to the World" was followed with Annette Dobson's stunning rendition of "O Holy Night," which provoked a range of disturbingly odd behavior.

Some people were weeping, some praying, some fell on their knees. The sound of her voice gave me chills, and it literally felt like I was being torn in two as I listened to her sing.

Her voice cut into me in waves of notes. But something was deeper at work inside me. Somewhere deep in my body, the rage was bubbling again.

Evil thoughts surfaced in my mind. I was filled with the cruelest intention to harm someone. The thoughts only grew as I looked around and saw the mesmerized lunatics hanging on Dobson's song.

"Take a hostage. Fight your way out of here," I heard myself say. Kill them if you have to. Just get out!

I began to fantasize about the whole scenario. I could jump the guard, take his weapon, and start beating anyone who got in my way.

Die! Die! Die was the battle cry in my head as I looked around. But the notes of music simultaneously attacked the other side of my psyche.

I nearly wept at the beauty of Annette's voice, the poetry of the lyrics, and the simplicity of the love being poured out in the majestic chapel.

The sounds, the murals, the stained glass, and picturesque statues seemed to soften my heart, while my head hardened with malice.

And right when I thought I was the only person so dualistically divided, this guttural scream ripped through the microphone. A shriek of terror came from the same voice that seconds before had been saturated with such purity.

Innocence vanished. It was replaced with shrills of fear crying, "They're killing my baby! They're killing my baby!"

Before Dobson could run off the stage, Rev. Billings subdued her and within a minute, Nurse Evans brought Kevin into the chapel.

Dead silence filled the room. Heels clanged off the marble floor, echoing off stained glass as she brought the baby up the aisle to the altar.

The baby's misery hung like a cloud. A thick presence filled the air and sobs of pain reverberated off the stained-glass walls. Disturbing shrieks and moans rifled out like cannons toward the altar, and a chilling breeze swept across the aisle, blowing out the candles on the altar.

As baby Kevin was brought up, Rev. Billings addressed the room.

"It is imperative we enter a spirit of worship and prayer. We must prepare ourselves to fight the enemy and put on the whole armor of God," he ordered.

The prayer warriors positioned themselves around Kevin. That's when I recognized that guy from the post office. His name was Earl, the old guy with the eagle tattoo. What was he doing here? Was he part of the setup?

When he put his hands on Dobson, she dropped down to the ground like a rag doll. The others formed a circle around Kevin, and his crying was hushed as passionate babbling resounded beneath the melody of a violin.

Rev. Billings joined Earl and prayed over Annette. She looked like a corpse. Billings had his hands on her stomach, babbling something when she gagged, then popped straight up.

Everything fell into a hushed silence and the single string of the violin screeched across the bow, before hushing into a sour note. Then silence. Complete silence stirred in the air. All eyes were fixated on Annette, waiting for a response.

After what seemed like minutes, she broke into laughter, releasing the cloud of tension that hung over the room.

She looked like she was crying and laughing at the same time. It was an undeniable release from something that weighed heavily upon her.

Within moments, this incredible smell filled the chapel. It was like rose petals and violets. Lavender, ginger, cinnamon, and jasmine. Like a fresh forest after the rain, or a cool clean autumn morning in the mountains. All of it rolled into one essence. It was hard to describe, but it was so intoxicating.

Everyone was peaceful and joyous, but my nerves signaled something was wrong. I scanned the room. Then— *bam!*—reality hit me!

What if the drugs were being tested in gas form? Inhalants carrying psychedelic hallucinogens, nerve gas, nitrous oxides, Yopo snuff. For centuries, drugs have been used by shamans and incorporated into religious services. Why not here? Why not now?

I tried to slow my breathing. I placed my shirt over my nose and scanned the room to plan my exit.

With all attention up front, I managed to slip out and slowly make my way to the rear of the chapel unnoticed.

I got to the exit, but the door was locked from the outside. We were trapped. Those drugs were going to work their way into my system one way or another. I could feel them in the air.

I felt dizzy. My eyes got watery. The pressure of the migraine began to throb in my head again. I tried to control my breathing, but my eyes rolled back in agony.

My head felt squeezed so hard on the inside that it dropped me to the ground. The next thing I remember, I was on the floor looking up at that old guy Earl.

He was praying over me, smiling as he said, "Choose life." Then he helped me to my feet and hugged me.

"I took care of your package like I promised," he told me reassuringly. "I'll always be a friend."

And in that moment, my headache was lifted and everything became clear. But this intoxicating euphoria only lasted about five minutes, then within a fraction of a second, in the pulse of a thought, the pain shot through me like a bullet, and angst filled me again.

I saw Annette holding Kevin peacefully in her arms. I'm not sure what it was, but it really bothered me. Perhaps it was because my million-dollar story was flaunting itself in my face again, and I had no way to expose it.

I felt this desperate agony cling to me. And just when I thought no one else shared my pain, I glanced over and saw Donald staring at me.

Our eyes locked. He smiled sadistically, his lips trembling and eyes fluttering. It silently spoke across the room that our agony was shared.

Billings disrupted the moment bellowing out in an authoritative voice.

"'If it is by the Spirit of God that I drive out demons, then the kingdom of God has come upon you.' Let us repent from the evil in our hearts, our iniquity, the impurity in our minds, and give no place for the devil to live. For he roars about like a lion, seeking those he may devour. The lies, deceits, vanity, promise of fulfillment, all return empty. But God says His word will never return null and void of its promise. So on that word we stand."

I don't know why I remembered those words so clearly. Maybe it's the echoing voice of a higher power begging me to listen. A voice directed at me from various angles, people, and places, designed to help me off this ledge.

I am overlooking the bottomless pit, the place of nothing I journeyed through before. Whether this is the death of my soul under the black light and neon glow of seduction, or the passing of life in the lividity of seclusion, the death card is speaking to me again.

Perhaps it beckons me to realize my last shot at redemption.

Is this the new beginning my beautiful oracle foretold?

Or is it the finality of my physical life, mercifully reflecting light on me, so I can see my inescapable future?

My window of life is closing like the wings of that vampire bat, sucking me into the vortex of eternity.

What reality awaits me on the other side?

I lay my head back in this pale, barren room, accompanied only by the muttering of a lunatic in deep sleep.

At some point, I too will close my eyes and fall into the waning hands of the unconscious, clinging to the hope that tomorrow I will awaken to a renewed light of hope.

Or maybe the dark, cloudy skies of my inevitable future will play themselves out in the cards I've been dealt.

JOURNAL ENTRY:
WEDNESDAY, DECEMBER 22, 2010 – 3:33 A.M.

At exactly 3:33, I was jarred out of a deep sleep. I don't remember what I was dreaming, but it felt like I was choking. I rose up, gasping for air.

That's when I saw Rudy hovering over my bed, naked, staring down at me.

He was in this deep trance, a lurid dream. His face was locked in torment, like Santiago's. His eyes were wide open, but it looked like he couldn't even see me. He was locked into the darkness of his soul, poised over me, emitting this gruesome energy, ready to attack.

He was palpitating, shivering, unconscious to this world. All I could see were the whites of those detached eyes locked on me.

It was deeply perturbing. An intrusion, which sent a rush of defensive adrenaline through me.

My reaction was fast and furious. I rolled back, tucked my knees to my chest, and shot my legs out hard at him, punishing him with a kick beneath the jaw. It knocked him off the bed and cracked his skull off the floor.

With a raging menace, I leaped out of bed and flung myself on top of him, throwing two jarring left hooks to his face. I was ready to pound him into submission when I saw his eyes roll back, and I realized it wasn't his conscious body trying to attack me.

He was defenseless, hurt, bleeding. And in that instant, my mind transcended back to the dark woods so many years ago, where my ruthless demon first reared its ugly head.

My fist was positioned to strike a finishing blow, but something stopped me once again. I heard people running around frantically, doors slamming all over the ward.

I jumped off Rudy and ran over to the window. Bodies crossed the great lawn toward Ward B. The whole asylum was on high alert as the alarm sounded.

Rudy was lying on the floor, still not moving, blood slowly gathering around his head.

I quickly peered out the door to make sure no one was coming our way. Then I dragged Rudy into the bathroom and threw him into the shower.

I turned on the cold water. Spit and blood washed across the tub, and he flopped like a fish out of water, awakening from his daze.

Rudy had no idea what he did or how he got there.

I told him he hit his head sleepwalking, and I got up to help him.

"We need to go to the nurses' station for help," I said.

So I threw a gown on him, and we made our way downstairs. When we got there, patients were scurrying about frenetically.

A security guard was stationed at the door, making sure no one got out of the building unauthorized. It was chaos.

I looked for an escape route, leading Rudy toward the back stairwell unnoticed.

As we descended to the basement, I briefed him on our next mission. I told him he broke the code open, and it activated everyone into the game.

Now his mission is to find Annette Dobson. "This is top secret," I told him. "You get ten points if you find her."

We made our way down the back stairwell into the laundry room. I remembered a window by the air conditioning vent, which led outside. I squeezed Rudy through, giving him a final warning about the secrecy of our mission and the penalty for revealing it.

Now my mission began. I made my way back to my room, avoiding contact with the staff.

I rummaged through Rudy's possessions to get additional information on him. Anything that might help me understand his reason for being held in Uphir.

Other than medications, underwear, uniforms, there was nothing. Just a picture of him with his dog, a Bible, and a checkerboard.

JOURNAL ENTRY:
WEDNESDAY, DECEMBER 22, 2010 – 7:45 A.M.

I'm tripping out. Rudy never returned to the room. I think I finally fell asleep around four, after things died down in the ward.

At seven on the dot Nurse Regan barged in for wake-up call. She drilled me hard about Rudy's whereabouts.

I told her he probably got spooked when the alarms went off and got lost in the commotion.

She gave me a dirty look with her puffy black eye that said she wasn't buying my story. A pool of dried blood next to my bed didn't help.

"I don't know how it got there," I explained.

Regan continued her inquisition. None of the security guards at the exits or any cameras detected Rudy leaving the building. Now for some reason, it's my responsibility. Apparently, as the last person to be seen with Rudy, I am now a suspect.

"Dr. Haworth will see you immediately after breakfast," Nurse Regan warned as she continued digging through my room for clues.

JOURNAL ENTRY:
WEDNESDAY, DECEMBER 22, 2010 – 9:25 A.M.

Everyone's eyes were fixated on me as I entered the cafeteria, like I held the answer to some riddle. Quiet whispers replaced the ceremonious shrieks from the night before.

As soon as I looked at someone, the eyes, they would turn away in fear and the murmuring began.

Remnant voices circulated throughout the room, groaning about demons coming back for vengeance, demons taking control and planning an attack.

Finally, I heard a coherent voice beckon me.

"You're the one. The one who killed Rudy," said Donald with a seditious tone. "Not like he didn't have it coming."

He stared at me with an intense glare. It held the same venomous grin from last night's service. He kicked out a chair so I took a seat across from him and set my tray down.

"Why would you say that?" I asked.

"I saw it with my own two eyes," he answered. "You confessed it in your dream. I saw you."

I remembered the look he gave me in the chapel, the way he shuddered in pain. The way he seemed detached from his body. I wasn't sure how to answer.

"In my dream?" I asked.

"Well, *dream* is a strange word for someone who dwells inside you. Don't you think? … *Think,* that may be the more appropriate word. You think with me, because we are one."

Donald went back to ravaging his eggs, scooping them up in his hands. He was so focused on eating, he didn't even look when I asked, "What's inside us? Parasites? Demons? A virus? Are we diseased? Poisoned? Did they inject us with something?"

With him still ignoring me, I said, "Don't pretend it's not happening. It's like someone sticking a knife through your eyes!"

He ate faster, ignoring me, so I pushed harder to get through.

"We need to stick together. We can get out of here before this disease takes over. Before we end up like Tyler."

"Like Tyler!" Donald stopped. "Before we end up like her."

He looked over as Annette Dobson entered the cafeteria and picked up a food tray.

"That bitch is in denial. Pretending. Pretending," Donald groaned, digging his fingernails forcefully into the table. "Pretending that God will wash away her stain. Lying to herself and acting like the Virgin fucking Mary."

"That's what I said." I met Donald eye to eye, finding common ground.

"Then we're the only ones who know the truth. And the truth shall set you free, right? That's what the priest said, ET!"

"He did," I replied, glued to Donald's gaze.

"Then set her free!" Donald demanded.

He continued devouring his food, humming to himself in contentment as Annette took her seat two tables behind us.

Donald shucked me a knowing glance, and I felt a wave come over me. The hairs on my arms stood on end.

I knew! I knew intuitively, the time was now! This was fate.

I got up and walked toward Annette. I could hear Donald start whistling in these sadistic tones, whistling a song that seemed so familiar.

Annette smiled warmly as I sat down next to her.

"Good morning, Annie. You sang beautifully last night. Like an angel," I said, touching her hand.

She pulled back from me a little frightened. Her whole body tensed up.

"What's wrong?" I asked.

She looked at me with fear. "He's crying again."

"I'm sure someone is watching him, right?"

"Yes," she murmured without confidence.

"Someone you trust?"

"Yes," she replied nervously.

"Like Keron. Keron can be trusted. You should listen to him when he talks to you. You still hear him, don't you?"

"No!" she answered with tears taking form in her eyes.

For someone who believed in truth, I could tell she was finally able to lie. It was time to end that false religious pretense and truly become herself again. I touched her arm.

"You can, Annie. You hear him now," I told her.

"No, Eddie. He's not real," she said, trying to convince herself of her own words.

With that, something kicked inside me. Keron was very real. I could feel he wanted to tell her something. And for the first time, I began to realize that there was something unseen working in this place, and perhaps working in me.

I felt awakened, driven to find the gateway into Annette's soul. I scanned the room, looking for the answer. And like a bolt of lightning, my mind lit up, and there it was, right in front of me, so crystal clear.

A picture inside my head envisioned me opening the gateway. It was a symbol that transcended time.

"Look at all that delicious fruit, Annie," I said, pointing to the cart. "My favorite is that apple. It's so shiny and red. It's almost glowing."

"Yes," she answered, staring at the apple.

"Doesn't it look delicious? It's calling your name. Annie. Annie. Come eat me," I joked with a cartoon-like voice that made her giggle.

"It is glowing."

"Because it's for you. Want me to get it for you. It will make you feel better."

"Okay," she said, staring lustfully at the fruit. "It looks so good."

I walked over to the counter. When I picked up that apple, this feeling of euphoria came over me. I grabbed the plastic wrap beneath it, and wrapped it shut, trapping in its life force. The anticipation of Annette touching this was intoxicating. It made me tremble with excitement.

I returned to the table, seeing her innocent little face light up as she gazed at the fruit.

"Here, sweetheart," I said. "I kept it fresh for you."

"Thank you, Eddie."

"Unwrap it," I gently instructed.

I watched her cautiously dig her fingernails into the plastic, and this orgasmic, radiant energy filled me.

I put my hands on hers, and we pulled back the wrap in unison. It felt like making love.

"Feel that," I said. "Feel the plastic. It feels like home, doesn't it? Wrapped around the little baby. It's so good, isn't it?"

"No," she moaned.

"It's your life. You and Kevin. Your babies. Remember. Remember Kevin?" I said, keeping her hands glued to the plastic as we suffocated the apple together.

I could hear her gasping. I felt Annie resist, trying to push her hands back.

"No," she cried as I locked my grip tighter, peering into her eyes. "Please stop."

"See him, Annette. See Kevin Dobson. Your husband. I want you to see him. Picture him. Tall, brown hair, brown eyes, wearing that tuxedo with the pink bow tie. How you loved pink. He looked at you with such love in that old church, the bell tower was ringing as he said, 'I do.' You can see him now, can't you?"

"No! No! I don't," she cried.

I could feel her hands gripping the plastic wrap. I knew she saw the same thing I did. Our minds were one. As Donald said, we were one. One in spirit.

A new picture emerged on the pallet of my mind. I saw Annette wrapping plastic around her child's face. I could see her in that cold, dark room, pulling back the plastic tightly, suffocating the child.

I grabbed her hands tighter and forced them along the plastic, feeling its shiny surface slide between our fingers.

"Remember how we put the baby to sleep?"

"No," she muttered.

I smell the defeat in her. I tasted the victory of her giving in to my voice. She couldn't deny who she really was any longer. She saw it too.

I felt her fingers get sick satisfaction from the touch of plastic, but her eyes feared this new discovery. The forces in the room worked harder. I could feel their presence invade the air around us.

The room grew dry and cold. I saw my breath exit my lungs, molding the plastic around the apple until it took the form of a baby's face.

I watched reality sink deeply into Annette Dobson's mind and a chorus of voices ushered in the vision.

Donald began the song I knew deep in my heart. The others followed. Eight voices distinctly singing...

> *"Bye, baby, Mama's here.*
> *Rocking her little baby so dear.*
> *Angels guard you while you sleep.*
> *Hush now, baby, do not peep.*
> *Oh! Bye, little baby, bye oh.*
> *Bye, little baby, bye oh."*

The despair in Annette's eyes was glorious. Tears rolled down her cheeks. The truth was finally released into the frigid air, ringing out from my lips with fervor.

"Annette Dobson, Executed Offender 381. The state of Texas found you guilty of murder in the first degree of six of your children.

Miranda Dobson, February 14, 1997.

Richard Miles Dobson, July 4, 1999.

James Edward Dobson, April 1, 2002.

Bridgett Dobson, Christmas Eve, 2004,

Kenneth Kennedy Dobson. Ken-Ken! You strangled his helpless body on Halloween night, 2007.

And your last victim, Anthony Dobson, baby Tony, murdered on your own birthday, March 1, 2009!

Now it's time for Kevin!"

"No! God, no!" she cried, clutching the apple in agony, realizing the veil was broken. She crashed to the floor. She needed to see the truth for what it was. FREEDOM!

I continued with unbridled passion.

"I showed you six little graves last night. Six little graves while you were singing. Six little graves where your children lay sleeping!"

She fell to her knees, sobbing uncontrollably. It was a sweet melody to my soul.

Donald walked over like he had just knocked out an opponent in the boxing ring, gloating over her fallen body.

"Where is your God now?" he said. "Do you think He loves a murderer, who covers her sin?"

Donald glared at Annette on the floor. Her sobbing was so deep, it punctured me. Then this energy passed through me. The powerful feeling I had moments ago was gone, and my stomach kicked back hard. My heart sank deep in my chest. I couldn't look at Annette suffer like this anymore.

What did I do?

Before my next thought could generate, two nurses helped Annette off the ground. Security grabbed me, and I flopped over lifelessly.

I didn't have the strength to fight. They restrained me and dragged me out of the cafeteria to this holding room in Ward B.

I still hear Annette crying. She's completely broken, and they have her on suicide watch. It's disturbing to hear someone crying so loud for so long.

The strange part is that all this insanity quieted the voices in my head. As if they gained satisfaction from my actions.

But it left me physically drained. I feel weak, cold, detached. Chills run through my body, and my mind keeps blanking out. My body is growing numb.

It's hard to focus on my computer, and the bones in my fingers throb in pain as I stroke the keyboard. I read through my journals to make sure they make sense. But I don't remember writing sometimes.

It's like I go into another dimension, staring at the screen, and when I recover, I look down at the monitor and everything is there, clear and concise.

Something is stirring inside me. Moving in and out of the deepest places within me, that I didn't know existed.

Is it my spirit? Is it my soul that I am finally in contact with? Or is it an alien presence invading this sacred place within me?

Is this a disease? Or some kind of tumor affecting my brain? Is contaminated blood pumping through my veins, filled with toxins and drugs? Is this all a reaction to the foreign substances that fill me with this poison?

Or is it a demon?

Could a demon possibly be living inside me?

For the first time, this question begs consideration.

I don't feel like myself anymore. Maybe I'm detaching from the consequence of my actions to justify what I did.

Maybe I need to put the blame on someone or something else. Anything but me.

Could I become so desensitized to the evil that lurks within me?

Is this the defense mechanism that lies to protect us from a perfect God? That's what Billings told me about sin. And now I'm questioning if anything he said could have a measure of truth to it.

What have I evolved into?

Why would I purposely aim to destroy someone, or in the worst-case scenario, kill them?

If I killed Rudy, I don't even remember it.

What happened with Annette was so vague, but this force comes back and brings all these deeds clearly to my mind. I relive each moment as if it were happening all over again, like it's haunting me.

My mind becomes this projector, playing movies on the walls inside my head. Sometimes I open my eyes and I'm still inside this theater of my soul. The darkness plays tricks on me. I'm not sure if I'm dreaming or hallucinating, or even living for that matter.

Reality is lost. Time stands still. And the replay of mortal consequence is on auto-play, looping through my mind.

It's exhausting. I'm freezing up. I want to curl into a ball and sleep. I want to forget everything. I want to go back in time. Go back before life accosted me and slew its vile vision of my future into this universe.

JOURNAL ENTRY:
WEDNESDAY, DECEMBER 22, 2010 – 1:40 P.M.

After waiting inside the holding room for a while, I was brought to the infirmary for examination.

My body temperature plummeted to 94 degrees. I'm suffering from hypothermia. They gave me an IV of iodine and warm tea.

Nurse Evans wrapped a heated blanket around me. I'm trying to keep my sense of humor, but the way she looked at me, I could tell something is wrong.

I'm sick. Sick in the head. Sick in the heart. Sick of this place. Sick of my thoughts. Sick of the voices that torment me.

I'm sick of Haworth and Billings.

I'm sick of mentally ill patients.

I'm sick of hearing Annette Dobson cry over her demented life.

I'm sick of being blamed for everything.

I'm sick of losing.

I'm sick of being rejected.

I'm sick of failure.

I'm sick of IVs feeding me drugs.

I'm sick of everything.

I'm just sick!

I can't stay here any longer. I can't entertain these thoughts anymore. I can't even move my body. I'm nauseous, dizzy, exhausted, but inside, I feel like I am going to burst open and watch my guts spill over the floor.

VIDEO LOG:
WEDNESDAY, DECEMBER 22, 2010 – 2:03 P.M.
ENTERED BY MELODY SWANN

I received this file in the mail, along with a note that said more material was on its way to me so prepare myself for what was about to happen.

The note was signed from "A Friend" again, so I don't think it came from Eddie. It's been eight days now since I last talked to him. I'm really worried.

Carl is convinced the tapes Eddie sent me of Annette Dobson are authentic, and he paid me for them. He's helping me put all these notes together to turn Eddie's story into a book.

This video has the time and date on the bottom. December 22 at 2:03 p.m. It looks like security video from a hospital room.

Eddie's lying on the bed, hooked up to an IV. He looks horrible. His skin is pale, white, and pasty. He's unshaven. His hands shake, and he's banging his head off the back of the bed, grunting like a wounded animal.

They restrained his arms and legs. He's going in and out of consciousness as his eyes open.

They look black. His eyes look black! Something's wrong. He's kicking, flopping on the bed, saying something. He's trying to say something.

> *"Daemones mihi vivere. I ad eas pertinent. Et videbis credidisti! Capiam Dei solium dominabitur homines nequam."*

Holy shit! I swear I just saw Eddie's body lift off the bed. It looked like a magic trick, or some video effect, but it wasn't. I know it. That was real. His whole body lifted or something pulled him up off that bed.

What if he's having a heart attack? What if he's hurt?

The worst thing is I can't help. I don't even know where he is. Why is no one helping him? He's alone.

I've got to talk to Carl. We need to go to the police.

AUDIO LOG:
WEDNESDAY, DECEMBER 22, 2010 – 5:48 P.M.

"This is Eddie Hansen. It's Wednesday, I think. I don't know. I can't move. I'm strapped down on this bed.

"I'm in the hospital at Uphir Behavioral Center in Uphir, Texas. If anyone gets this, please help. I need help. I may be infected with a parasite or virus. I've been given non-regulated, experimental drugs. I'm the victim of—

"Hey, who's down here? Is anyone down here? I know you're watching! I see the camera. C'mon. Help me!

"Hey! Hey! Nurse Evans. Come here. Please… Let me loose."

"I can't Eddie," she told me, playing with my IV.

"What are you doing? What is that?"

"It's dopamine. You went into shock. Remain calm. Just stay still."

"I feel like my chest is going to explode," I told her, feeling nervous as she changed the bags of medicine feeding me.

"I know. Just relax. This will help. Think happy thoughts."

"About you?" I said, looking for relief.

"Sure. This will help you sleep. Breathe deep. Relax."

"My laptop? Who took it?" I asked, trying to get up.

"Don't move, Eddie. It's here, on the chair behind you. You can't move, please. It can be fatal. I'm taking this. "

"No. No. No!" I said as she attempted to take my audio recorder. "Please."

"You need rest. I'll leave this right next to your hand, right here, okay?"

"Okay."

"Close your eyes. If you feel your heart racing or you need me for anything, just hit this button. Understand?"

"Yes."

"Good. I'll be back later to check on you."

This is the second video from the package I received from "A Friend."

Eddie is strapped down on the bed, sleeping. The fluorescent lights above flicker on and off.

Maybe there is something moving in front of them. It's hard to tell. A big shadow keeps moving around Eddie.

Someone may be in the room with him. I can't see them, but I see this shadow moving in front of his bed.

No, wait! That shadow is over the bed, right on top of Eddie. What is it?

Something's hovering over him, moving lower. It's getting close, but he can't see it. Oh my God. It looks like that shadow is trying to cover Eddie, wrap around his body.

It opened! Opened like it had wings.

What is it? A bat. It's too big. It's ready to latch on to him. I can't watch this…

He's helpless. I don't even know what I'm looking at. Something is wrapping itself around Eddie like a dark blanket!

Eddie's eyes roll back. I can only see the whites of his eyes. His mouth is hanging open, gasping for air.

I hear his sick, painful moan…

He's not moving. Oh my God, he's not moving!

His body froze up. I can't tell if he's breathing.

I don't see his chest or mouth moving. It's rigid. There's this shocked expression locked on his face. He's paralyzed…

I think he's dead! Oh God. I think Eddie just died...

Why would someone send me this? Why would they want me to watch Eddie die?

This room feels cold. I can't describe the chill running through me, seeing Eddie's lifeless body.

Get up. Please, Eddie get up… Let me know you're alive. Eddie!

Oh God! Something's crawling up on him. A roach or a spider, or some bug is crawling up his chest, but Eddie's not moving. Eddie! Get up!

It's climbing into his mouth. He's choking! Eddie choked! He's alive! He's still alive.

He's shaking. No, it's the bed shaking. The IV next to him crashed. Items are falling off the cabinets. Maybe there's an earthquake.

Eddie is lifting his head off the pillow.

He's saying something. That doesn't sound like Eddie's voice, but I think it's coming from him! He's saying something. I can't decipher.

> *"Deus miserere mei. Recede! Egredere de me.*
> *Eo Consumam. Edam corporis."*

The nurse runs in to help. She's at the bed.

Holy shit! Something shocks her. An electric shock.

Eddie pops up, breaking one of his restraints. She's trying to hold him down, but Eddie knocks her away.

It's hard to see. The lights are flickering. Eddie is shaking violently. He rips his IV out and jumps out of bed.

Two security guards rush in to restrain him. Eddie's going nuts. He picks up the bed like it and smashes it into one of the guards. He's tearing up the room like an animal. They are trying to corner him.

The nurse runs out screaming. Eddie runs after her, but a guard jumped on his back. He tasers Eddie on the neck, but that just got him madder.

Oh my God! Eddie spins around and grabs the guard by the neck. He picks the guard up over his head and throws him against the wall like a toy.

Now Eddie rams into the other guard, knocking him against the wall. He pushes the guard down, grabs something off the floor and runs to the door.

He smashes his fist through the window, reaches through the broken glass, unlocks the door and runs out.

AUDIO LOG:
THURSDAY, DECEMBER 23, 2010 – 3:33 A.M.

"They are killing me! They're trying to kill me! Melt me from the inside out with their drugs. I feel it crawling inside me. Whatever they injected me with.

These fucking monsters are trying to destroy me, but I got out!

I don't know how I did it, but I made it out of the asylum. I summoned the beast. I knew if I didn't make a move, they would have killed me on that bed.

I was paralyzed, trapped in this nightmare. And I felt everything slipping away.

Death was coursing through my veins. Liquid death, absorbing me, slowly eating through my insides.

Those sick fucks wanted me conscious so I could experience their madness, feel my life slip away. But I'm stronger than them.

As I walk deeper into these woods, I will not let anything devour me. I'm going to keep walking and keep walking and keep walking until I see the lights of freedom.

I will not feel the cold.
I will not feel the pain.

I will not feel tired or sick or weak.

I will keep walking.

Walking through the black trees until I'm free.

I saw the guards gather at the gate, organizing a search for me. But they never saw which way I escaped. I cleared the grounds and made my way up here.

There's a cemetery on top of this hill.

Under the moonlight there's rows of graves. A resting place for the poor souls who let Uphir devour them. I will not be one of them.

I ducked behind a grave for a few minutes to cover myself from the frigid wind.

I wanted to find something to cover myself with to stay warm, but there was nothing here but the dead.

I will not become one of them.

I'll continue deeper into these woods. The road is a few hundred feet below me. I'll make my way down when I clear the asylum.

I can't think about giving up. I've got to keep moving, no matter what.

My steps are getting a little harder because of the cold. I feel my blood getting thicker, freezing up inside me, but I've got to keep moving until I get over this crest. I'm almost at the clearing.

I'll keep talking, keep moving. Stay with me. I'll stay with you.

Down below, it's there. The greenhouse. It's there. Sitting so beautiful. The large glass building glowing beneath the moonlight. The frozen river beside it.

I'll warm up inside and figure out an escape plan.

I need to save these batteries, so I'm turning this recorder off until I get inside...

Damn it! There's nothing here. No plants, no trees. Broken glass. Everything's dead. It's been closed for a long time.

I've got to find something to cover myself with. Protect myself from the cold. I don't know if I can make it until morning. I've got get out of here, keep moving...

What a joke. The only thing to cover myself with is a plastic tarp. Is it fate to wander back into these woods wrapped in plastic like one of Annette Dobson's victims?

Look at me, wrapped up, walking down the road, watching my breath pour into plastic. Watching my hands turn purple. Feeling my feet go numb.

My face tightens, my body constricts, my lungs clamp in. I feel my heart beat slower and slower.

Each step is more difficult, and this road stretches into blackness. Endless mountains greet my eyes in every direction.

The moment I stop moving, this patch of frozen earth becomes my grave.

I've got to keep pushing. I can't let my muscles freeze.

I can take another step.

I can take another step.

I can take another step.

I can take a--

JOURNAL ENTRY:
THURSDAY, DECEMBER 23, 2010 – 9:06 A.M.

Am I thinking or dreaming or dying? Am I lying to myself or digging inside myself to find my deepest truth? Will I find a core of evil, rotted from years of abuse, neglect, and harassment?

Or deep in my heart, will there be some hope of light, a remnant that has not been contaminated with this blood of death?

Within me, I feel this sense of loss and the loss of sense. I smell nothing, and the frozen air, which fills my lungs, leave my body void of feeling.

Have drugs left my tasteless breath forming the shapes of my tormenters as I exhale, so I recognize my murderers as I begin to drift from myself?

Has the intoxication of chemicals, fetid food, and contaminated water nurtured something within me that I cannot no longer bear to live with?

A monster destroyed me from the inside out slowly deconstructing my organs, before lulling me into this false and final sleep.

The last thing I remember was seeing my body on the road. I was looking down at myself, screaming to get up.

But it felt like I was moving further away from my body. I saw lights rushing toward me, blinding me until everything disappeared.

My thoughts are the only thing I have left. A lifetime of memories stashed in this hard drive of my brain is now driven by a decreased heartbeat and frozen mind.

Is this my last attachment to this world? I am void of feeling.

My heart no longer beats, my blood no longer flows. I see my final breath leak out and realize it is no longer my mind dreaming. I am leaving this body.

The substance of the earth fades from my consciousness, and the noise of life quiets itself in preparation for my departure. My final gift of life is my last thought separating me from my body. I think of— THOSE I LOVE.

I love Melody, but my heart ran too shallow to really express that love. The pain of heartbreak created a shield around me that wouldn't let her see the love I should have offered.

I love Kennedy. This kind of love is enduring. It's not shattered by years. Not yielded by memory. Not tested by time. That love lived in my very own blood, and it carries itself with me because a part of me will always live in my daughter.

I call her by name. My lips mutter "Kennedy." The faint vision of her face comforts me as I slide into this timeless horizon.

There are so many things in my life that I could never bring to mind until this moment when the totality of my life's journey is laid bare before me.

Those things were locked away in this box of unconscious memory, hidden until now. Little moments of pain, neglect, suffering. Dark moments I inhaled and kept within me while I exhaled the freely given breath of life and did not appreciate its simple majesty.

And so this dark moment, this little thought slipped inside me and burrowed itself deep within the walls of my heart unnoticed.

All those thoughts, those words were alive. Tiny organisms of demonic blood that grew and fed off each other.

The bitterness, the jealousy, the envy, the pain, the hate, the rage, the doubt, the fear, the wrath, the lust, the uncertainty; they all feed and grow, and like a pregnancy, the embryo of this monster begins to form within me until the entity is conceived. The parasitic seeds of a demon.

A fallen angel. An evil spirit that contaminates my blood and grows within me unnoticed.

And I morph into this new species, part human, part God, part demon, my evolution begins as I depart from this life.

I am conscious. I feel fully alive, but I am no longer in my body. I'm inside this void, the chasm I entered in my dream, or as I clearly see now, my nightmare.

It is this black emptiness without sound or light, without form or texture. Without smell or taste. Without life!

The most terrifying part of this place is that I know time does not exist in the way I experienced on earth.

I could be stuck alone in this void for eternity, or however long I am held prisoner here, to reflect on my past life.

It's terrifying, This feeling penetrates my core. This reality forces me to writhe in torment.

My life no longer belongs to this planet, but it does go on. There is more, and I am going to witness it for another lifetime or longer. I have no idea. No conception of how long this can last, waiting to find something to pull me out of this pit, toward anything!

I cannot bear the thought of nothing any longer, of being alone in this void. This paralyzing fear penetrates every fiber of my being, or whatever life I am still experiencing.

There is feeling without senses.

There is reality without experience.

Every part of me screams in a voice I cannot hear, trembles in a body I cannot feel, cries from eyes I cannot see.

And I realize that there is no taste to death.

There is no sting. Only transition.

And like a butterfly in the cocoon, when I break this shell, I will find life on the other side.

But for this moment in time, I linger in the depth of this womb. Everything I was is nothing. I am merely an embryo again.

But what is carrying me? What is going to birth me?

What if I am in the belly of a demon about to be conceived into eternal torment?

Would torment be better than emptiness? I don't know. I honestly don't know.

It's an agonizing crush on whatever part of me is still alive.

I need to fill the void. I need to take hold of something. I need to feel something. Taste something. See something. Hear something. Smell something... Anything!

Anything to ignite my senses. There has to be something in this universe to cling to. Something to give me hope! There can't be nothing forever!

In this fraction of this moment, inside the abyss, the silence was broken with a voice.

A comforting voice entered this womb, and I felt it divide the darkness, awakening me inside.

It was soft, without judgment or anger; but it had unlimited power. I knew that voice could have spoken and shattered me. It could have crushed me into nothingness.

But instead it opened like a beautiful flower, and these words filled me, saying:

"You're not going to die. You have a lot to learn."

In the nothingness between life and death, something became clear, the totality of my life's journey.

I saw how an innocent child became a haunted man, and I began to drift toward a light.

This light was not the cold fire of torment, nor was it the warm light of pure love. It was the light of my former life, calling me home to see things from my new reality. I can see my body lying on the hospital bed.

Demons wrap themselves around me. Their blackness covers me like a cloud, and my face is stuck in the realization of my nightmare. I am able to see this dimension. I see needful spirits craving my body, my soul, to survive.

How can I describe this? My soul. I see a small light buried deep in my heart that's still burning. Inside a beautiful box it holds my life's memories and how I let them define me.

The box is my mind, my intellect, and my emotions are like a bow wrapped around this box, like a Christmas present.

My soul is a wonderful present I received with my life.

But those monsters are feeding on the bow, trying to unwrap me and get inside the box. I need that gift inside, my soul, to take to my next life, or those demons will claw in and take it.

But what is this part of me that is still alive watching this? The part of me that lived in the box, but is now awakened and living outside my body?

Is this my spirit?

Is this the part of me that lives on forever?

Is this the reflection of myself I saw in the mirror that stretched to eternity, but I could not recognize it?

Is this the part of me I hear in words that live long after I am gone. Words that speak to me in this state?

"For now we see only a reflection as in a mirror; then we shall see face to face. Now I know in part; then I shall know fully, even as I am fully known."

I look down on my body. Is this knowledge a fraction of something greater that I must witness face-to-face?

Who is the other face?

Before I could even decipher this thought, the next words came to me as I gazed down on my body.

"And now these three remain: faith, hope and love. But the greatest of these is love."

I heard those words before. All this, I heard it all before. Those are the words Annette Dobson parroted to me in her room with such conviction. I felt the words had power then, but now they live.

Words do have power. All my words, all my life were constructed to define me. The words built my box.

Why did I let those negative words grow and not feed off words that bring life?

Inside this nothingness that seemed so abandoned, so empty, there were three things unseen that remained with me the whole the time. *Faith. Hope. And Love.*

This is the love that Annette spoke about, the love that had no motive other than to give life, heal and restore. When those words became part of me, they rescued my body. They brought warmth and heat and light back to me.

In that instant, I was no longer looking down at myself, but was back inside my body staring into a light that was dividing the blackness over me.

I began to rediscover my senses.

My feet were frozen. My hands were stiff. My eyes felt heavy, but as received those words of life, a rush of heat entered.

My blood began to flow. I could feel it awakening every part of my body again. I knew I would live.

The blackness over my eyes dissipated. I could see the room again. Fluorescent lights kept me company as I stared at the ceiling.

As my fingers regained sensation, I could feel my recorder still in my hand. I forced my fingers to hit record as the footsteps grew louder. With all the energy I could muster, I twisted my head as far as it would go, and saw Dr. Preston approaching.

AUDIO LOG/JOURNAL ENTRY
THURSDAY, DECEMBER 23, 2010 – 10:07 A.M.

"Good morning, Eddie. How are you feeling?" Dr. Preston asked.

I wanted to talk but my body still couldn't mutter words. Preston looked into my eyes with a light, observing me carefully. "Do you remember anything from last night?"

"Dreams," was all my lips could spill out.

"You went into shock, Eddie," said Dr. Preston, examining my chart. "Your heart stopped beating and… well… you… clinically, you were dead for three minutes."

I tried to move. Dr. Preston must have seen my shocked expression. Still no words could be spoken.

"Relax," he told me. "You need time to recover. You're lucky you're alive. We found you on the road, a few miles away."

I watched him thumb though my charts.

"It's miraculous. Your body temperature is almost normal. There's no brain tumor. No damage or sign of trauma. Someone's looking out for you."

I felt dizzy, but I forced myself to lift my head to see him checking the machines I was attached to.

"You may still experience side effects from hypothermia, so we need to monitor you a little longer to make sure that you are in stable condition."

Dr. Preston walked back toward me, touching my hand, then my head. I was calm and listened, smiling as he told me, "I'm going to take these restraints off. Promise me you will stay still won't get up. Keep your IV in, okay. Or we will restrain you."

I nodded. I could feel the blood loosen in my body and begin to flow again. The energy I was so desperate for was slowly returning.

"I'll come back to check on you. If everything's fine, you'll be released."

What did he mean, released? I needed to know. I summoned all of my strength to ask.

"I can go?"
"If you're healthy."
"Go... Home... I can go?"
"Eddie, you're not a prisoner," he responded, as if he knew nothing of what was really going on here.

I summoned all my energy to say it again to make sure he heard me clearly.

"Home?"
"I need to review all your tests results first, okay? Then I'll be back and we can talk about your release."

JOURNAL ENTRY:
FRIDAY, DECEMBER 24, 2010 – 7:45 A.M.

That was bizarre! I'm hoping Dr. Preston was telling me the truth. He doesn't seem like the lying type. I'm not sure what his motive would be.

He told me later that he would sign my discharge papers when I recovered. Was he trying to provoke a reaction to get me excited about my freedom? Was he testing me to see how I'd react?

Thoughts began pouring into my head.

The whole night started coming back to me as if in a vision in broad daylight. This was a strange, vivid trip into death, and it feels surreal even writing about it.

Sitting on that hospital bed, I watched my dream replay itself in my mind, spinning out the reels of film.

I didn't feel like I was writing. I felt like I was a conduit or court stenographer recalling a witness's testimony.

My fingers moved across the keyboard, documenting what I heard and saw playing back in my head.

Reading this back, I'm not sure how I wrote it all. Everything that's happened. Not just to me, but Dobson, Tyler, this whole place. It's all so peculiar and distant, and yet I'm right in the middle of it, struggling for control.

This whole investigation played tricks on my brain, like I was warned so long ago.

I've lost sense of my surroundings. I felt like I was dreaming again. When I came back, I found myself where I started, inside my cottage.

Everything is placed in the same position like the day I left or the day I arrived. I confuse the two, not fully comprehending this perception of time.

My days, my nights, even weeks have merged as one. It seems part of me has been here for eternity; like this place holds part of my soul.

I look through the triangle window like it's a portal in time or a portal to another dimension.

The leopard statue stares at me, warning me of my place here, while guarding the gates of the portal.

I close my eyes and try to think.

I vaguely remember Dr. Preston returning and giving me a clean bill of health. I'm holding his signed discharge papers, so I know that's a fact.

Scanning the room, I see my clothes, my camera, audio recorder, USB drives, lenses, my wallet. Everything is organized like I left it. And I would never have known time had passed, had I not looked into the mirror.

There, I saw a different man. My face is buried behind weeks of hair growth. My skin is pale, dry, my eyes look bruised. My fingernails are uncut, long, and dirty. I feel dried blood, dirt, hair, and pieces of skin beneath them.

I taste acid in my stomach, bubbling up in my breath. I smell the odor of my unwashed body.

But for the first time since I arrived, I feel some sense of control. I can change what I see.

I pulled out my electric razor and began to peel off the matted hair. There were scratches on my face that burned as my beard fell into the sink. I discovered war wounds hidden beneath my hair as I began shaving my scalp.

The sharp, stabbing pains in my head were no longer a mystery. Shards of broken glass wedged into my skull from when my car hit that tree.

My long, dirty fingernails were like pliers, plunging into glass and skin, digging out the bloody pieces.

My mangled nails were next to be cut as they held on to remnants of my battle.

Stepping into the hot shower was a sadistic mix of pleasure and pain. It was soothing yet burned at the same time. My muscles ached from the restraints.

I felt rigid and tight moving around in the shower, and it brought stabs of pain to various parts of my body. My muscles had been constricted, because my body was subjected to an incredible volume of stress.

But the water began to awaken my senses, and I took pleasure in feeling pain because that meant I was feeling something.

After experiencing the void of death, any feeling became a positive sign that there was life in me.

Once I cleaned up, I began to feel some semblance of normality, and emptying my mind through writing made me realize it was time to regain control of this situation.

I put my notes together and organized my data to see where I stood in my investigation. The true beauty of it all is that all my files are here, untouched.

My credit card thumb drive is full of information and videos. I'm ready to go home with what I have from this investigation.

Along with Dr. Preston's discharge papers is a signed consent form from him, Dr. Haworth, and Rev. Billings that allows me to bring my camera to my exit interviews.

The three of them will conduct a tribunal, where each one will give me a final assessment. Once I pass, they sign me out.

With Dr. Preston already signed, my next meeting is with Rev. Billings before closing out a session with Dr. Haworth.

A consent to film means I'll have all this on tape, proving the authenticity of my claims.

Looking through these files, I have the institution on tape. I have escaped death-row prisoners Annette Dobson and Timothy Tyler. I have the birth of Kevin Dobson. I have Billings, Preston, and Haworth's interviews proving their existence.

The only claim I can't back up is proof of any unregulated drugs, a greenhouse, or any video of Annette Dobson's exorcism.

I still have no idea who is in control of this experiment, who funded Uphir or why.

These are the last pieces of this puzzle. But there is no sense in taking unmitigated risks at this point. Nothing could be worth the hell I just went through.

On my way back home, I'll look for the greenhouse. I'll videotape my journey and leave a path of breadcrumbs back to this place in case of emergency.

JOURNAL ENTRY/AUDIO LOG:
FRIDAY, DECEMBER 24, 2010 – 1:45 P.M.

"For though we live in the world, we do not wage war as the world does. The weapons we fight with are not the weapons of the world. On the contrary, they have divine power to demolish strongholds. We demolish arguments and every pretension that sets itself up against the knowledge of God, and we take captive every thought to make it obedient to Christ. And we will be ready to punish every act of disobedience, once your obedience is complete."
2 Corinthians 10:3–6

"This is Eddie Hansen. It's December 24th. I'm with Rev. Billings at the Uphir Behavioral Health Center in Uphir Texas. Rev. Billings will confirm that this meeting is part of my unconditional discharge from the institution."

"Yes, Eddie," Billings replied. "We will study this verse, because your life depends on it."

"Why would you say that? Is that a threat?"

"No, Eddie. I said it because I care what happens to you, and whether you like it or not, we are heading into a battle for your soul."

"You hear that ladies and gentlemen? This is what I deal with here. The Battle Royale for my soul, in the Uphir octagon, only on Pay-Per-View… How did you come to this conclusion?"

"The same way you did, in a dream. 'In the last days…I will pour out my Spirit on all people. Your sons and daughters will prophesy, your young men will see visions, your old men will dream dreams.'"

"That old guy, at the post office. He said that," I replied. "I saw him at the chapel. Are you two conspiring together?"

"No, Eddie. The word of God goes beyond death. You learned that last night. You heard my prayers. 'And these three remain: faith, hope and love. But the greatest of these is love.'"

"How did you get my journal?"

"I didn't. I feel the Spirit of God telling me things, so that you believe. God wants you to know Him. Come to Him. Let Him release you from the demon that torments you. You can be free. That's your story. It's Annette's story. It's my story. Tell that story to the world."

"I can't... You know what's really going on here. It's my responsibility to report the truth, without bias."

"Yes, Eddie. I know what's going on. Eight demons returned here to find a home. They will destroy everything that opposes them. I need to lock them in a vessel, inside Ward E, before they kill someone else."

"Kill?"

"Yes. Kill. Rudy Martin's body was found yesterday outside the basement window behind Ward C. This morning Donald Lambeck committed suicide after he tried to kill Kevin Dobson."

"What?"

"Donald apprehended one of the guards, then stormed into Ward B threatening to kill the baby. When I dealt with the spirit directly, Donald turned the gun on himself and fired. When the spirits came out of him, they said that they were coming for you!"

"Don't fuck with my head!"

"Eddie. This is why you need to take every thought captive to Christ. Don't listen to me! Listen to God!"

He crossed the line. I can't let him drag me into his game. I feel powerless, but something is at stake here. He needs me as much as I need him. Billings continued his final assault.

"Without the filter of Jesus Christ, the thoughts that plague your soul go unfiltered into your heart. For out of the abundance of the heart the mouth speaks.'"

"You really want to hear my heart speak?"

"I do. But can you filter your thoughts. Allow the spirit of truth to separate the lies that allow demons to influence you. It's life or death, Eddie. Which do you choose?"

"I choose to leave," I said gathering my things.

"Is that what you really want?"

"Yes! I want to go home."

"You're free to go, but I can't guarantee you'll make it home. And even if you do—"

"Are you are threatening me?"

"I'm protecting you."

"You're protecting Haworth and his experiments. You're protecting your concept of God, not me. Want to protect me? Let me go. I don't have to believe the things you do."

"You don't… I'll sign your discharge."

"Thank you."

"But before we see Dr. Haworth, I need you to see something."

VIDEO LOG/JOURNAL ENTRY:
FRIDAY, DECEMBER 24, 2010 – 3:33 P.M.

"This is Eddie Hansen, Friday, December 24th, 3:33 p.m. I'm with Rev. Billings and Annette Dobson. I have permission to videotape this conversion."

"Of course," said Rev. Billings.

"Yes, Eddie," Annette Dobson told me as she extended a smile. But there was something underneath it that made me wonder.

"I just prayed for you," she said.

"Thank you," I answered back, knowing something was bubbling beneath her surface. Extending her hand to me she said, "I understand your pain."

Then Billings intervened, putting me on the spot.

"Is there anything you'd like to say to Annie? Before you leave."

Before I could get a word out, Annette intervened.

"He can call me Annette," she said coldly. "I know who I am. I know what I did. You showed me, Eddie."

"I'm sorry. I know I hurt you," I told her.

"Hurt. You shattered me," she said sitting upright. "You wanted to see me suffer."

"I didn't… I don't know why I…"

"Felt the need to destroy me."

"Annie, don't let your thoughts take control," Rev. Billings instructed. "What do we do with our thoughts?"

"Take them captive to Christ."

Turning back to Billings, she cried out. "Look at him! Look! He doesn't care what I went through. All he wants is his story."

"Annie, I'm sorry. I don't remember saying anything."

"How would you feel, Eddie? If you suddenly realized an entire different reality to your life existed? The worst part of you, your worst nightmare was true?"

"I'd be hurt…and confused," I told her, sitting down at the edge of her bed.

"And sick. Sick to death. I felt like my heart was going to explode. That I deserved death for my sins. I killed my children, and for the first time, I saw it with a clear head and had to deal with it. I had to look into my son's eyes and promise myself that I was a new creation. That I'd never do that again. I begged God to forgive me. I cried, for days. I cried for mercy on my soul."

"God forgave you, Annie. All things are new," said Billings.

"Then why do I hear voices telling me to make him suffer like I did?" Annie groaned. "Why?"

"Temptation, Annie," interjected Billings. "Remember. Test the spirits. Take control."

"Look at me, Annie," I told her, moving closer. "I've suffered immensely."

"I'm Annette to you. I see it in your eyes, Eddie. I hear it in your voice. You want my story so you can glorify yourself, while the world judges me. What will they do to me, Eddie? Will I ever have peace if you leave?"

That question stopped me cold. Was she trying to keep me here? Could she? What if they don't want me to take my story with me? What would this story do to Annette Dobson if I published it? What would it do to Kevin, husband and son? What would it do to me?

Looking into Annie's eyes, all I could ask was, "Do you have peace now?"

"Had peace," she moaned. "I had peace, until you came here. Until my tormenters returned sevenfold to weigh my sins against me. Until a man stormed into my room, threatening my child before killing himself in front of us. Now I have to fight for peace with every breath. Get down on my knees, pray that I can be strong enough to hold off my attackers," she said, moving closer with each word.

Then she grabbed my arm, digging her nails into my skin, saying, "I feel eight demons pressing against my head, against my heart, trying to get in an open door. I hear each of their voices reminding me of each and every sin! They beg me to revenge your offense and harm my son."

I could see something burning in her eyes, in her soul.

"But I refuse to listen to those lies anymore," she told me as we met eye to eye. "I forgive you, Eddie. I can live with myself now. I forgive you. Go! Do what you feel is right. But may God be merciful with your choice."

"Thank you, Annie," I said, getting up. "You are Annie now."

After that, I had no idea what to say. There was an extended moment of silence where we all observed each other. A gust of cold air blew through the room sending a chill down my spine.

Then Rev. Billings spoke, sensing something was taking place in invisible realms.

"Annie? Eddie? Is there anything you want to express before we leave?"

"I'm good," I responded, trying to take it all in.

"These demons won't be staying with me any longer," Dobson said coldly.

I could see her breath. The chill was lingering on my skin. The air crawled with invisible forces. It was dense and becoming arid. I wanted to leave. Even if I couldn't see it, I knew what was there. Billings did too.

"Would you like to pray together?" he said.

"I'm ready to go"

This wasn't the time for any of Billings' games or demon parlor tricks. I needed to get out. I could feel the cold pressing into my skin. It was forceful and deliberate. I turned back to Annie, making one last offer for a peaceful resolution.

"Annie, I promise no one will come here for you. I won't tell, unless you want me to let Kevin know—"

"Eddie!" Billings interrupted, glaring at me with a strict stare that said "watch it."

"Let's go!" he said. As Billings dragged me out of her room.

I'll never forget the look of regret and sadness that lined Annette Dobson's face. I guess I stunned her again, reminding her of the love she left behind, that might never be mended.

As the door was about to close on my chapter with Annette Dobson, she spoke.

"You know what Ose just told me?" she said, smiling seductively. "They're coming for you, Eddie. Good luck with that!"

JOURNAL ENTRY:
FRIDAY, DECEMBER 24, 2010 – 4:48 P.M.

Why'd she have to say that?

Of all the things to leave me with, I'm not sure I want the demons of Annette Dobson following me. My nerves are raw with emotion. I feel rattled, like a snake coiled up ready to strike. That's because I need to defend myself, because of the venom within me. It's all I have left to strike down my enemy.

I'm trying to focus on writing, as I wait outside Haworth's office.

He and Billings have been chatting it up for a while, keeping me on edge. To complicate matters, my old friend Curtis is guarding the door, making sure I stay put.

He was released from Ward D yesterday, retaining his guard duties, while Timothy Tyler will undertake his final descent into Ward E.

According to Curtis, Rev. Billings made his third and final attempt at an exorcism with Tyler, but it was unsuccessful. They feel there is no chance left to deliver him.

Curtis said he got delivered and he's going to abide by the rules, so I don't have to worry about him killing me.

I'm supposed to believe that, like I believe Dobson is sending her demons to me for a meet and greet.

At this point, I'm too close to home to instigate any more problems. Even if I have to fake typing and say nothing, I'm going to focus on this computer and forget that Curtis is staring me down. I'll wait for Billings and concentrate my thoughts and energy on getting out of this hellhole.

The door finally opened, and Billings came out with my signed discharge. I'm all Dr. Haworth's now. My final assessment before freedom.

VIDEO LOG/JOURNAL ENTRY: FRIDAY, DECEMBER 24, 2010 – 5:13 P.M.

I'm waiting in the conference room. Haworth excused himself and left me with photos of exorcisms performed at this institution.

The before-and-after pictures of these people are pretty astounding.

I don't know what he's trying to make me think. But he wants to play with my mind. I know this because the last picture I looked at is of me from a few days back.

I'm in the infirmary, lying on the table. I look like an animal. Unshaven, eyes dilated and black, my hair matted, and my mouth bleeding.

There's no after picture of me here. I know I must look pretty bad. Shaved down, battered, bruised, scarred, broken. I'm a shell of what I was when I entered this asylum.

Haworth returned with a DVD in hand and sat across from me, giving me permission to start recording this assessment.

"This is Eddie Hansen. It's Friday, December 24th, 5:13 p.m. I'm with Dr. Alan Haworth at the Uphir Asylum, and I have permission to videotape this conversation as part of my unconditional discharge from this institution."

"Health Center, Mr. Hansen. This is a behavioral health center. And yes, you are correct about your release. Shall we begin?"

"Sure."

"First, I'd like you to tell me your observation of Annette Dobson today. How did she appear to you on your visit?"

"She seems like a different person," I said, watching Haworth jot down a response to my answer.

"Able to function in society?" he asked, still writing.

"I guess."

"Would you say she's rehabilitated?"

"That's not my area of expertise. I'll leave that to you. I'm just a reporter."

"You've seen these pictures," Haworth stated, sliding them back in front of me. "You've watched tapes, spoken to her. I'm sure you have an opinion. Do you feel that she should still be punished for her crimes?"

"I don't have that power," I told him, feeling deception behind the question.

"If you did, what would you do?"

"Why are you trying to trap me into pronouncing judgment on her?"

"You want to release your story, correct?" said Haworth as he got up and walked over to the video monitor. "In some sense, isn't that judgment?"

"An unbiased account. Based on facts."

"What are the facts?"

"Everything on my recordings. We'll let people make up their own minds. She had an exorcism; she feels better. Is that what you want me to report?" I asked, feeling the room close in around me.

"Can you report the truth about what you've seen, and what you are about to see?"

"Yes."

Grabbing another picture from the pile, he slid it to me asking, "What about Timothy Tyler's condition? What do you feel about him?"

"Based on my limited encounters, I'd say he's deranged and confused."

"In what manner?" Haworth asked in a chilling, calm tone.

"He has no ability to distinguish reality from fantasy."

"Would you detain him here, based on that assumption?"

"What are you getting at?"

"Do you think he speaks from reality or fantasy?"

"Fantasy."

"Why do you think that, Mr. Hansen?"

"I just do. There's no consistency to his claims."

"What claims?" Haworth asked, in a demanding tone.

"Nothing. He just rambles about nothing. I don't even remember half the shit he says."

Haworth then picked up the DVD and put it into the deck. He turned on the monitor.

"If you need help recalling anything, we have it recorded. Are you missing anything you'd like to remember?"

"I'm good," I said, sensing him making his move.

"Then may I ask about your ability, Eddie? Do you feel you can distinguish reality from fantasy?"

"Of course!"

"Who are you?"

"Eddie Hansen."

"Your birth date."

"November 7, 1977."

"Where were you born?"

"San Diego, California."

"Today's date."

"The twenty-third. I mean fourth, December 24th."

"Of which year?"

"2010. Why are you doing this?"

"What if it weren't December 24th? Would that alter your perception of reality?"

"No. No. Everybody gets days confused. You get busy, lose track of time. It's normal."

"To be confused," Haworth stated, pushing the file in front of me.

"I don't understand what you are getting at!"

"To lose track of time, not being able to distinguish reality from fantasy, unable to remember one's actions, violent attacks on others. Does this seem like normal behavior to you?"

"No."

"But that's your behavior."

"No. It's not. I'm fine. You can't keep me here."

Moving back to the monitor, Haworth continued. "I'm about to show one of our tapes, Mr. Hansen. Pay careful attention and tell me what you recall."

He hit play and the video began, showing security cameras from around the institution. To my shock, this video was of me sleeping in Ward C, in the room I shared with Rudy.

I was twitching and groaning, as if I was having a nightmare. I looked like that picture I just saw: disheveled and sick. Then Rudy walked up to my bed naked and stood over me. I remembered the tormented look on his face. From this vantage point, I could see myself sleeping and Rudy hovering over me, growling.

Suddenly, I was jarred awake, coiled my body back, and struck him with my feet, as I remembered.

Then I charged at Rudy as he lay on the floor and began punching him in the face, bashing his head off the floor.

It was an incredibly violent moment I witnessed, but from a different perspective. This is not what I recalled.

It gave me chills to see his unconscious body lying on the ground as I continued to assault him with unmitigated rage.

I watched as I dragged Rudy's body into the bathroom and began to clean up all the blood. I wrapped him in a gown and carried him out the door over my shoulder.

A camera in the basement stairwell showed me dragging his limp body across the floor.

Finally, the camera in the laundry room showed me hoisting Rudy's motionless body into the vent area before pushing him out the window. I looked back at Dr. Haworth, speechless. Was that really me?

I can't believe I killed Rudy. How did I conveniently forget the brutality of my assault?

Dr. Haworth walked over, gloating over my defeated body. "I'm not here to punish you, Eddie. I'm here to get to the root of your problem. Would you like to do that?"

"Do I have a choice?" I asked, feeling fate seal me in like the wings of that creature.

"You can report everything or nothing. You can leave here or stay and get help."

"I want to leave."

Haworth sat down next to me, stating coldly, "If you publish this story, all our tapes will be included. With certainty, they will all find a way to the police and your newspaper. Unbiased reporting is what you wished."

"And if I don't publish anything. I can leave, right?"

"On one condition."

JOURNAL ENTRY:
FRIDAY, DECEMBER 24, 2010 – 6:17 P.M.

I'm alone in the morgue in the basement of Ward B, below the infirmary, down the hall from where I had my MRI done. No wonder death felt so close when I was inside that machine.

Like the triangle window in my room, like the cocoon of the MRI, or the isolation of seclusion—all pointed toward a new dimension. A place beyond this present life.

And now with the pain of seeing my onslaught on Rudy, I am forced to face my victim to ask myself where his final resting place may be.

Rev. Billings escorted me here on Dr. Haworth's instruction, to inspect the remains of Rudy Martin and Donald Lambeck.

I'm now standing at a table filled with various embalming tools used to perform autopsies and prepare the bodies for burial. I can't even think about these tools ripping through my body.

The bodies of Donald Lambeck and Rudy Martin are on gurneys, covered in bloodstained sheets.

Three more unidentified bodies line the outer wall of this room, wrapped in plastic, bound with rope. They are planted on shelves about to be transported or buried somewhere in these remote hills, never to be discovered.

I can't help but think how many bodies have been processed through here.

This room is cold. I can see my breath. I'm sure it's like this to preserve the bodies, but damn it's cold! The air punctures my lungs, freezing me to the bone.

My final assignment is to report what I feel is the last thing they saw while remaining in their bodies, or the first thing they saw after leaving them, much like I had experienced.

Billings said this is an indicator of where they are going to spend eternity… What was that?

A knife fell off the table behind me, scared the shit out of me when it bounced off the floor.

I could never be a mortician; but I've got to do this.

Haworth's orders prevent me from videotaping. He said it was to protect the families of the victims, but I'll bet it's to protect this place and what might happen to me in here if I ever showed a tape. They don't want any witnesses.

Everyone is protecting someone here, allowing them just due for their sins. It's never been more obvious than now. I'm about to unveil the corpses to complete my journey here.

Rev. Billings allowed use of my audio recorder, so I can bear witness and never forget this moment.

AUDIO LOG:
FRIDAY, DECEMBER 24, 2010 6:25 P.M.
RECEIVED BY MELODY SWANN

"This is Eddie Hansen, Friday, December 24th. I'm reporting from inside the morgue at the Uphir Behavioral Health Center. I'm standing between two corpses, covered with blood stained white sheets.

"I'm about to examine the first body belonging to Donald Lambeck. He was pronounced dead earlier this morning after allegedly committing suicide after an altercation in Ward B. "I'm pulling back the sheet to identify him."

Eddie pulls back the sheet. He drops something. I hear him gagging.

"Shit! That's foul! It smells so bad. That smell" That's Donald Lambeck, if that's even his name. Another prisoner who slipped through the system and found his fate here. His eyes are still wide open, even in death.

"His face reminds me of Rudy's, the night he stood over my bed, His mouth is open. I see the bullet hole and exit wound through the back of his head. I'm going to examine him."

Eddie lifts the body. Something slides across a table and crashes.

"Fuck! Donald's arm, it moved. I thought he was alive for a second. It lifted up at me like it was trying to grab me.

"I saw it. I saw the whole thing. I saw Donald killing himself. I saw him pointing the gun, pulling the trigger. I saw his brains splatter out the back of his head. I saw baby Kevin crying.

" I don't know why? But I just saw this whole thing flash through my head."

Something smashes again.

"Shit! What was that?

"A pair of scissors fell off the table behind me, next to the wrapped bodies. How'd they fall that far? Like they were thrown at me.

"I just want to get this over with. Get the fuck out of here. Blood is frozen on the corpse. Right through the hole in his head. I'm done. Done with Donald"

"Here goes. I'm taking the sheet off Rudy."

I hear something humming, like a loud turbine, scraping across the floor. Eddie pulls the sheet off the body. Something hit the ground hard!

"Fuck!"

Maybe Eddie fell. He's panting hard. Something's moving.

"I did not do that! They tore him to pieces! His body is spread out in pieces on the table. Bones and muscles everywhere! Ripped off him, like an animal!

"I did not do this! I put him outside. He was in one piece. You saw it on the tape!"

Something is moving. Or Eddie threw something. I hear something smash.

"What did you do to him? His arm's missing. His guts are ripped out. Three scratches ripped through him, from his chest to his waist, completely torn open.

"No way I did that. No. No. No!

"His face. Want to know about his face. It's the same as Santiago's, same as Donald's. All the same face, the same fucking face. They're scared!"

Something bangs hard again!

"What the fuck you want? What? What!"

There is a loud thump!

"Mother fucker! A body fell off the rack behind me, wrapped in plastic. Fell off the rack and rolled toward me.

"It moved. I swear. It moved! Inside the plastic, it moved. Something is in there."

"Shit! Shit!

"It's moving across the floor. The bag's moving! Something's inside. You sick fucks are burying people alive. What the hell's wrong with you?"

I hear something ripping through the plastic. Eddie bangs on the door, screaming.

"Let me out! Somebody let me out! Hey! Hey! Something's in that body bag, clawing to get out. C'mon!"

The generator sound is getting louder. Eddie is banging and screaming.

"What the fuck is in there? What are you doing? Let me— Ahhh!"

What was that? It sounds like an animal, attacking, devouring. It's gurgling, regurgitating. Eddie's groans are muffled under some engine churning. I can't hear him. I can't hear him.

The door opened. Someone came in.

"Eddie? Eddie? Are you okay? Eddie!"

It's that minister, I know his voice.

"Eddie! Eddie! Can you hear me?

He's doing something to Eddie. I can't tell with all the noise.

"Ose, if you are in him, I command you to speak.
In the name of Jesus, Ose, I command you to speak!
'*In nomine Iesu praecipio tibi ut relinquat!*'"

I hear another voice. A disturbing, gravelly voice:

"*Consummatum est!*"

That's it. The tape went blank. That's it.

JOURNAL ENTRY:
SATURDAY, MARCH 12, 2011 – 3:19 P.M.
ENTERED BY MELODY SWANN

That was the last time I heard from Eddie. I received these tapes February 21, 2011, almost two months after his last contact with me. In accordance to Eddie's wishes, I went back to the lingual institute to have these journals translated.

Eddie's last words were spoken in Latin, *"Consummatum est!"* which means, "It is finished!"

Moments earlier the minister had commanded something in Latin, saying, "In the name of Jesus, I command you to leave."

Who or what he was talking to remains a mystery.

I traveled to Dell City in late January, when Eddie was reported missing. I never found Uphir, nor would anyone in town talk about it. There were no hotels to stay at, and by sunset the town sheriff asked me to leave.

I made several requests to the Texas State Police to set up a rescue mission for Eddie, but nothing materialized at the time of this publication.

A month later this last batch of tapes and journals arrived in my mailbox. They had no return address or postage. They were simply signed "A Friend."

I still hope other tapes or journals appear in my mailbox, since I know that there is more to this story.

I beg the person who calls himself "A Friend" to come forward and tell me the truth about what happened to Eddie in Uphir.

I write this with the sincere hope that anyone with information regarding Eddie's investigation will contact me at melodyswann@gmail.com. Your cooperation will be kept strictly confidential.

This journal is published in memory of Eddie Hansen. I pray someday we see each other again.

TRANSLATIONS FROM THE RECORDINGS.

In accordance with Eddie's wishes, the following transcriptions from the Beverly Hills Lingual Institute are provided to add clarity to these recordings and help make sense of Eddie's story.

"Ego animo habitant quemadmodum habitarunt hoc recording" is Latin, meaning "I will inhabit your soul as I inhabit this recording."

שלי היא שלך הנשמה is Hebrew, translated to "Your soul is mine."

"Avertir Hansen qui Ose est ici" is Latin, meaning "Tell Hansen that Ose is here!"

"Ego eómai o Theís tou myaloó sas. Tha Eúmai pínta mazá sas," is Greek. It translates to, "I am the god of your mind. I will always be with you."

"Daemones mihi vivere. I ad eas pertinent. Et videbis credidisti! Capiam Dei solium dominabitur homines nequam," is Latin, which translates to, "The demons live in me. I belong to them. You shall see and believe. I will storm the throne of God and rule over wicked men."

"Deus miserere mei. Recede! Egredere de me," is Latin, which translates to, "God have mercy on me. Depart. Get out of me."

"Ego Consumam. Edam corporis," is Latin, which translates to, "I will consume him. We will eat his body."

ABOUT THE AUTHOR

SEVEN-X is Mike Wech's debut novel and the first in the forthcoming SEVEN-X series.

As a writer, Mike strives to bring a unique edge to his work and tell stories in creative new ways. He loves thinking outside the box to create art, which captures the imagination and engulfs the audience in the experience.

As the survivor of a near death experience, a debilitating car crash and a career in Hollywood, Mike has maintained his persistence to overcome obstacles and pursue his passion for telling stories.

As a professional filmmaker and film editor, Mike has worked with some of Hollywood's top talent and he has been innovating new technology to create an immersive theatrical experience for the SEVEN-X film franchise.

Mike has teamed up with Award-Winning engineers, technicians and producers to bring Next Generation 3D Film to the big screen with SEVEN-X.

Horror fans get ready for a creepy, unsettling ride into your worst nightmare!

For more information on the SEVEN-X Franchise visit:
http://www.seven-x.com
http://www.desertrockentertainment.com
http://www.datangmovie.com/en

Follow SEVEN-X on Facebook
https://www.facebook.com/SEVENX.media

Follow Mike Wech on twitter:
http://www.twitter.com/mikewech
@mikewech

52465105R00163

Made in the USA
Charleston, SC
14 February 2016